J.F CANNON

Behemoth Strides

First edition

Editing by Lillian Boyd

This book was professionally typeset on Reedsy.
Find out more at reedsy.com

Contents

Acknowledgement

Thank you to my wife for her love and support, and for illustrating the cover you see on the front of this book.

Thank you to my friends and family for plodding through my early drafts and for being helpful and supportive throughout the entirety of this project.

Prologue

Sweet silence.

Lorne Ambrose, industrialist, serial entrepreneur, and possessor of a cool few hundred billion dollars sat alone in his newly completed home. The endless slew of personnel he had hired over the past few years to design and build his dream home were gone at last, and even Lorne's wife was away on business. He could finally enjoy the quiet tranquility of his home without having to share it with a soul.

The conversations with one architect, several designers, and a team of Swiss art dealers had become increasingly tedious the longer the project had stretched on. The interminable meetings seemed to forever forestall the day on which he could enjoy his personal, bespoke sanctuary. As early in the process as he possibly could, he had set up shop in the unfinished structure to better monitor and supervise the property's precise finishing touches. The constant movement and incessant noise of the hordes of carpenters, movers, electricians, and gardeners made him feel confined and under siege within his own space.

This September evening, Lorne stood in his living room, which had been designed to comfortably seat an intimate party of twenty-five. He ran his fingers along the custom-built bookcases that lined the room. The serene quietude of the bookcases' soft eggshell paint was matched only by the gentle calm of the whisper-white armchair underneath. He looked at his collection of books with satisfaction. It had been his idea to have every single one of them custom bound and embossed with an off-white leather book jacket to match shelves, carpet, and furniture.

Expecting cool night air, Lorne stepped through double doors to the porch balcony overlooking his courtyard garden. Instead of a crisp September breeze, unseasonable warmth lingered in the air, blanketing the man as he surveyed the garden. Meticulous arrangements of seasonal annuals decorated the surrounding borders in geometric patterns. The blossoms formed a halo surrounding the garden's crown jewel: a small grove of mature cherry trees Lorne had paid to have extracted from their original location in Japan. The fiery glow of the setting sun glinted through thousands of pink-white petals on their bobbing branches. It had cost a small fortune to have mature trees dug up, sent on an oceanic voyage, and replanted by crane to accommodate their massive root structures, but it had been worth it to have the garden completed at the same time as the house.

Lorne basked a moment more in the beauty and genius that was his property. The (at-the-time-unknown) architect he had chosen had become an instant celebrity after the public had learned of Lorne's hiring him for the project. Lorne had paid the architect an exorbitant fee to never again produce another residential property; his home would be truly one-of-a-kind.

The heavy air became oppressive as the soft sounds of the evening faded into the blanketing silence of the night. A thin film of sweat formed on the back of Lorne's neck. He grimaced and wiped it away before stepping back into the cool, crisp, conditioned air of his haven.

Lorne spent his evening alone with his television. The TV opened to financial news, as it had been programmed to do by default. Coverage of the mega-storm that had just battered the East Coast dominated the airwaves. Newscasters stood in front of the grandiose home of his friend and social rival Charles Lavosse. The mega-mansion's roof had been ripped off cleanly, almost surgically, as if some vengeful god had taken a scalpel to Charles' hubris.

The door hung off its hinges, yawning open to reveal the swirl of debris scattered throughout the home's massive foyer. A huge vase of freshly cut red roses imported from France stood absurdly untouched on the marble table in the center of the wrecked Venetian marble floor. The image set itself upon Lorne's mind: a home besieged by fetid moisture, soon to be beset by mold, algae, and the decaying stench of beached sea life. A thalassic invasion onto a perfectly curated and tamed property.

The thought wriggled like a maggot in his head. *If it could happen to Charles, it could happen to anyone.* Lorne's head spun in shuddering fear as he assured himself that his custom shelves, antique rugs, and immaculate garden were all intact. He feared the impermanence of his sanctuary. A veritable Sword of Damocles of grief and loss dangled above him, waiting to split his skull like an overripe melon.

Of course, he *could* have everything reproduced and rebuilt, but he feared the process of doing it all over again, the waiting, the phone calls, the talking that seemed to stretch into infinity, the dealing with his lessers that he had had to put up with to get it done, the unfortunate necessity of planners and workers to realize his vision, the *hammering,* the *yammering.* Lorne's stomach turned and bile rose in his throat.

His hand flew to the remote, and he changed the channel to a mindless action movie. Before getting up to pour more than a few fingers of scotch, attempting to calm his mind and let sleep find him. Alternating cycles of dozing and jolting followed. Every time his eyelids slid shut, infernal images of Charles' waterlogged property pricked and prodded the base of his skull. The snapping beams in his dreams were suddenly the support beams of his own bowling alley basement. Rivers of stinking sea water befouled the intricate mosaic tile floor of his custom chef's kitchen. Mold crept up the drywall of his personal movie theater room, and every single custom all-wood cabinet in the house swelled, cracked, and splintered behind his eyelids. At a quarter past three a.m., panic overcame inertia. Lorne picked up his cell and made a call.

A sleepy engineer, one of the many head engineers at one of his many companies, answered in a dazed state. Lorne, near-crazed with paranoia, barked a frantic scheme into the receiver. On the other end, the engineer moved into another room for fear of waking their light sleeping, heavily pregnant wife. Lorne talked over the sounds of sleepy footsteps and the fumbling for pen and paper on the other line.

After the plan had been communicated, Lorne had the last word, as he always did. First, a forceful question:

"Can it be done?!"

A thin, raspy voice offered up a tired yes.

"Good. Cancel all other projects and begin work immediately. This is top-priority." At this ungodly hour, it was clear that sleep was out of reach for this tired engineer as they booted up their laptop and began the work.

Chapter 1

Many years later

Vance O'Brien stared daggers at the video on his screen. The backlight from his monitor cast a hazy glow across his face in an otherwise dark room. Through this video feed, Vance saw through the lens affixed to the drone he piloted. The machine's eyes were his eyes as Vance commanded its every flit and flutter with well-honed keystrokes from an empty room a great distance away. Vance's two eyes were one of the few pairs of eyes permitted to see the outside world in all its ruin, his lips of the few permitted to keep secrets deemed too terrible and too frightening for the civilian populace.

A flashlight beamed from the top of the machine, illuminating the pitch black hallway. Falling flecks of aerosolized dust floated downward, the only motion in the abandoned hotel where Vance had pried his mechanical nose.

The vessel in which he explored the outside world hovered, its engine humming near-silent. Its engineered frame spread three-by-three cubic feet in size. Spherically shaped, it possessed an array of small propellers affixed equidistant around its carriage, permitting its omni-directional flight. Vance had remote-piloted this technological marvel into the empty hotel through the labyrinthine rubble of the collapsed parking garage next door.

The drone held its course and hovered down the forgotten hallway toward the hotel's presidential suite, past cracked wallpaper and over dry-rotted carpet. The drone's microphone picked up little clicking and pitter-patter sounds as it floated down the hall. A pop-up window on Vance's display identified the highest probability source for the chatter. BROWN RATS: 4 ESTIMATED.

As the vessel came to the hallway's end, Vance sat up straight in his chair. He brought his face closer to the screen. A deep gut feeling animated his psyche. He hoped against hope an untouched trove of old-world luxuries lay just beyond the door ahead. *Please let there be something expensive and lightweight beyond this door. Something that will do well at auction. Lizzie's daycare bills will only get more expensive in B Sector.*

Vance tapped out a short pattern on his keyboard. A mechanical tentacle ending in a dexterous, clawed appendage telescoped outward from the drone's undercarriage and grasped the rusted doorknob in its many-fingered grip. The mechanical pseudo-hand twisted the knob gently and slowly to the right.

The door clicked and Vance pressed forward. It swung open on silent hinges as the drone explored the suite. Wonderful old statement pieces abounded-beautiful, classically styled furniture, oil paintings in still-intact frames, and above the fireplace a pristine, faceted mirror reflected the drone's flashlight beam from within its gilt frame.

Vance perused his short list of requested items. The mirror sat high on many of the "most wanted" lists for A and B Sector persons that frequented artifact auctions. *There's Lizzie's next month of daycare right there.*

Vance decided he would come back later with Vickers and Santoro. With multiple drones, they could work in concert to retrieve some heavier items, but for now, the mirror was his singular target. It was small, about a foot tall, and appeared light enough that he could abscond with it solo.

Vance keyed in a code and the tentacle's hand shifted. The claw tips rotated into the hand and came out with little felt tipped ends on the fingers. Ever-so-carefully, the claw lifted the delicate mirror off of its spot above the fireplace. Vance sat back and breathed for a second. He couldn't believe his luck. *Burning the midnight oil paid off this time.* Item secured, Vance manipulated the controls to begin the drone's return journey. Red letters flashed on Vance's display and a blaring alarm beat through his headset.

BIPEDAL SOUND SIGNATURES DETECTED! Vance reared the drone back from the wall and spun around. His own headphones picked up what before only the drone's augmented sound detection system had perceived. He heard footsteps. He heard running.

The door to the adjoining room flew open. Vance saw the unmistakable visage of two Lingerers fill his screen-bulging, yellow eyes ,veins pulsing through semi-translucent skin, a snarling, pained face and hunched, animalistic posture. The two figures burst forth and split into two different directions. Vance readied combat controls.

The first Lingerer lunged toward the drone, hand holding a hammer ready to smash apart everything in its pain-induced rage. Vance swept the drone up and to the left, just out of arm's reach of the monstrous figure. The hammer's head just missed the mirror dangling from the tip of the drone's felt-fingered tentacle. Vance keyed a command. A dart shot from the drone's frame into the neck of the once-human, mutated thing.

Vance piloted the drone up high. Its top hovered below the room's vaulted ceiling for two second's more: one, two. The creature fell, smashing through the nearby glass-topped table. Glass splinters ricocheted out in every direction.

A second window on Vance's screen popped up. It read:

No pulse detected. Hostile biological life form euthanized. Count +1.

Vance readied a second shot. The dart struck the second Lingerer attempting to retreat. Vance counted another few seconds. *One, two.* The dead thing fell to the ground.

Familiar words scrawled across Vance's screen.

No pulse detected. Hostile biological life form euthanized. Count +1.

Vance sat back in his chair. His screen showed him everything the drone saw. *Dear God. How did it all come to this?*

The deceased figure's mutated face held still in its chilled agony death mask. Vance trembled. Beneath the monstrous layer, he could still see the semblance of what used to be a person. Rage, sadness, and despair boiled and pulsed beneath his eyes and temples. He stared at the screen and tried yet again to harden himself against the pain. No tears spilled forth. They shook him from within. *I've seen this so many times. Why do I still feel this way?*

Vance remembered the first day he had been authorized to pilot a drone. Superior officers had taken him to an unmarked room and showed him a Lingerer corpse. *The wretched thing.* They had said he must know the truth, must be prepared. In that unmarked room, they had revealed the truth. The thing lay dissected, its corrupted organs splayed out for all to see, all contained in an airtight glass tank. The image of that corpse had always stuck with him. He'd always hated it, and now, he had created two more. Through the drone's eyes, Vance stared at two dead Lingerers.

Humans not on the arc had been reduced to this. *A slow lingering death. A shambling echo of humanity. Was this better? Putting a wounded creature out of its misery? It was merciful, at least.* Vance had circled through this logic countless times. He'd done it again just now. He knew through his actions, he'd ended the suffering of these victims and he protected everyone on the arc from the truth of this cruel, sick terror.

Still, it hurt. Death was death. Vance was only human. In this dark room, alone, lit only by the screen's backlight, Vance still held back tears. Now, he felt the price of his silence; the secret only he and a handful of the highest security officers on Arc Ghost knew burned him from within.

The photo framed on Vance's desk brought a glimmer of reprieve. His one year old daughter's messy blonde hair flopped in front of her face. Her smile beamed a big, goofy, mostly toothless grin. Lizzie looked so full of life like she'd wriggle right out of her mother's arms, right out the photo. Kayla just held tight and smiled her same smile. That smile always brought Vance peace. Lizzie and Kayla. *I don't deserve them.* Vance steeled himself from doubts and pain. His trembling lessened. He could shoulder this burden. *I have to shoulder this burden. For them.*

Vance got back to work, ready to bring the mirror back. The switch always got to him a little, the incongruity of his two appointed tasks. Ending pain in a dead world and bringing back trinkets and treasures. *Still, these treasures keep people happy and distracted. New shiny things to beam about and buy. New things to put on walls to impress people at parties.* The bits and bobs he found kept people from looking out toward the horizon and having to bear the burden of its horrors. In a twisted way, these two halves of Vance's job served the same function.

Lizzie would have another month of daycare. And one day, a good school. Vance guided the drone out of imminent danger, out into the open air. He set it to autopilot. It and the mirror would return to a decontamination chamber on Arc Ghost. A few days later, a drone would load the mirror to its drop point, ready to be picked up by cargo drones and taken to Arc Alpha where it would be stored until auction. Hopefully the software designers, resource managers, and boardroom-sitters would drive up the auction price enough to *really* make Vance's commission worthwhile. Might even pay for two months of Lizzie's daycare.

Vance turned off the computer and shut off the screen. He left the pitch black room and returned to his barracks. It was late now. He looked hard at the barracks phone and decided to use his one weekly call now. He needed to hear his family's voice.

The phone rang. After a moment he heard his wife's voice.

"Hey, it's late. What's up babe?"

Vance smiled. "I Just wanted to hear your voice. Is Lizzie still up?"

"Oh, babe, I'm sorry." Kayla's voice betrayed that she was dog-tired, but to Vance, it was still the most beautiful voice in the world. "I just put her down for the night."

Vance stiffened. He had just missed the chance to hear his daughter's chatters and babbles. *Again. Just a few more weeks and I'll see them. She'll be so much bigger by then.*

Kayla spoke again, interrupting his train of thought.

"How was work? What'd you do today?"

Vance sighed. "Nothing much," he lied. "Just ran security logs and did some training with the new recruits."

The rest of their conversation continued the way most of their conversations went: easy laughter, gentle reassurances. Vance was feeling burnt out and ready to come home; Kayla was struggling with her nuisance family. A pause.

"I love you."

"Love you too, babe, but I'm exhausted. I've gotta get to bed. Goodnight."

Vance lay in his bunk trying to sleep. The pained expression of the Lingerers he had put down flashed every time he closed his eyes. He jolted and thrashed, trying to force the images from his consciousness. He conjured his daughter's smiling face and his wife's sweet voice instead.

Goodnight.

Thoughts of their faces and voices chased away the horrors he would

CHAPTER 1

never tell them, everything he never wanted them to know.

Goodnight. It was a good night because it *had* to be a good night.

Chapter 2

Two weeks later

As the sun set, a man pried both hands under a dry-rotted, hollowed out log. Bereft of all moisture, the dead wood felt light enough to heave with minimal effort. The log bashed against a nearby boulder and shattered into soft, fibrous splinters. They curled and bent, more like rubber than wood.

The man scoured for little glints of light in the sun, searching for his quarry. Sure enough, the shiny hides of night crawlers reflected the burgeoning evening light. The creatures' wriggling frames stood out, stark white against the dull, dusty browns of the earth around them. The man picked as many as he could find, and with a well-practiced pinch of the thumb and forefinger, ceased their squirming.

He swallowed three of the grubs whole and dropped the remaining protein filled bits into a small satchel attached to a crude belt of tattered rope tied loosely about his waist. Next to the satchel hung a knife hewn from bone, an emptied animal bladder for carrying water, and a deer skull with only the nub of one broken antler protruding from its crest. The grubs bounced around against the roots, shoots, and nuts that lined the bottom of the satchel. The man continued his trek.

Amidst the dying forest, he marched through the heat of late summer. Its sparse canopy gave little shade, but the abundant light made the sourcing of grubs easy at least. Yellow-and-brown leaves, dead long before they'd felt the cool embrace of fall, crunched beneath the man's feet with every step. He trudged through a carpet of desiccated mulch that, without any blessed rain, had become the dust that blew away in hot winds. Too little moisture for fungus, the fallen bark and limbs dry-rotted. Trees leaned as lignin skeletons, leafless and bare, casting gaunt shadows across the ground. Sun rays besieged all the rest of the earth, scorching the forest floor's already-exhausted understory. Drought and baking heat hastened erosion. Plant roots grew too shriveled and weak to hold their last scraps of earth. The cracking, crumbling soil dwindled to dust light enough to blow away in the wind.

The man lifted the one-antlered skull from his waist cloth and glared deep in its empty eye sockets. He asked in a quiet voice between a whisper and a prayer,

"Are you sure this is the way?"

"L I S T E N."

The man dropped to the ground. Calloused hands swept away the carpet of rubbery twigs and papery leaves. A pocket of bare earth lay before him. The man lowered his ear to the uncovered patch. Heeding the skull's command, he listened.

A dull, trembling, crashing racket swept deep under the earth in rhythmic waves of sound and silence: Crash, silence, crash, silence, crash.

"I should not have doubted." The haunting rhythm lent assurance in the direction of the man's feet. He tied the skull back with his belt cord and resumed his journey. Hills of fallen timber stood between him and that metronome sound.

He climbed over them and under them. Rare, still-standing trees poked out from the arboreal graveyard. He marked his travel, passing these landmarks that seldom materialized across the ever-stretching horizon.

The man knew that in time, these lone trees would fall as well. The

13

brutal, unending, silent force of drought would one day render the remnants of this forest into a featureless ocean of desiccated wood. All animals save for the wood-boring insects would flee. They would overcrowd, migrating to the few oases of green vegetation hidden far away within the vast seas of dust and hard-baked ground. The man knew this, but he knew he would reach his target before those last trees fell.

Voices and feelings stirred within him. He could no longer ignore them. He could no longer run. He would find what made that sound.

In a matter of sun-bleached, grub-fueled days, the man came to the edge of the forest. Before him stretched a great prairie plain flanked far to his left by the hulking husk of a city's skyline. The ghostly, distant metropolis sent a slow shiver that started at the base of his spine and ended as a pressured pain surging through his temples.

"N E V E R T H E C I T I E S . O N L Y V I O L E N T G H O S T S A N D C R A C K I N G C O N C R E T E." The man patted the skull soothingly on his waist cord. Well did he know its warning against the cities by now, and he had no intention of braving their winding streets.

The prairie ahead was heavy with clay. Its smooth particulates shrank from an unending want of moisture, leaving deep ravines that spread from inches to feet. Gashes ripped through the earth at disorderly angles. The prairie ahead appeared as an endless stretch of shrunken-down mountain ranges- jagged, crumbling, and uneven.

Only the hardiest grasses and thistles still held purchase on these brick-hard dunes. The sound that the man had been chasing was louder here. In moments of perfect silence, he could hear that rhythm of low crashes for the first time without his ear pressed firmly to the ground. Little bits of sediment broke apart and rolled into the ravines ahead in tandem with those crashes.

The man scaled the first summit with practiced ease. He dropped to his hands and feet and crawled across its cracked clay peaks. This unforgiving terrain would have snapped the legs of the uninitiated, but the man knew the importance of his every hand- and foothold. For hours, he crept across crumbling peaks, the sound growing ever-louder and the strata growing ever-more active with every distant emboldening bellow.

He finally reached the prairie's edge. The ground began its gentle slope downward. It followed a gradual decline. The edges of a dust storm dwelt far away, whipped up by blistering-winds, winds that swirled around that reverberating bellow's maker.

Within the depths of that near-opaque cloud, the barest silhouette of a behemoth figure stepped. Across the horizon, the figure appeared small. The man knew from its distance and its sound it was anything but. The silhouette shuddered and moved into the heart of that distant storm. Unsure if it was a trick of his eyes, the man swore the storm followed that distant giant, the rhythmic crashing echoing across the plains their loudest yet.

The man crouched. So close, finally in sight, he sought just a moment to rest his aching limbs. The sun crested high in the late afternoon and was now beginning its descent to mark evening. A broad wash of light crept over the land, illuminating its gray-and-brown features in brilliant orange. The man once again lifted the skull off his waist cord and placed it gently on the ground.

"LISTEN."

The man attuned his hearing and listened. A nearly imperceptible pitter-patter scuttled along the nearby ground. A few feet from where he knelt, a fat, hairy tarantula plodded across dusty earth. While the man watched the creature's trek, a slight rustling sounded nearby. A coiled shape in the shadows lengthened slowly at an intercepting angle to the unaware, fat spider.

Suddenly, the shape straightened. Piercing fangs punctured the arachnid's carapace with a small pop. The arthropod was dead in seconds, and the reptile began to swallow the creature whole. The man seized upon this unique opportunity. Stealthily, he picked up the largest rock he could find. The throat of the reptile stretched as it choked the arthropod's many jointed legs down its elastic gullet. The man hefted the weighty, flat rock above the unassuming serpent. The rock's shadow loomed over the feasting creature.

Suddenly, the serpent learned too late. The man's prey tried one last-ditch effort to slither away from impending doom, but its body, still weightily filled with its last fresh meal, could not escape the stone crushing its body. A crashing *thunk* was the last sound the arachnid's predator heard as the rock flattened its body into the ground. The slithering creature's tail wriggled. The man pressed more weight onto the broad, flat stone. The tail's wriggling ceased.

The man removed the stone and lifted the reptile's carcass out from its tomb. Crushed remnants of the well fed arachnid fell from the creature's flattened jaw. The man severed the carcass two inches down from its smashed head. He returned his bone-hewn knife to its familiar place on his belt and raised the severed opening up to his lips holding its tail high above his head. Dripping drops of blood, water, and pulverized tissue sloughed down between his parted lips. The man ate and drank steadily as he squeezed the carcass inch-by-inch from its tail to its headless front.

He heard the voice from the one-antlered skull again.

"S T R E N G T H F O R O U R B O D Y F O R W H E N W E F I N D I T."

The man tossed the reptile's corpse onto the prairie ground. A small gust blew away its paper-thin corpse, emptied of everything that had once allowed the serpent to hunt and slither. The man's gut did not tremble once. He had long grown accustomed to the rough morsels of this waste.

The silhouette within the dust cloud towered ahead, crawling away beyond the horizon. The man picked up the cervine skull and trudged

16

forth. That silhouette grew large and its crashing steps grew louder. Distant memories swam through the misty fog of the man's mind. The one antlered skull hung proudly above a small hut's threshold. Nearby, other huts stood in rows. Beyond them, sun-hardened and sinewy men and women sat around the crackling coals of an evening fire. A woman fashioned tools from bone and wood. A man counted seeds in the voice of a prayer.

The memory twisted, shook, and bent as a final image trespassed through the man's mind. All these living, sun-hardened and sinewy bodies lay completely and totally still. Their eyes were glassy. Their chests drew no breath. Their corpses vibrated gently to that haunting distant rhythm: Crash, silence, crash, silence. The memory faded as a boy scarcely older than a child ran from that sound.

Drawing back to the present, the man stood. He knew now that he would run towards that sound. He knew he had no choice.

The man's gait grew faster and faster and fastest of all as he hurled himself into the swirling dust cloud's storm. His eyes squinted shut. Sandglass swirled around his face, cutting his cheeks.

There, for the first time it towered in its full presence. The man bent his neck back as far as he could to glimpse up high. A city, like those the one-antlered skull forbade him to enter, perched atop a massive, incomprehensible metal structure. A bulbous, round body like a fattened tick heaved beneath that impossible skyline. The body stood supported by six behemoth legs that stepped forward one at a time: Crash, silence, crash, silence. The slow strides lurched the mass ahead step-by-incomprehensible-step.

They left great craters in their wake and the deafening echo of crashing sound. The man followed that stride and followed that sound. He peeked through near-shut eyes into the depth of a crater where a titanic foot had stepped moments before. He saw the smashed remnants of a tree flattened into the clay earth. Through the dust cloud under the behemoth's body, the man saw other figures of similar shape. Not as grand, they followed the largest structure like pups follow a mother wolf.

The man stood still. Incomprehension and sublime, awestruck terror rooted his legs to the earth. Crash, silence, CRASH, silence. The rhythm filled the depths of his being. From the bubbling recesses of his memory, to the deafening cacophony that surrounded him, that sound became the totality of his existence. In an instant, a booming voice pierced through his trance.

"I T I S H E R E."

The man crouched into a sprinter's lunge. He waited for the moment of silence that settled every time one of the feet rested after its stride. A foot sunk deep in the cracked clay ground. It rested holding up the structure's unfathomable weight. In that pocket of silence, the man broke into a dead sprint toward the metal foot. He leapt onto its platform width and began to climb.

He climbed *fast*. His arms and legs were well-accustomed to the unplanned spontaneity found in natural cliff faces. They found an easier time in the mechanical predictability of the hand-and footholds that comprised this metal structure.

His body flew up the triangular metal bars that came together to form the structure's titanic legs. The man was already fifteen feet up before he felt the sharp pain of an object pierce the back of his neck. His heart rate exploded and his vision blurred. His grip and coordination slackened. He hit free-fall. He used his last moment of muscular agency to brace for the fall.

His limp body slid off the platform foot and rolled down the rock onto the hard ground, tumbling weakly into the depth of a newly formed crater. He lay there paralyzed, unable to move as a massive shadow slowly blotted his view. An uncaring, unknowing, behemoth foot continued its stride. It was ready to follow the step of the leg that had preceded it, into the space the previous foot had occupied, the very same space where the man now lay dormant. His last conscious thought was of the snake flattened by his broad, flat rock.

Chapter 3

Earlier that day

Delaney Quist-Laney, as she liked to be called woke up with the hard agitation of a springboard. Her eyes, still heavy with sleep, roved to the tablet on her nightstand.

"Another beautiful day on God's Grey Earth," she muttered to herself as she got onto the floor and began to stretch. Deep back-bends, near-180-degree trunk twists, and ass-to-ground squats jump started her sleep-logged muscles. Still, she couldn't chase away the nagging fatigue felt deep within the tissues of her work-worn body.

She drank exactly eight ounces of water with a double-dose of caffeine by way of two small, white tablets dissolved in her glass. She slinked into her coveralls branded with the company logo (Arc Interior Solutions) and slung her climbing harness over her shoulder sauntering out of her quarters up the stairwell to the Arc Alpha Promenade.

Few others were out and about at this hour, save for a few bleary-eyed night shift workers returning to their humble hovels. Laney exchanged polite nods and rote waves to those that crossed her path. She could reach the auxiliary cargo bay faster if she didn't head up to the promenade before descending back down, but seeing the sunrise and spending a few more minutes not confined by the hull's steel walls made being slightly late to work an even more enticing option.

Laney surveyed the horizon. The sun had barely risen high enough for its rays to weave through the shade sails draped above the arc's main deck. A man looking to be in his early fifties wore the green uniform of Arc Repair Professionals. He balanced atop a high ladder, making repairs to holes in one of the shade sails. The sight reminded Laney of a giant green grasshopper trapped in the world's largest spider web. She gave a half-snort to herself and continued her commute.

Midway across the deck, Laney passed a few empty tables and benches outside a tropical-themed synth-coffee hut. The fake-flower-and-grass-adorned seating spaces sat empty for now, but they were sure to be filled soon with packs of loud white-collar types conducting business at prime boasting volume. They would no doubt discuss various dips and peaks in projected verch sales.

A tired-looking woman turned on a neon OPEN sign as well as a larger colorful sign reading *Coconut Joe's Coffee and Bar*. The weary woman spotted Laney as she rolled up the metal cage protecting the main bar area.

"Hey, Laney!" she called out. "Magda says she owes you a drink for how you helped her last week. She's working tonight, so be sure to come on by after your shift today!"

Protesting was futile. Laney knew how Magda was: never one to leave a favor unreturned and always insistent on paying it back in person. She gave a quick thumbs-up to the sleepy barista and shouted "I'll be there!" as she quickened her gait.

Crossing the remaining two hundred feet or so, Laney descended the winding network of stairwells down to the arc's bottom deck. She came to an iron barred door marked *AUTHORIZED PERSONNEL ONLY*. Laney lifted a chunky piece of white plastic hooked to a carabiner on her belt loop and held it against a sensor on the door. The guts of the machinery churned and let out a loud buzz, then familiar *click* as the door unlocked. She stepped into her work home, Auxiliary Cargo Bay C.

It was a warehouse turned upside-down. Everywhere dangled orange scaffolding repurposed into shelves with plywood and screws. The rows and rows of shelves were welded directly to the underside of the arc's hull. The first level of storage was accessible via the suspended maintenance walkways that spanned the length under the Arc Alpha's hull. To access anything below this first level, Laney had to hook her climbing equipment and rappel up and down the ramshackle shelves to retrieve items of import. For the past few years of her employment at Arc Interior Solutions, the tensile strength of a cable tether and the gripping skills of her limbs had been the only guardrails against a precipitous drop and a sudden, untimely splatting death upon the earth's surface.

Laney walked to a nearby console and eyed the delivery manifest for her shift. *Another auction is coming up soon- gonna be a heavy couple of days.*

13K5 14lbs.
   19E5 61 lbs.
   5F 9 154 lbs.
Laney mentally mapped out the most efficient pathway for retrieving the items. In the midst of her planning, the nearby console chirped twice. A robotic voice hummed out,

"Retrieval Manifest Received. Retrieval Manifest Received. Retrieval Manifest Received."

She looked at the contents of today's delivery requests. Over twenty new items scrolled across the screen on each docket.

"Starting early today," Laney muttered to herself. *Hope Helen doesn't make her way down here to interrupt work with any of her "productivity wisdom" talk.*

Laney tightened her harness and hooked her tether to the guardrail. She made her way to row thirteen and vaulted over. After falling about thirty feet, she deployed the cable's braking mechanism, which added just enough friction to the system for Laney to slowly slip another twenty feet to level K. She gripped the cord attached to her harness and thrashed her body in precise concert. Her muscles worked in a wave from her legs through her core until her undulations built enough momentum for her to swing herself over to the desired shelf. She caught a scaffolding crossbar and pulled herself in.

Here we are. Laney undid the cables that bound the package to the scaffold. Laney shook the parcel gently and it made a muffled rattle. *Wooden jewelry box with pearls inside. Headed to an unlucky wife whose husband is cheating on her. The pearls are nice, though.*

Making up little stories about the items she retrieved was one of the small ways Laney passed the time at work. Clipping the parcel to her vest, she started the climb back up the scaffold to the top, placing her weight only along the joints where she knew the welds were strongest. She climbed the fifty-five feet back up and placed the package in the crudely taped-off corner of the walkway marked 'outgoing delivery.'

Laney proceeded for the next several hours detached, focused on the physicality of the task at hand and all the fantastical little stories she imagined for the item's eventual recipients. She finished the remainder of her shift with her mind disengaged from worry. The last item Laney needed to retrieve was an ornate, mahogany desk, weighing one hundred seventy-five pounds, being shipped to one of the manors in District A. *This desk will be the writing space for a book the author will never finish.*

It was near the end of Laney's shift, her traps, abs, and hamstrings burned, and she was feeling a little less charitable in her thoughts. *Ninety percent of the people on the arc live shoved together in a tin can, and the rich have still got the space in their mansions for antique furniture.* A tag stuck to the desk read 'INTENDED FOR AUCTION.' *If I ever saw that auction, I don't know how I'd cope. Room full of richie riches throwing a money fight over some old, dusty stuff a robot pulled out of a dead world.*

Hilarious!

Laney clipped hoist pulley straps under each desk leg for a balanced load. She rocked the desk lightly testing the strap's grip. She felt something rattle inside. She opened the desk's drawer and remembered the little gilt mirror that came in recently. *Gotta find a new place for this.* Laney stuffed the small mirror in a nearby box filled with a stack of old paintings and returned to the desk.

With many pulls on the hoist cable, she sent the piece back up to the top of the walkway before clipping the brake, ensuring the item would not fall back down. Laney preferred to save the hoist mechanisms only for pieces she absolutely could not move with just her strength and ingenuity. She slipped a dolly under the desk and wheeled it over to the outgoing delivery area, then tapped her hand on the solid old planks that comprised the piece. *Wallace and John will take you to some under appreciative yuppie's home in A or B Sector.* Laney thought of her delivery team coworkers.

We have robots to carry every ounce of cargo, but the last leg of delivery has to be hefted by a meat machine. Laney thought. She remembered the words her boss Helen always said,

"Only a human touch could properly complete the Arc Interior Solutions experience."

Wallace, who actually handled the deliveries, maintained a different theory: nitpicking a faceless robot over finicky minutia just didn't have the same magic to it for someone so thoroughly bored with their life.

By the time Laney finished shift, it was nearing sunset. She started the trudge of her commute in reverse, making her way back up the various winding staircases that led to the promenade. She remembered Magda's offer of a free drink and the heaviness in her steps lightened as she walked up the last few flights imagining the flavor of a fresh, cool beer.

Laney stopped at Coconut Joe's, as bidden by Magda. *Coconut Joe's*

Coffee and Bar. Terrible name, good drinks, better service, Laney thought to herself. The scene was much more crowded than it had been earlier that morning, just as Laney had expected. The watering hole held the regular crowd of maintenance and service workers getting off shift, plus (Laney's smile soured) a couple of well dressed-professional types from A and B Sectors. *No doubt they're slumming it here in order to "change up the routine."*

A broad, brassy woman with graying red hair leaned over from behind the bar. Her booming voice lit a smile on Laney's face, as it did every time.

"Glad you could make it, kid."

"Good to see you, Magda."

Magda pulled the leftmost tap at the bar and expertly poured exactly one pint of Laney's favorite choice with the perfect ratio of liquid to foam. She paused, winked at Laney, and poured a little bit more before slapping the glass down on the aged laminate and sliding it Laney's way. A tiny amount of foam sloshed over the top of the overfilled glass as the beverage slotted perfectly into Laney's work-tired hand; neither Magda nor Laney paid the little spill any mind.

Magda leaned over conspiratorially and spoke in what she considered a whisper, but would still have been quite loud in any setting other than a crowded bar.

"Can't thank you enough for helping me with my little...issue. They've just finished inspections in my branch of C Plus Sector apartments, sooo..." Magda looked knowingly at Laney, wiggling her eyebrows, clearly trying to covertly convey her unspoken request.

"I'll get it back to you next time I go on shift," Laney answered with a laugh. Magda beamed, full of excitement.

"Thanks, kid, you're a real treasure."

A couple of the clean-cut, sweat-free yuppies started complaining loudly a short distance away about not being served promptly. Magda and Laney exchanged exasperated looks.

"Duty calls," Magda said as she left to attend to the situation. Laney sat enjoying her beer. The crisp full-bodied amber liquid hit better than she'd expected. Twenty minutes of nursing the tall glass later, the hairs on the back of Laney's neck stood up. A voice shattered her sense of peace.

"You know, you are *way* too pretty to be wearing coveralls all day. You could easily move up the food chain around here if you wanted." Against her better judgment, Laney looked over, eyes already rolling. As expected, one of the yuppies had broken off from the pack and occupied the bar stool next to her, ready to try what he thought was an original line that Laney had of course heard at least a dozen times, if not more. She scrunched her nose unkindly in non-reply before turning away. To her horror, the man continued his impotent attempt to chat her up. She heard him as an irritating insect whining in her ear.

"Wyatt Corgan. Junior non-fungible virtual merchandising programmer. I have a very nice balcony apartment in B Sector. It overlooks Boutique Street."

Laney slow-blinked her eyes, hoping that by the time she opened them, this annoyance in khaki slacks would be gone. She opened them, but alas. *No such luck.* There he sat, more mosquito than man, uncomfortably tugging on his starched collar that wilted in the pressing heat of the crowded bar.

Laney batted her eyes and looked at the man. She stood up, smiled, and spoke.

"I'm..." the khaki slacks mosquito man hung on her every word, his face contorted in palpable excitement, "a person with somewhere else to be."

Laney downed the rest of her beer, scanned her inc card to pay, and sauntered away from the dejected occupant of business casual clothing. She lamented that she could not think of a more elaborate prank to pull, but the quick bait-and-switch would have to do. Leaving the noise of the bar, she began her walk back to her below-deck apartment in C Sector. Taking the first step down the stairwell, her subterranean apartment felt like the wrong place to be. The man's comments irritated her. *Too pretty for coveralls. Move up the food chain. Every person at every moment, reduced from who they are to just what they do.* That's the way things were on the arc. Laney was used to it. *But it's a shitty thing to have to be used to.* Laney thought of the man himself, puffing up about his tech work and his possessions to strangers. *So glad I left that world.*

Lost in thought, Laney turned and walked abruptly in the opposite direction, away from her apartment. She didn't feel like retiring for the evening, not just yet. *Let's not end the night on a sour note. May as well retrieve Magda's package early.* Her voyage down to the auxiliary cargo bay proceeded as it always did save for the very end where she reached the electronically locked, iron-barred door marked *AUTHORIZED PERSONNEL ONLY.* Laney broke into a running start and leapt. She caught the top of the gate with cat-like grace and pulled herself through a small gap between the gate's top and the ceiling above. She looked at the unopened gate and smiled to herself. *No paper trail.*

Back down below decks in the upside-down, hanging warehouse, Laney put her harness back on and dropped to the bottom level. She grabbed a small plastic box wedged in between two steel crates and opened it. There it was, the small bag of green organic matter that would have given Magda so much trouble. Cheddar-grass, a mild, non-addictive drug, possession of which was functionally prohibited for anyone with residence less than B Sector.

Laney stowed the bag in a zippered pocket of her coveralls next to a small plastic pocket lighter she'd no doubt absent mindedly grabbed from Magda's place one day. The pocket's interlocking metal teeth kept the contraband snug and hidden. She began to climb back up, but some urge stopped her. Some force deep within just did *not* want to return just yet. She didn't want to sleep. She didn't want to usher in the next day. Laney instead looked out to the earth below, a dusty surface scored with countless spider webbing cracks.

It was oddly beautiful. Not in a traditional sense, but serene, something everyone on the arc had lost. In this vista of wasteland, Laney longed for something she'd never known.

A home that doesn't move. The feeling of something under your feet that isn't metal. A wide-open space where there isn't anyone around for miles. To grow *with* a place instead of in spite of it. To have roots.

Laney unclipped her first tether from the top rail, and clipped a second tether to a spare bar of scaffolding on the very bottom level of the hanging shelving. She descended down the line to just hang from the bottom of the arc. She swayed gently with the movement of the giant behemoth's stride, alone and at peace. This was it, the farthest she could possibly get away from the terrestrial, metal cruise ship, the city that had always been her home. The irony that she was literally tied to the arc was not lost on her.

The earth was gray and lifeless. The cracked ground faded, losing the last of its color in vanishing evening light. Everything her schooling on the arc had ever talked about all came back to one foundational message: *The earth went sour and died, and we should be so grateful to live on the arc, where humanity could persist forever. Thanks to Lorne Ambrose, we were the lucky ones.* Laney swung from her tethered cord bobbing with Arc Alpha's steps. *The lucky ones.*

Her thoughts were interrupted by an unimaginable sight: a human figure climbing up one of the arc's legs.

Laney was utterly shocked and transfixed by the figure. She watched it ascend a few handholds before it let out a loud shriek and fell. It hit the arc's massive platform foot, rolled, and fell limply to the ground.

"Shit-fuck!" Laney yelled. "What crazy bastard gets their jollies trying to spelunk down the arc's legs?!" Her thoughts raced even as she flew into movement. *I've got to help whoever that is!*

Laney flew up her tether. She grabbed every length of rope she could find and a second harness. She dashed down the walkway roughly a few hundred feet above the mystery man's limp body.

Back, down, the body laid still, sloughing down into a crater, a crater left by Arc Alpha's front foot. *Fuck! In less than a minute… the mid section leg…*

Laney suppressed her panic. She clipped her tether to a hoist pulley and vaulted over the railing. Down, down she fell with lightning speed. Laney tapped the brake mechanism just as details of the still body came into view. A wiry-framed man, clothed in rags and with a long dusty beard and an animal skull tied to his waist.

"What the fuck?"

Laney's feet touched the surface of the earth for the first time in her life. She had no time to process the feeling of dirt beneath her soles. She dove down into Arc Alpha's craterous footprint. Her hands ripped the man's limp limbs through the straps in her spare harness. She tightened the buckle. The mid-section leg hovered above the pair. Laney hooked the man's harness to her own, threw him over her shoulder, and scrambled out of the crater. The gargantuan metal foot hovered mere feet over the soon-filled footprint. Laney yanked hard on her line.

The pair rose up just as the giant metal foot crashed down into the space they had just occupied. Laney's arms went into overdrive, sending them up the hoist pulley's line. She climbed like a spider speeding up its own thread. The man was *heavy*; she was tired, but adrenaline rocketed through pulsing veins. She reached the top. She saved the stranger.

Laney flung the unconscious man's body over the railing and collapsed beside him, chest heaving. Terrified, depleted lungs sucked in air like a black hole sucked in light. Laney glanced at the man's body and saw his chest rise and fall with breath. *Alive, thank God!* Laney gently tapped the man's face. He did not stir. Laney wracked her brain trying to remember Magda's old EMT stories, scouring them for anything useful.

He's unconscious. Check him for injuries. Laney searched. No obvious wounds or physical traumas manifested in Laney's investigation. She breathed out. The man's appearance struck her. Everything about him was alien, from the strange material of his clothes to his mass of long hair and dust filled beard. The animal skull held tight tied in knots on his belt cord.

Only one massive, reality-altering possibility loomed before Laney. She didn't breathe it out loud. It wracked her brain from within.

He's not from here. Everything she'd ever learned became a lie in an instant. *There are still PEOPLE out there!*

A tiny object entered Laney's view, nestled within the long locks that draped over the back of the unconscious man's neck. She gently rolled him over to discover more. A thin dart protruded from the skin. She recognized it instantly: a tranq dart used only by arc security.

"Motherfucker!"

Chapter 4

Laney's heart felt like it would burst through her chest. A million questions zipped around her brain like a cloud of buzzing insects. She struggled to tame them into anything resembling a coherent plan, with no luck. She took in a deep, steadying breath and gripped the nearby railing tightly with both hands, but it was no use. Her head was already spinning and she felt like she might float away, harness and all. She forced out a series of quick exhales and dropped into a deep squat. The powerful feeling of the posture cleared her head, grounding her and giving her a small sense of control. It assuaged the enormity of the situation just enough to allow her to think.

If this man is from off-arc (the word *off-arc* sounded strange in her head) *and had a dart in his neck, that means arc security knew about him, shot him, and left him to die. Arc security is not friendly on a regular basis, but this - this looks like attempted murder. Fuck fuck fuck.*

The still-breathing-but-comatose man she had saved lay at her squatted feet. *Shit I'm in possession of unconscious, living contraband. Maybe whoever shot him saw me save him. Maybe they're gonna come after me. They could track him by tracking me...*

A dreadful thought entered Laney's head.

Do I really owe this man anything? Maybe I should just leave him...

The horror of this selfish impulse jump started the rest of her mind into high gear.

"No!" she said audibly. A new resolve overtook her. Her fist clenched to a white-knuckle pallor as she reached up and tightened her grip on the guardrail. *Maybe they just shot him and left. After all, no one knew I was down here. They wouldn't assume he'd have survived that fall, and even if he had, the arc's foot would have taken care of the rest. I mean, no one would expect someone on-arc to save someone off-arc. I didn't even know there WAS anyone off-arc until three minutes ago.*

No! I can't assume that. *Too many unknown variables. Who is this man? Why does arc security want to kill him? Are they tracking him? Did they see me save him? Can they track him by tracking me? Are they watching now?* Laney's head spun. No sounds or sights appeared out-of-the-ordinary for a regular evening trespassing in Auxiliary Cargo Bay C.

Better to assume the worst, prepare for the worst, and hope I'm wrong. I've got to hide him while he comes to. That's the best chance he has. It's the best chance I have. Laney paced a short beat up and down the warehouse.

I can't take him to my place. If they saw me scoop him out of that hole, my place would be the first place they'd check.

Laney patted her breast pocket and remembered the delivery she'd promised to take to Magda's. *Guess we'll see what Mag's thinks of all this. That might work.*

She got to work. Her brain cobbled together the least-bad plan it could think of. She didn't have the luxury of a good plan right now; least-bad would have to do.

Magda always said the tranquilizers that security uses were pretty serious business. The unconscious man's breath rose and fell out of a body little more than skin and bones. *He's small, a real lightweight.* Laney pulled the dart out of the man's neck. *That dose might hit him harder. Optimistically, I've got a couple hours. Might be just enough time to help him.*

Laney rummaged through a nearby closet and grabbed a pair of coveralls. She slipped them on the unconscious man, mentally apologizing.

Sorry Wallace, I'll get you a new pair. The coveralls absolutely swallowed the man's lithe frame. *Better than rags and dirt, but it still won't quite do.* She pulled at the loose fabric and twisted, taking out some of the slack, then took a nearby zip tie and cinched the bundle of fabric to make the ill-fitting clothes drowning the man's skeletal frame a little less obvious.

She found a pair of sharp scissors, against all odds, and did the absolute best she could to trim the man's hair and beard into something approaching the business-like short styles every other man on the arc sported. She untied the one antlered deer skull from the man's belt and hid it under a nearby tarp. *At least now he won't stick out like the world's sorest thumb. Maybe the second-or third-sorest.* That was about as much as Laney could hope for.

She searched desperately for anything else of use. She saw a large, rectangular reinforced cardboard box and a moving dolly. *That'll have to do.* Muscling the limp-but-lightweight body into the box, Laney taped it up and levered it up onto the dolly. She eyed the freight elevator, but thought better of it. *A work zone elevator in use outside of work hours would surely draw suspicion from any suitably bored or overzealous security personnel.* Stairs it had to be.

Laney came to the electronically locked door that stood as a cold sentinel between her and the stairs. In what was fast becoming a habit, she made a snap decision she hoped she would not later regret. Laney reached through the bars, unscrewed a side panel on the electronic lock, and disconnected a wire that connected the door to the rest of the arc's security system.

She took out her pocket lighter and held the open flame near the machine's sensor. After a few seconds of waving the flame, a small black-and-white display flashed '*FIRE MODE*'. The door unlocked. *Thank God Akash taught me how to do that before he moved up to B sector work.*

33

Laney waited for the display to return to normal, then rewired the lock. *Should be easy enough to pass the old tech off as malfunctioning, picking up fires that aren't there. Better that than have my key card traced, pinging me at this door when I'm not supposed to be here.*

Laney walked backwards, pulling the dolly toward the stairwell. With enough heft, the wheels caught the top of each stair. She muscled the unconscious man's weight up, step-by-step. A minute later, she breathed out a heaving, tired gust. *One flight of stairs finished —don't think about how many more to go.*

Laney felt tired. Her muscles were shot, but enough residual adrenaline pumped through her body to fight through the throbbing discomfort. She pushed through one stairwell after another. Out of breath, Laney made it to the top of the stairwell up to the deck level. She stopped and caught her breath.

She surveyed the promenade, her next hurdle. It was crowded. Today was a shopping day. Stores were freshly stocked from the previous shipping day and everyone from C to A Sector was out in the evening, looking to stock up on provisions, verch codes, or this month's new phys-goods.

Laney ducked her head, grabbed the dolly, and made a beeline back to Coconut Joe's. She tried to walk in a way that did NOT say "I'm transporting contraband." The watering hole was even more crowded than usual and Laney's heart fell into her stomach as she spotted two off-duty arc security personnel knocking back shots at the bar. *Yep, I'm definitely going to prison. Fuck it.* She ducked behind the cabana-style building, and parked the dolly and contraband cargo next to a few boxes. She hesitated, then put an empty box on top of her box in a feeble attempt to camouflage the situation.

Laney gingerly opened the bar's back door, trying to be as quiet as possible. She hid in the break room waiting for Magda. *Come on, come on, come on.* Several minutes passed before Laney heard the loud, brassy voice she was listening for.

"I'm going to the back. Somebody else take over!" Magda yelled. The voice got louder and slurred a few off-key notes as Magda walked into the back room. Laney put her finger to her mouth in a shushing gesture as she slowly stepped out from her hiding spot to meet Magda's gaze. With steel nerves at the best of times and now pleasantly buzzed, Magda did not make a sound. The barkeep keyed into the severity of the situation and took the surprise in stride. Laney's deep-brown skin blanched with a pale clamminess. Rampant sweat beads dripped down all over her face and body. Immediately, Magda knew. Something was obviously, deeply wrong.

Laney spoke first in an urgent whisper.

"There's a situation... I-I can't explain it now, but I need to make your delivery to your place RIGHT now...it-it's... Laney nearly hyperventilated but choked through the words. "It's important. Give me your apartment fob and your code and I'll make the drop-off NOW."

Magda paused for a second before answering. She had never seen Laney so severe. Magda knew her friend was in deep with something.

"Is this gonna cause trouble?" Magda asked.

Laney shook for a second before replying.

"Probably."

Magda pressed a key fob into Laney's hand and whispered her apartment code.

"If we're gonna be partners in whatever crime this is, I want my code name to be Red."

"Thanks, Red." Laney gratefully mustered up a laugh and backed out of the door. She picked up the still boxed-up mystery man and wheeled him toward C+ Sector. Laney entered the residential elevator in Magda's building and punched the button for Magda's apartment. The old elevator shuddered alarmingly a bit and Laney began to panic about maximum capacity loads. *Relax, you're nowhere near the limit. Its just that nobody bothers to maintain these buildings.* When the elevator finally started up and began its ascent, she breathed a silent prayer of relief.

The short remainder of the journey into Magda's apartment went without a hiccup. Laney wheeled her John Doe across the threshold into the living area of the studio. Inside, C+ Sector apartments were the same as C Sector except that, being above-deck, they had windows that opened to the outside. Laney opened the box and laid John Doe onto the couch that sat across most of the room. The man had not stirred.

Laney sat on the floor, entirely too tired to bother to situate herself more comfortably in a chair. She waited. The adrenaline had worn off and she felt exhausted, but anxiety kept her awake. She sat on the floor nervously rocking back and forth. Her eyes scanned around, noticing the few personal objects Magda had peppered throughout her small living space. A silver badge hung above a metal mantel, commemorating Magda's time as an EMT. A harmonica sat on a small end table next to the bed. The VerchLife projector helmet, ubiquitous in every home below A sector, sat tucked in its charging bay. Laney looked out the C+ sector window. Her view consisted of the front face of a building identical to the one she currently sat in.

What felt like hours passed. More than a few times, Laney thought she heard a murmur or saw an eye-twitch from the unconscious man. She looked back to his still, silent body and convinced herself it was just the anxiety. Laney had no idea of the real time that had passed when the front door opened.

Magda stepped in. She held a steel canteen in her hand and smelled of ale and sickly-sweet vape pens. She stood frozen on the spot. The elephant in the room, the unconscious, unknown, and unnerving man, drooped passed out on her sofa.

"You said you were making a delivery," said the barkeep.

"I did make the delivery," Laney said. Laney pulled the cheddar grass from her zipped breast pocket and dropped it on the ground. Silence filled the room until Magda couldn't stand the tension.

"What happened?" Magda asked.

"He's from the surface...from..f-from..." Laney trailed off, trying to find better words before blurting, "He's from off-arc, out there, and security tried to kill him!"

Magda dropped her canteen. The metal bottle clanged against the floor. Hoppy-smelling, amber liquid pooled around Magda's well-worn shoes. Magda sank into a nearby chair and lamented,

"Surface. Holy shit! This is-"

Before Magda could finish her sentence, both women's eyes drew toward the same grunting, coughing sound that precedes someone waking up from a long, hard sleep. The deep, sunken eyes of a withered and wild face opened and stared hard at the pair of them. John Doe was awake.

Chapter 5

"Where am-who are-what?" The man spoke a slurry of incomplete questions. His eyes were still glazed-over somewhere between waking and sleep. He twitched his arm and stiffened his back struggling, unable to move into anything but a reclined position. Magda looked around the room and back at the now-semi-conscious John Doe. She whispered in Laney's ear.

"The tranquilizers designed by arc security are designed to wear off slowly in stages. While you're under, you regain cognitive and speaking capabilities before you get motor skills and ambulation. Eases interrogation."

"Shit, shit, shit, what do we do!?" Laney asked.

Magda grabbed Laney by the shoulders and stared directly into her eyes. Her large, forceful hands held Laney in place, calming her frayed nerves, commanding her attention.

"We have got *maybe* thirty minutes to convince this man who's never been on this arc! Who has no idea where he is or who we are! Who is clearly wanted *dead* by security *not* to get up and bolt the second he regains control of his legs. If we don't and he gets loose, most likely arc security will finish the job, kill him, and *we*," Magda looked even sterner as she pointed at Laney and herself, "will both be in deep, deep shit!" Laney breathed out before sucking in a quick gulp of air.

"Understood."

Laney crouched before the man and opened her hands. She splayed her fingers with her empty palms, facing him. She spoke in the calmest and most measured voice she could summon in this dire situation.

"Someone tried to hurt you," she corrected herself, "to *kill* you when you climbed the arc." At the mention of the arc, the man's eyes narrowed, distressed and confused. He thrashed a little, shaking his full body. His leg extended fully from the knee and both women saw the man's ankle flit about, looking for purchase on the sofa. Magda's volume rose.

"Shit, that kinda muscle control is *not* supposed to happen that fast! Better cut the clock in half to fifteen. Laney, how fast can you make a friend?"

Laney changed tactics. "I am Laney. This is Magda. I saved you. We want to help you."

The man writhed, unaffected by Laney's words. Between incoherent grunts, Laney finally caught a word she recognized from the thrashing man. "Where? Antler... one...skull?" Laney's eyes lit up. She remembered what she'd thrown under a tarp in auxiliary bay. She bolted towards the door.

"Magda, *trust me*, I will be right back."

"Where are you goi—"

Before Magda could protest, Laney was gone. The front door to Magda's apartment slammed shut with a decisive *thwack*.

Magda stood up and eyed the squirming man. A leg and an arm flailed, fighting through numbness and muscle spasms, becoming more practiced and articulate by the second. Magda briefly considered restraining the man, but figured that would likely end any chance of convincing him she didn't wish him harm. She hoped against hope that Laney knew what the hell she was doing, and more importantly, that she could do it *fast*.

Laney bounded. Her powerful legs pumped in a practiced rhythm.

Wind whistled past her ears. She flew out of Sector C, across the promenade, down the stairwells, and over the gap in the fence. She found the inauspicious tarp thrown over an animal cranium tucked in an unassuming corner of aux bay. Laney found the one-antlered skull. *Hope to God this works!* Sides in stitches and heaving, Laney grabbed the skull and flew back up the stairwells. She pressed through the pain, and reached the top deck unimpeded. As Laney stepped out onto the deck and began her stride, a telltale mosquito voice stopped her dead in her tracks. It whined through her ears, drunker than when she'd heard it last.

"Where you headed, gorgeous?"

"What the hell?" The words fell right out from Laney's lips as she turned around.

The mosquito man continued, drawing closer, eyeing the one-antlered skull. "What have ya got there?" he asked pointedly.

Shit! Laney cursed inwardly as she hid the skull behind her back. *Why did I not grab that fucking tarp?*

"Nothing!" Laney lied. Out of options, she stood waiting for something brilliant to come to her. *This pissy fucker would be exactly the type to turn me in for suspicious activity. Myself, Magda, and Mr. John Doe Mystery Man, would be entirely fucked.* The mosquito man leaned in, eyeing the skull. Laney blurted.

"Oh, this! This is a wall decoration from the aux bay. We're gonna install it in an A Sector house next week. I do storage and requisitions for Arc Interior Solutions. I also do touch-ups on the side, and this one's broken." Laney gestured to the cracked-and-broken nub on the skull. The mosquito man swayed, regaining balance in his loafers before he answered.

"Oh, always on the grind. I like that. I'm afraid we may have got off on the wrong foot earlier and I can't help but feel like the setting might've had something to do with it." He delivered his lines with practiced, well-oiled ease. "Call me. We'll go to a nice quiet place in B Sector. Much more refined than some public corner of the promenade." He handed Laney a thick business card with his apartment phone code printed on it.

"Will do," Laney lied. She sensed any other response would add precious seconds - seconds that she could *not* afford to spare to this already unnecessary conversation. Luckily, he let her go. Laney speed walked across the promenade until out of sight before she shifted back into a full sprint. She sped back to Magda's.

Laney flung open the door. She saw John Doe press his body up from the sofa and stand in an awkward, unbalanced stance that nevertheless held his weight. He took a step forward, and then another.

Magda shouted to Laney,

"He's almost out of here! Do something!"

Laney thrust the smooth, worn animal skull into the man's hands. His fingers gripped its cranium.

The man stilled and fell silent. Magda and Laney watched as John Doe collapsed to his knees, and Laney heard a small voice murmur.

"Thank... you."

He trembled for a moment before speaking again. "You... brought... it. You... brought... them." Deep pauses filled the air between his shaky words. Syllables sounded labored, as if they were fighting their way past a lump in his throat. The man wrapped the skull tightly within his arms and held it against his chest as he lay on the floor.

Them? Laney questioned.

Magda, confused, looked askance at Laney.

"What just—"

Laney cut her off violently, waving her arms to shush her as she drew their attention back to their stowaway.

Silent tears of exhaustion and pain spilled from the man's face as he sat on an unfamiliar floor in this strange, unknown place. He cradled the only familiar thing he had in the world.

Laney closed in and put a hand on the man's shoulder. That was all it took. Emotion finally overtook the man, tears streaming down his ridged and weathered face as he released muffled, strangled sobs. Laney wrapped her arms around the man's shoulders and squeezed gently as he held the skull and cried. For the first time, Laney got a good look at his face: He was beat to shit. He had dark-circled, deep-set eyes that looked like they had seen hell. Unspoken pains and tribulations etched themselves across his face in haggard lines and misshapen scars. His skin was deep-tan, rough, covered in dust, and had many small pock marks.

Laney stayed on the ground with him, giving the best gesture of comfort and sympathy she knew how to give. She held him until his shoulders stopped shaking and he took in and let out a few long shuddering breaths that slowly evened out. The tears fell from the man's face slower and slower until they stopped.

He looked up at Laney and Magda.

"Sorry...I-I thought...I...was last...last one...none left...alone."

He took the deer skull and stared into its empty eye sockets before looking again at the two strangers. His shaking hands slowly placed the skull on the coffee table before reflexively reaching back to grab it. He performed this same series of actions two times more. Laney watched this curious set of movements and understood. She spoke softly to the man.

"It's okay. Everyone has their familiar treasures and comforts. This is obviously very important to you. Hold it as long as you need to."

Watching the scene unfold, Magda decided to do what she did best in times of great stress: dole out drinks and comfort in equal, generous measure. She set her electric kettle to boil and grabbed three mismatched cups. She opened a small tin on her mantle and pulled out three pinches of dried leaves, dropping each pinch into one of the cups. As she stowed the tin back on the mantel, she heard the friendly electronic chirp that let her know the water was now boiling. She poured hot, steaming water from her kettle into the mugs. The warm, sweet, flowery smell billowed from the steam. It wafted through the air, filling the room with a pleasant scent. Magda occupied the minutes spent waiting for the tea to cool to a drinkable temperature by searching her pantry and mini-fridge for a suitable meal. It had been a few days since she'd bought anything on a shopping day, and all she had left in the mini-fridge were Nutri Logs. She pulled shrink-wrapped packaging off of a solid gray stick and slapped it on a small ceramic plate. The tube wriggled for a second or two after its plating, as it always did.

Magda placed three mugs of tea on the coffee table before taking the inaugural sip. She sipped slowly and deeply as she flitted her eyes between Laney and the now tranquil-mystery man. Laney sipped carefully, and the beleaguered man took one hand off the skull to take his mug. His eyes closed tightly and he tipped back the insulated mug, trying to drink the whole thing in one speedy gulp. The hot liquid on his lips and tongue stopped him, and he placed the mug back down on the table and smelled its steam. His eyes watered, and his nose wrinkled. Magda laughed in a way that was too good-natured for anyone to think she was laughing *at* them.

"It's alright, there's plenty. It's not going to leave you." She herself slowed down, taking an exaggeratedly gentle sip of the hot beverage to get the point across. The man watched intently and followed suit following the slow sipping motions of the women.

Something in the warm floral taste of this drink brought him back to something buried deep within his memory— something he had forgotten he'd forgotten. Images of a little hut and a pot with bubbling liquid drifted into his mind. People who looked like him sat around a little fire, drinking and laughing. The newly summoned memory felt cloudy. It faded away, like the steam rising from the cup in front of him.

Magda got up and returned to the kitchen area. She placed the plated Nutri Logs in front of the man. Before she could hand him the taste fork, he had scarfed down the whole log. Laney retched slightly at the gray tube's consumption and Magda chuckled.

"Must've been *really* hungry to eat one of those without properly fooling the senses first." Magda repeated the unpacking-and-plating process of another Nutri Log, this time catching the attention of the man.

"Slow, like the tea," she said. She grabbed a fork with a black plastic handle attachment and pushed a button labeled STEAK on the handle. The fork hummed, a buzzing low-voltage electrical current running through the tips of its tines.

Magda switched on the projector mode on the VerchLife helmet and pointed it toward the Nutri Logs sitting on the plate. A holographic projection of an eight ounce filet enveloped the pale, gray tube, obscuring reality in its virtual facade. She then used the fork to carve off a bite of the "steak," to show the man how to use it more than anything else. She handed him the buzzing fork. He took a bite, this time with all the trappings of this bizarre custom. He ate slowly with this utensil that felt foreign in his hand.

The taste was both there and not there. Fleeting, ephemeral, like the negative violet-and-green remnants one sees after closing their eyes against a bright light. Still, this phantasmal approximation of haute cuisine opened entirely new sensations of taste and richness for a man who had grown accustomed to the lean and rotting wild stuff of an Earth turned to waste. Magda laughed again as the man's eyes widened and he ate with increasing speed.

"It's not the same as the real thing, but it's better than the stuff on its own." Magda poured the man another cup of tea and the three drank as he finished his food. The atmosphere settled. It seemed, for now, that the man would stay. Laney and Magda no longer worried about his immediate departure.

"What is your name?" Laney asked, unable to resist the question, as hungry for knowledge as the man was for food. The question hung in the air in heavy silence before the man started on an answer.

"I... "used to be Uli. Those that called me Uli—" The man paused for a good long while before finishing his sentence. "Gone." He seemed like he wanted to continue. Laney felt a pang of sympathy.

"Take your time," she said with an attentive and gentle smile.

His words fumbled out, unsure of themselves. Syllables tied up and bumped into each other.

"I...don't. Don't want to be Uli...anymore. Name...hurts. Others... called me Uli...but others... gone... I... Need... new... name"

"Others!" Magda blurted, surprised. "Who are the others you are talking about?"

The man's face, lightened by the tea and the food, fell noticeably. He regained a pained expression and shifted uncomfortably, making himself smaller as he averted his eyes. Laney shot Magda a side-eyed glance. Magda threw up her hands in an affable and apologetic gesture.

"Sorry, sorry! Never you mind. There'll be time for all that later. Meantime, we have to call you something." She crossed her arms, resting her chin on the ridge of her fist. "Let's think about what we know about you— which ain't much admittedly.

Laney jumped in.

"When I first saw you, you were climbing up one of the arc's legs. That probably makes you the first person to ever try to climb the arc."

Magda eyed the strong, lithe frame of the man. "From the looks of you, you probably would've made it all the way up there if you hadn't gotten pricked in the neck by arc security."

The man brought his hand to the spot where the dart had pierced his neck and he shrugged. Magda uncrossed and crossed her arms again. "Heard the name Tenzing the other day at bar trivia. Sounded cool, seems like a good climber's name."

The man sat in silence, closing and opening his eyes several times before he spoke.

"Tenzing...will...do. I like Tenzing." The trio sat for a time and sipped their tea.

"How old are you?" Laney asked, taking in Tenzing's weathered face and body. Bolstered by a new name and soothed by the forces of hospitality, Tenzing answered with more confidence.

"I don't know. I lived in the village for thirteen years. Lived outside the village alone for that long. Maybe longer." The hard lines on his face and sunned, scarred skin suggested a man at least ten years older than that.

"You've lived hard for a long time, then," Laney sighed.

Tenzing stiffened.

"I lived. Stopped thinking of hard or easy a long time ago."

Everyone sipped their tea and the silence in the room billowed like a slowly filling balloon, that was finally burst by Laney.

"It's late," she offered lamely to the room, looking toward Magda expectantly with raised eyebrows. Magda got the hint and turned toward Tenzing.

"You can stay here for a while. It's safe enough. We've got food, water in that jug over there, and a place to sleep that's not out in the sun."

Tenzing nodded and Laney felt his eyes pierce right through her

"Why do you help me?"

Magda and Laney sat looking uncomfortably at each other, and then back at Tenzing. Laney spoke first, words tumbling out awkwardly as she tried to put voice to the rapidity with which she had been thinking during the whirlwind rescue.

"I...I saw you about to die and I did what came naturally. I mean, I *was* technically trespassing when I saw you, and authority being what it is...well, and then I saw the dart, so I knew it was the authorities who had basically just tried to *kill* you, and...well I guess I just had to help. It seemed like the right thing to do and...and I'm gonna see it through. *Plus,* I and *everyone else* on this big fucking tub of lies have been told that the *only* people left on the planet are on this arc! That anybody left in the wasteland died out decades ago. Obviously, you're proof enough that that's not true, and I need to make sure you stay alive long enough so that I can figure out what else I've been lied to about my whole life! And why."

Tenzing studied Laney's face as she finished speaking, searching for signs of subterfuge and finding none. Her face seemed natural and earnest.

Magda decided it was time to offer her own explanation, and her booming voice filled the room.

"Me, I'm getting old and bored, and anything that fucks with the plans of the people who run this shit can is alright to me!" She rasped out an infectious laugh, and it wasn't long till all three of them were chuckling. There could certainly be no doubt about the older woman's forthcoming nature.

Tenzing brought his head down and folded his hands. He looked again at the pair who had saved his life.

"Thank you." His words felt surer than ever. *It feels good to speak to people again.* Even as the thought occurred to him, he looked back to the deer skull reflexively, awash with a strange sensation of guilt and embarrassment. *It feels even better to be spoken back to, really spoken back to.*

Despite his joy at being able to converse normally for the first time in over a decade, Tenzing felt an overpowering wave of exhaustion cresting on the horizons of his subconscious. He handed his mug to

47

Magda, lied down on the sofa, and passed into a deep sleep with the practiced ease of someone who'd learned to fall asleep fast, never sure how many hours of sleep they would be allowed.

Magda and Laney huddled together to plan. They decided Magda should entertain and see to their guest during Laney's day shift, and Laney would do the same for Magda's evening bar shift. Laney would stay here for the night in case anything happened.

After settling the logistics for their nascent fugitive-harboring plan, the two retired for the evening, Magda in her bed and Laney on a cot in the corner of the room facing Tenzing on the couch. Laney lied down on the cot and fell asleep almost instantly, her body and mind desperate for rest, exhausted from both a full day's work and a full night of saving a man who should not exist, according to her official education.

Magda washed everyone's mugs and retreated to her bed to smoke half a pipe of the cheddar grass Laney had retrieved. Her usual aches and pains lulled themselves into a pleasant, buzzy, numbness as she mused—, *Ah, great stuff, and it was the whole reason Laney was in exactly the right place at exactly the right time to save Tenzing. Everyone who said I should quit this stuff is an idiot.*

Tenzing's body lay catatonically still in his slumber. For the first time in longer than he could remember, the wild man of the waste, newly christened as Tenzing the arc climber, knew *comfort* as he slept. Speech and a desire to be among humans had returned to his psyche faster than he'd ever thought possible. The smell and taste of warm tea and non-rotting food plus the warm comforts of hospitality and trust had stripped away the edifice of animalistic stoicism that had encased him for far too long. Gone was the concept of survival as the only motivator, a mental prison that he had worn for so long, like clothes that protected and shielded but still fit poorly.

For all the time that Tenzing had lived alone, he had never fully succeeded in casting out the hope that he would find other people somewhere. Some small part of him could never give that up. Now, he'd found them. Real people. Kind people. He had spoken with them out loud. He smiled in his sleep. That small part of him, that part of him that never went away, had been right.

His peaceful sleep was interrupted by a choir of voices. He saw in his dream the one antlered skull, gigantic and floating, wreathed in white mist. It stared down at Tenzing, its eye sockets filled with a spectral flame of green that filled the space of its missing and broken antlers.

The green turned from fire to flowering vines. It spoke in a multitude of voices all at once. Tenzing remembered the voices— voices of those bodies that trembled and shook from the vibrations of gigantic, behemoth footsteps. Voices of bodies that lay still, never to speak again, their laughter around fires never to be heard again. The voices of bodies he had left to that terrible sound as he'd run away in fear.

Tenzing trembled. He shook, powerless to hear anything else but the multitude of disparate voices falling from the skull's skeletal maw. They commanded him in otherworldly harmony.

"DONOTFORGETWHATTHEYDIDTOUS"

"DONOTFORGETWHATYOUMUSTDO"

Chapter 6

Laney's body woke to the rhythm of her routine. Her mind would have preferred sleep, but aux bay employment called.

She pulled on her coveralls and tiptoed through Magda's apartment, careful not to wake either of the other occupants. She looked at Tenzing, still sleeping, and noticed he had turned his deer skull still sitting on the coffee table in the center of the room, at precisely the angle where (if it had had eyes) it could have kept watch on both Laney and Magda in the night.

An imaginary deer eyeball transfixed as a sentry upon each one of them. Laney recalled a nature documentary of Old Earth she'd chanced upon in VerchLife media archives. Deer eyes, like many prey animals, dwelt far to the side of the skull, to keep watch for predators stalking from angles outside a forward view.

Predators. Prey. Was this how Tenzing thought of us?

Hard to blame the guy for being a little paranoid with everything he's probably been through. Real trust comes slow. Laney poured herself a drink from Magda's water allotment container. She gulped it down and set off on her commute.

As she walked, Laney kept her eyes forward and spoke to no one. The arc drifted away ,and she stayed in her head. Her body and mind limped, emptied from the tumult. To muster a passable greeting was a task beyond her current capacity. The thought of Tenzing's life held in her hands scraped up and down her nerves, little cuts unseen on the body but nevertheless causing injury. She didn't know how long she could maintain a facade of normalcy were she to engage in everyday pleasantries. A wrong "good morning" or strange "hello" might doom an already-doomed man.

Laney turned to other matters. The whole "harboring a fugitive '' situation was kind of like staring at the sun. It was just too big and too much to think about, so it was easy enough to push those thoughts from her mind. The worrying remained, shifting to the small stresses of her shift that really didn't matter.

So and so is missing their lampshade, Mr. Whats-It's desk came in damaged, a chair's legs are damaged and it wont stand up. Trivial matters kept pinching her like an ever-replenishing cloud of gnats. Irritated by this odd contradiction, Laney drew nearer to aux bay, praying that today would be a light day, knowing full-well it wouldn't matter. Without fail, every time she *really* needed a break, the A and B Sector crowd would all the sudden "*really* need their things today," and her job requirements would amp up. *If I am ever in a position where the requisition of old-world furniture and knick-knacks becomes an emergency to me, my life must be pretty fucking good, and I would never complain about another thing.* Resigning herself to the day it would be, Laney tried hard not to think about much of anything as she descended the final stairwell to auxiliary bay. *Let's get this over with.*

Arriving, she saw two unfamiliar faces standing outside the security gate. One wore green maintenance coveralls with the Arc Repair corporate logo on the back, and the other preened about in the black uniform of arc security with a lapel pin reading *Harold Harkness: Senior Security Officer* affixed front and center to his chest. The security officer marched toward Laney.

Act normal, play dumb, Laney thought.

"Hi how are ya?" Laney offered to the pair of men. The man in maintenance coveralls said nothing and busied himself fiddling with the door sensor module. The senior security officer addressed Laney with an unblinking stare. He thumbed his notes on a tablet before speaking in a low, sticky drone. The voice sounded to Laney as if spit-up chewing tobacco had developed an enthusiasm for speech. She braced as the words drip-dropped from his stained, toothy mouth.

"Miss Quist, is it?" He looked up from his odd, circular tablet and waited for Laney to nod. Laney hated that security personnel had the right to employee records for every business on the arc. "We are doing an inspection on this door module. There have been some irregularities with the sensors that warrant an investigation."

"What's the problem?" Laney asked.

The spit-up chewing tobacco voice continued,

"It is sensing fires where there are none. Now, fires are not typically subtle affairs. If there were a fire here, wouldn't any of the other doors on this deck have picked up something like that? Wouldn't we see any soot, or char, or some kind of remnants of there having been something burning? It's odd that it'd malfunction like this in just this manner. Wouldn't you agree, Miss Quist?"

Laney matched the officer's stare, watching every pronounced syllable trickle from his lips. She deciphered everything about Harkness from that slow, syllabic trickle. The man loved to talk, loved an audience, loved to make them squirm.

Laney would not squirm. She responded,

"You know, weird things happen with old tech. Maybe somebody snuck down here for a smoke— no camera down here and all." She watched a near-imperceptible wince within the officer's eye and knew this last line about no camera would really dig under the man's skin. The man grumbled through gritted teeth.

"Yes, the area is under proprietary information of Arc Interior Solutions. No cameras."

"You should have seen the NDA I had to sign to move these chairs around in the first place. Designers are ter-ri-fied of their inventory lists getting public before they announce them," Laney said as she squared out her shoulders and took up more space.

"Assets may be proprietary, but employee IDs are not," the officer returned. "I will be speaking with Misters Wallace and John after I've finished with you, Miss Delaney Quist."

Ooh full name. Again. The line about cameras must have gotten to him. Laney eyed the officer up and down. He had a slovenly appearance uncharacteristic of most Security personnel—a grizzled patch of graying stubble with only a hint of black flecked the bottom half of his face. He sported a slight paunch and leaned heavily on his truncheon and the nearby railing. He had a strong odor of cologne, masking a fainter smell of some heavy alcohol just below his breath. Only his uniform and the perfect placement of badges and pins displayed any pride or upkeep. Laney thought he looked comical.

Then she saw his eyes; a hatred lurked in those eyes. Laney understood from those eyes that this man would do any savage, violent act if just given permission.

Laney took a step back as the security officer clenched the truncheon he carried and twisted it against the top of his black leather boot. He bared his weight down and rested his thumb atop the baton just in reach of the switch that could electrify the weapon's end with a thoughtless flick. He spoke between clenched teeth.

"Maybe your smoke theory is correct. Maybe not." The security officer chewed on the words as he drawled. Syllables took seconds each to spill like slow molasses from his smirking lips. "Miss Delaney Quist, I will go speak with the delivery team for this auxiliary bay now."

He pored over his circle shaped tablet and made an exaggerated display while checking personnel files. "They should arrive any second. Arc Interior Solutions' auxiliary bay has been open for three minutes now, but this file states Wallace and John Danvers are guilty of perpetual, habitual lateness. Perhaps I can run into them on their way here. Please do be careful and watch out for anything out-of-the-ordinary. Remember, the arc strides on when we *all* do our part."

The old adage every authority figure repeated to every child since birth. It rolled right off Laney's brain like always, a cliche rendered useless and annoying through endless repetition.

Laney thought of the security officer with his comments on her coworkers' lateness, and his using her full name. She looked over toward a bay full of furniture and knick-knacks. *Fucking chairs get more legal privacy than employees.*

Laney watched the oily security suit depart. She crept up and checked around the corner to see the elevator doors close behind him. Laney returned and spoke to the man in green coveralls.

"What's your name?"

"Aaron Gonzales," the man squeaked. Laney noticed his hands shook as he struggled to tighten the last face plate on the door's sensor module.

"Are you okay, Aaron Gonzales?"

Aaron spoke without making eye contact.

"That guy made me nervous. Kinda scared the shit out of me. Whole thing was weird, like *really* weird for security to be involved. Especially someone with such a high rank for something like this."

"Weird indeed," Laney agreed, her eyes distant as she thought. She looked back to the terrified repairman suppressing a still visible shake. *He didn't need any of this. He's just fixing things.*

She fumbled in her pocket and grabbed an old coupon for Coconut Joe's Magda had given her a while back. She unfolded the crumpled, slick plastic-paper and pressed it into the man's sweaty palm.

"Take this—, one drink on the house. Talk to the loud woman with red hair. You can't miss her. She's a friend. A good friend."

Aaron's face lightened.

"Thank you," he said. He finished the last screw on the door module's OK and walked off. Laney wondered what douchebaggery Mr. Chewing Tobacco Voice performed to scare this innocent third party so much. *No telling. Maybe his eyes were enough.* Laney prepared for work. She lifted her key card to the newly serviced door module and stumbled into the aux bay, head swelling with thoughts. Laney ran through the facts of her recent encounter with security.

They don't have a corpse to ID, so they figure their wanted man ran off or still got aboard the arc. Probably think the latter since they're obviously still looking for him. Given the layout of the arc, this auxiliary bay is one of the only places someone could see the arc's legs. They figure if their fugitive made it aboard, somebody had to have helped him and somebody working this bay would be the logical first place to look. So they start cracking heads here.

They don't have anything concrete to say it's me— other than the imaginary fire I conjured, there's nothing too out-of-the-ordinary in my key logs. I went to Magda's last night, so there's no record of my return home last night, but that could just be a social visit. Nothing that screams "red flag"...

But many repeat-visits to Magda's place might put it under the microscope. Top priority needs to be figuring out a more permanent place to hide Tenzing. Laney reached this resolution as she heard a familiar voice.

"Laney, what the fuck is going on? Some hopped up prod-pig in a security jumper just stopped us on the way here. Kept asking what we knew about the damn door and seeing if we knew about anything out-of-sorts."

A second raspier voice piped up from a slightly taller, significantly lankier body offering only a corroborative,

"Yeah."

"Hey Wallace. Hey John," Laney said. Wallace, a mountain of muscle built like a human fist cocked his head at Laney's non-answer, clearly waiting. Laney sighed at the pair.

"You know arc security. Any excuse to shit on somebody with less than them."

This brief diatribe satisfied John who walked away from the conversation and put on a VerchLife helmet. Wallace yelled toward John.

"I keep telling you bro, you're not gonna get anything in life if you've always got your head plugged into that damn fantasy helmet."

Wallace stopped. He realized his younger brother could not hear him, already plugged into some virtual world, doing God-knows-what. Laney felt a twinge of guilt seeing the exchange as her eyes rested on John. Her thoughts ran through a familiar, rehearsed loop: *I tried to stop it. They built it anyway. I can't beat myself up forever.*

Laney turned her head back to Wallace who spoke to her in a clear and tired voice.

"Laney, whatever you've got going on, I'm not gonna narc, but keep me out of it. I've got my kids to look after." Wallace glanced toward his younger brother laying on top of a nearby storage crate, nearly comatose in some virtual world. "And his dumb ass."

Laney saw real fear, real worry in her coworker's eyes ..

"I'm sorry," she said. "I really am sorry."

Wallace returned to the more casual tone Laney heard everyday.

"It's gonna be a rough day for you— aft loading dock was shut down for about two hours yesterday, so yesterday's incoming auction shipment got delayed. It's coming in *on top of* today's shipment."

Laney's brow furrowed. The back of her mind ran some calculations.

"That's weird," she mused, "they never shut down the loading bay."

Wallace didn't look up from his delivery manifest.

"Yeah, I heard from a friend of mine who works aft dock, there was some mechanical failure with the cargo bridge. Typical. Whole arc seems to fall apart more every day. Everybody was dismissed while they worked on it— security claimed some potential breach. Didn't let anybody near it."

Laney's stomach clenched.

"What time did the loading dock shut down?"

"Late afternoon, early evening. I know some B Sector folks were upset because it was shopping day and fresh oysters got left off and didn't make it to the menus." Wallace answered offhandedly as he dragged his thumb across his delivery manifest. He paused.

"Why do you—?" But when he looked up, he didn't see Laney anymore. She had left the conversation and paced to the other side of aux bay.

The realization struck her like lightning.

The time aft loading dock was closed would put it exactly within the margin Tenzing was shot. There are very few spaces on the arc with a sight-line of the legs, and the aft loading dock is one of them. That has to be where Tenzing's sniper took the shot. And if the aft loading dock was shut down...

Laney's mind stumbled at the implication. *This was not some rogue officer who just happened upon a wasteland straggler by sheer chance and decided it was a good opportunity for target practice. Only someone with serious credentials could authorize shutting down the whole aft cargo bay. They would need the blessing from the board of directors. This knowledge of people in the waste has got to go pretty high up the ladder...but why would they lie to everyone about this?*

A wretched beeping derailed Laney's thought-train. A nearby console squawked and sputtered,

"RETRIEVAL MANIFEST RECEIVED. RETRIEVAL MANIFEST RECEIVED."

She shuffled over and glanced at the long list of what she had to accomplish. Her heart sank as her eyes drew toward the first item.

With a deep sigh, she thought, *Solving a societal level mystery and saving a man's life will have to wait. Right now, I have to find someone's antique, hand-carved chairs.*

Chapter 7

Earlier that morning, Magda rose early. She ducked into her kitchenette and decided that an unusual day demanded a fortifying breakfast. Tenzing woke to a strange, unfamiliar noise. He pried himself up from his cushions and homed in on the source of the sizzling sound.

"What are you doing?" he asked.

"Making us breakfast," Magda answered. "As a privilege of my C+ Sector salary, I am allowed purchasing rights for eight eggs a month. This morning, we are eating four of them."

"Eggs from what?" Tenzing asked.

Magda scrunched her face for a second before she processed the question's meaning.

"Chickens. They're birds useless for about everything other than eggs, meat, and shit production. Last ones in the world, so they say. She shifted her eyes toward Tenzing.

"But they say a lot."

"Where are these chickens?"

"They've got a couple hundred of em slammed in a little space on Arc Charlie with some of the other animals." Magda flipped the pan, browning the underside of eggs over easy.

"Chickens probably can't live out where you were?" she asked.

"Fat birds, none-too-bright, can't fly so well?"

"No chance," Tenzing said. "Things don't live in the waste. They survive."

Magda pried the egg's corners with a spatula lifting the now-firm-but-flexible white-and-yolk mass onto two plates. Tenzing watched Magda's precise and delicate movements as she worked.

"Here ya go." Magda dropped the breakfast plate in front of Tenzing.

He leaned over the steaming egg on the plate. His mouth watered—the smell affected him unlike anything he could remember.

Magda opened a package from the pantry and pulled out two light-brown, grainy-textured circular lumps. She put one on each plate with the eggs.

"This is a morning biscuit. It's a sort of nutrient-dense thick cracker. I get them in bulk." Magda put the now-fully-assembled breakfast plates on the table and pulled out two forks with thick black plastic handles from a drawer.

She took one for herself and handed the other to Tenzing.

"Push the button that says savory breakfast spices—on there," Magda said with a mouthful of egg. Tenzing looked at the four little bumps on the fork and the strange symbols next to each. His eyebrows drew together and he offered a mile long stare.

"Oh, sorry... probably not a lot of things to read out there eh?" Push the button closest to the blunt end of the fork." Tenzing pushed the button. The same small humming current from the last time he ate bubbled and buzzed through the fork. He took an experimental bite and tasted the egg and a multitude of spiced, warm, pungent flavors for which he had no names.

"Tech on those taste fork's can replicate spices and seasonings better than it can replicate the whole meal. In short, real eggs with fake spice taste better than fake steak with fake spices," Magda said.

Tenzing nodded. He ate slowly, savoring the sensations of each mouthful. The white-and-yellow bits filled Tenzing with a sense of nourishment—food that could build him and give him real strength.

This food was different from the half-rotted or sickly proteins he could scavenge in the wastes.

"Eggs are good," Tenzing said. He stared down at the now empty-plate and a grin curled across his pockmarked, weathered face.

Magda smiled.

"Well, these pale-yellow yolks aren't anything like what you'll get from the heritage hens they keep for brunch plates in upper-sector cafes." She took Tenzing's now finished plate and beamed at his grin. "But they are more than good enough for a morning like today."

The pair sat in amicable silence, enjoying the sensation of full stomachs. Tenzing spoke.

"What is this place?"

"What do you mean? This is my apartment."

Tenzing stretched his hands out as wide as he could make them and asked the question again.

"No, what is this place?" Magda grasped his meaning and fumbled for an answer.

"Oh, this is the arc. It's where we live."

Magda had no ready explanation. She had never had to explain the arc before. It was something everyone just knew. They knew and learned from birth. She tried anyway.

"It's a city— err, a home for people, and the city moves about. It walks." Faltering a bit, Magda looked over to the VerchLife helmet, and remembered the *History of the Arc and You* program, the default media program for most of the older model devices. She set the helmet in projector mode and pointed it toward a blank spot on the wall, selecting her intended program. A shaft of light shone across the blank wall, filling the space with a projected image. Tenzing watched in silence, struck by the vivid images of the strange device.

A triumphant musical swell framed an aerial shot of the arc. A skyline atop a gigantic metal body supported by six titanic legs plodded through a deserted landscape. Smaller models of the same machine walked at a distance, following the largest arc like camels in a great caravan.

A soothing voice poured from the helmet's speakers, wafting through the room as the image cut back to the shot of the largest arc.

"This is Arc Alpha." The image crawled from the front of the arc to the back. Huge, individual, pristine houses gave way to towering buildings with a modern feel, followed by a huge open space deck full of people and smaller commercial businesses. The image shifted back to the whole shot of the arc without ever zooming in on its back half.

"Unless you have a job on one of the satellite arcs, this is probably where you live," the voice over said. The screen cut through images of laughing children playing on the promenade, arc security officers waving with kind smiles, and office and service workers dutifully performing their respective roles.

"When the earth's natural cycles became too dangerous for human life," the screen flashed images of floods, fires, hurricanes, failing fields of corn and wheat, and faceless crowds brawling in city streets flashed in quick succession, "the brilliant inventor, business magnate, and humanitarian Lorne Ambrose, our founder, hatched the idea that would save humanity and preserve a way of life we all deserve."

The image cut to a middle-aged man, thin and clean-shaven. Tenzing did not recognize him. Magda scoffed.

"Lorne Ambrose wrenched civilization and prosperity back from the impersonal drivers of chaos seeking to doom humankind. He and his engineers dreamed up the very thing you live on today! Ambrose Industries materialized what others were too small minded to conceive."

The image switched to the same man sitting at a tablet on a modern-looking drafting table inside a clean home. Blueprints of what would later become the arc sat staged in discrete, disorderly, yet maximally visible piles on his desk. He pored over the documents, pen in mouth.

A singular bead of too perfect sweat rolled down his brow. He wiped it with an off white cloth that matched the color of the room.

"Brilliant visionary that he was, Lorne Ambrose dreamed this arc and put all his companies' combined resources toward its completion. He was so committed to the arc and all of us, he decided to go all in and move his entire home onto the arc itself, becoming its first, full-time citizen." The image flitted through a few shots. A modern looking mansion was crane-lifted piece by piece onto the front of the arc's deck.

"Whereas other efforts to save humankind have failed, we on the arc have prevailed! We stand as the survivors of this harsh planet. The human spirit to defy and build a life of value among chaos continues in all of us! Where all others have perished, we persist! May the arc stride on forever!"

Magda studied Tenzing as she mulled over the words she had just heard. It had been since school she had last heard that video. The line "All others have perished" felt hollow and left a wrong taste in her mouth.

If that lie is a crock of shit, what else is? Magda turned off the program and sat back at the table in the kitchen. She fidgeted with a spoon in her hands and looked toward Tenzing. The man sat quietly on the sofa waiting for her to speak or do something else. Magda wanted to know more about the world outside the arc, to pull at that thread of lies she had swallowed her whole life. She chuckled to herself. *A million little "facts" repeated millions of times all her life to construct a truth. But all it took was one man who wasn't supposed to exist sitting very much alive on her couch to shatter the whole thing.*

Magda remembered her faux pas from the previous night. Tenzing tensed up and shut down when she'd asked about the others he was with, out in the waste. Magda thought of her ample time bar tending. *Whenever people want to talk but can't, they can usually talk around a subject. Perhaps an indirect question will do.* Magda pointed to the deer skull sitting on the coffee table and asked. "Where did you find this?"

Tenzing's tan face turned a slight shade of red as he rested his hand over the skull.

"It hung in the hut where we lived."

Magda's ears pricked up, hearing the word "we." She leaned closer to ask,

"Did you find it, or...?"

Tenzing looked back at the skull and spoke in a quiet voice.

"I did not find it. It was found by another. They hung it in the hut where we lived to make the hut home."

A memory flashed within Tenzing's mind. His father's sister hung the skull over the threshold of the hut where they lived for a winter. A much smaller Tenzing, back then Uli asked her,

"Why do you put that up there? It doesn't do anything."

The woman in the memory smiled and spoke.

"A home is where you keep things that don't have to do anything."

The young boy bristled at the answer. .

"Why do you keep something that doesn't do anything?"

"Because keeping things that don't do anything means your living is more than just surviving," she said. "A home is where you are when you live, not just survive."

Magda waved her hand in front of Tenzing's face, drawing him out of a deep, vacant stare. Tenzing jolted up and asked,

"Where do you find the food on this arc?"

"We just ate,"Magda replied with a laugh. Tenzing laughed along seeing the good cheer and kindness etched in the many lines of the older woman's face. He looked around and saw many objects for which he could discern no function. He remembered the deer skull's commandments from his dream and felt tension at the back of his neck when he looked at the kind woman.

Tenzing shook slightly and spoke again.

"No, where does the food come from on this arc?"

Magda noticed a strange twitch in Tenzing as he asked the question. She got the distinct impression that Tenzing wanted to change the subject away from his past. *Okay, we'll go question-for-question. Seems fair enough, she thought.*

"We don't find our food. It's made on one of the smaller arcs and shipped over here."

Magda turned the *History of Arc and You* program back on and silenced the voice over. *It's easier to show than tell, and they won't be able to bullshit the technical details as well as they can bullshit our collective societal history.* The silent video feed resumed.

EMERGENCY BROADCAST SIGNAL TEST! EMERGENCY BROADCAST SIGNAL TEST!

The voice burst through the VerchLife helmet, overriding its silenced status. Flashing red-lettered text displayed the same message in the image projection. The VerchLife logo sat small in the image's corner, gently rotating. Tenzing reared back, placing himself as far back on the couch as he could.

"It's okay. It's okay," Magda reassured. "Just a routine test. This happens every week. There's never been any emergency. Not even sure why the board of directors still run that test. Probably some kickback to VerchLife now I think about it." Tenzing sat back down and Magda regained control of the holo-reel. The test ended and the video resumed.

Magda fast-forwarded to a frame of a stationary Arc Alpha. A smaller arc stood behind it. Hydraulic, telescoping beams outstretched from the end of each arc and interlocked in the middle, and a steel ramp extended from either arc, connecting the two through a large platform bridge. A combination of automated freight, carrying drones and human workers, carried cargo across the bridge from the smaller to the larger. Among the hundreds of boxes of cargo loaded and unloaded, the image zoomed in on plastic crates filled with colorful, ripe produce. The image lingered on the bright oranges and deep reds of carrots and radishes glistening with dewy shine. The image cut to cartons of speckled brown eggs and ice-filled packages topped with a rainbow of different fish, Among and whole. The succulent orange-pink flesh of a salmon filet entranced Tenzing's stare.

As Tenzing watched, Magda thought of Tenzing's answer to her earlier question and her question-asking strategy.

Her earlier query did confirm that Tenzing used to live with at least some other people. *Not earth shattering news, entirely— it wouldn't be possible for a person to survive on their own since infancy, but still something.* Magda studied Tenzing once more. He sat attentively, consumed entirely by the images upon the screen. Magda watched the man and thought of what she knew of his story.

Although he was at least twenty-seven by the years he'd recounted, he had lived alone in formative years without socialization, education, friends, family, or anything. Alone to deal with pains I could scarcely imagine. Developmentally at least, he is stunted, stuck somewhere younger than his biological age would indicate. Nature without nurture.

Magda returned to the conversation at hand and attempted to contextualize the images Tenzing sat taking in with rapt attention.

"Don't get tricked by how the video makes it look. We only get two shopping days a week."

"Shopping days?" Tenzing repeated the phrase in a confused tone.

Magda breathed out and started her explanation. "Shopping days are where there are new foods and items in all the stores around the arc and you go pick them out and give the store owners your money."

"Money?' Tenzing asked in the same questioning tone.

Magda hit fast-forward on the VerchLife helmet speeding over this topic, realizing she had absolutely no ability to explain purchasing, money, or any concept of commerce to anyone, let alone someone who'd grown up in a wasteland, presumably foraging for all of their meals.

"Okay *this* is how they *make* the food." Magda stopped the video on an image of a large hangar interior. A massive aquarium full of different types of fish swam about. The image homed in on a singular speckled trout swimming amidst a school of identical fish. Magda turned the volume on the holo-reel back on. The voice over resumed.

"Food production on the arc was designed with maximum synergy in mind. The fertilized and cultured water from the aquaculture deck flows directly into our hydroponics factory." The video showed a wide shot of thousands of white plastic vats arranged on hundreds upon hundreds of shelves. Each vat sat connected to each other by hoses through which water flowed. A single larger hose connected from the ceiling above to each shelf. Every row of vats contained a different fruit or vegetable with the image of each item plastered on the outermost edge of every aisle. Workers covered in sterile white uniforms and gloves picked and packaged immature broccoli from a row of vats dedicated to the crop, placing the harvested food stuffs in white plastic trays.

The serene narration continued.

"Mr. Ambrose did not want people aboard the arc to have to sacrifice their way of life. As many considerations as possible were taken to provide the logistics to maintain a cosmopolitan lifestyle aboard the arc." The image cut to the same speckled trout, served steaming over a bed of wild rice and broccolini. Tenzing let out an audible gasp as he saw the fish dinner. The flaky, juicy meat nestled atop the steaming rice and vegetables drew every ounce of his attention. His stomach yearned and growled for the contents of the delectable image.

"Can we have that?" he asked.

Magda let out a deep sigh. She had forgotten how aspirational and unrealistic the arc's official educational materials were.

"For that meal, you need to have some job that is at least above a C+. Anyone less than that wouldn't be lucky enough to eat like that more than once a year. You will be alright watching this for a bit— learn what you can. You'll figure out what's real and what's nonsense soon enough. I've got to get this." Magda picked up her apartment phone.

Tenzing only heard bits of the conversation before it faded entirely into the background. It was full of words that meant little to him. He stopped listening, entirely transfixed upon the rows and rows of water vat-grown vegetation filling the images. He saw more food in a single framed shot than he'd been lucky enough to happen upon in a year. Bright colors he had never seen on food among the dull browns of the waste clouded his eyes before the video feed shifted to something he could not comprehend.

The white shelves and vats of plants were gone, leaving a large room covered entirely with a deep red irregular surface lined with little streaks of pallid, silvery-white. The shot zoomed in on the red surface that covered the walls and hung down column-like structures connecting the room's floor to its ceiling. The close-up texture of the red surface pulsed quietly about once every second.

Tenzing's eyes studied the red material. Its color and texture most closely matched the texture of skinned and butchered deer he had eaten as a child in the village. Workers clothed in plastic coveralls and masks carried butcher knives, making delicate cuts into the walled mass of red flesh. They carved out chunks of the red substance and set it on little white foam trays.

The voice over resumed. "Citizens of the arc do not even have to give up meat from their diet. Our top scientific minds have discovered a way to grow live muscle tissues en masse along a biological substrate scaffolding."

A worker peeled back a portion of meat, revealing a wired caged structure housing plastic tubes running the length of the scaffolding. All along the tubes, smaller networks of branching tubing secreted cloudy white liquids beneath the facade of living tissues. The previous serene voice over grew in excitement as it spoke. "For those whose carnivorous inclinations demand a more traditional approach, arc scientists have got you covered as well."

The image panned nearby as two plastic-clad workers pulled two hooves from an aperture in another nearby flesh wall. Each worker grabbed a hoof in a tight grip and braced their stances. With a deep crouch followed by a rocketing of the legs, the workers leaned hard in the opposite direction throwing their whole weight into their pull. Furred hindquarters slathered in viscous, translucent red liquid slid slowly out of the aperture. What followed was the rest of a fully formed infant cow. The just-born calf opened its eyes as one of the workers took the creature in their arms off-screen. The calf did not return.

"Arc scientists have developed specialized free standing multi-species wombs. With our library of stored animal genetic material, we can still produce bespoke protein based culinary delicacies without the need for maintaining herds. Between cellular printing— both mass and custom—and live animal generation, the arc can produce *any* meat-based dish the stomach desires!"

The two workers walked to a nearby smaller aperture and pulled out a slick, newborn bleating lamb. Off in the distance, a mechanical arm extruded the cloudy cellular fluid into a filet-shaped mold.

Tenzing reeled back and looked toward Magda with bewildered eyes. Still on the phone, she looked over to the visceral display of protein generation and the expression upon Tenzing's face. She put down the phone for a second, and noticed what was on the video. Magda retched and then turned to speak.

"Ah, shit, I'm sorry about that. This all might be a little too much too soon." Magda walked over to the VerchLife helmet and turned it off again. "Really very sorry," Magda said as she looked sheepishly toward Tenzing.

Tenzing stood up and paced the confines of the small room. Several times, he dropped to his knees, holding his head within his hands before resuming his nervous trot. Magda watched him and thought of his captivity. *Poor man has found a hole to crawl into with plenty of food, water and a roof, but is bound by four hundred and fifty square feet and four steel walls. Not really much better than any prisoner. He can't live like this forever.*

Magda and Tenzing whittled away the next couple of hours watching VerchLife helmet projections about the arc. Tenzing took in everything that he could while Magda put the glossy, rose-colored tone of the propagandized infomercial in its proper context.

The morning turned into afternoon; the afternoon turned into late afternoon; late afternoon turned into early evening. Magda left Tenzing to his own devices. He had tucked himself within the confines of Magda's small, empty closet and seemed to be having a private conversation with the deer skull he kept. She didn't exactly understand the nature of Tenzing's relationship to the item, but gathered it was important enough to let him be.

Magda stood in the studio, getting ready for her bar shift. *Laney should be back at any minute.* Magda thought as she pulled on her boots and tightened her laces. She heard a knock on the door.

Shave and a haircut. That's just like her, Magda thought as she walked to the door.

"Laney's back," Magda announced to the empty room as she went to the door.

Magda opened the door and did not see Laney.

Oh fuck! she thought.

The black jumpsuit-clad figure of an arc security officer leaned into the apartment entryway placing his upper body between the wall and the door so it could not close. He left his feet still outside the threshold.

The man spoke in a sticky drawl that tumbled syllable-by-syllable out of a stained mouth.

"Miss Magda Erdos. Have you had any contact with a Miss Delaney Quist?"

Chapter 8

Vance tucked his arms toward his rib cage. Three hundred and fifteen pounds lay cupped in an overhand grip supported by the practiced alignment of his palms, wrists, and forearms. He held the bar's crushing weight just above his ribs.

"Come on, lightweight! Come on, Blondie! Get one more!" Above him stood the towering frame of Officer Santoro, egging him on. Vance hated those nicknames, a fact of which he knew Santoro was well-aware. That nagging irritation pushed Vance just a little bit more. The bar started up.

Vance summoned force through every muscle and gritted his teeth. Air forced out through a clenched jaw with the force of a geyser as he let loose a guttural growl. His throbbing, spent arms fought past their failure point. Finding that last little gasp of energy, pushing harder than the crushing weight's sinking, the barbell rose up, slowly shaking as it climbed.

"Come on! Come on!" Vance heard the screams of his lifting partner as his head felt like it would burst. Every fiber of his body shook with violence as he pressed past the tipping point. Vance locked out his arms. Santoro took the weight from him and pulled it onto the guard behind the bench.

"Hell yeah, O'Brien. You're starting to move weight like a machine!" Santoro cheered and threw his arms into the air. Vance could hear little as his partner's voice faded in the background. He felt pressure in his head and a burn in his chest. He breathed in and his lungs, heart, veins, and arteries evicted lactic acid's muscle burn with sweet, sweet oxygen. Vance flipped his body up from the bench like a sprung mousetrap, surging with accomplishment. He sauntered to the heavy bag in the fitness room's corner and threw his leg like a spear into the bag's center mass. His heel dug in a few centimeters before the bag moved. It flew backwards from the impact. Vance turned around and embraced Santoro in a small side-hug. They patted each other on the back as the bag swayed noisily from its chain behind them. A quiet voice wafted into the room.

"Good to see my officers maintaining their physiques." A tall, gaunt, severe-looking man stood in the doorway. Santoro and O'Brien snapped into a stiff, formal salute.

"Squadron leader Strickland, sir!" Their shout echoed throughout the fitness facility. The gaunt man walked forward, addressing O'Brien and Santoro with a deep, sustained stare. The man's head stayed perfectly still and his eyes seemed not to blink as he held his gaze on the officers. His raspy voice slinked through the air.

"At ease, officers." Squadron leader Strickland never spoke in anything above a moderate conversational volume. He didn't need to.

The two men relaxed their postures but held their eyes forward in silence, waiting for the man to address them.

"Santoro, you are dismissed." Santoro exited the room leaving O'Brien and Strickland alone. Strickland walked to the back corner of the room, crossing it with an immense stride. He covered the distance in what seemed like half the steps it would have taken Vance and stood at an angle to the mirrored wall that covered the back of the room. Vance stared into the mirrored wall directly ahead of him, the identical counterpart of the one that lined the room's back wall. In his far periphery, Vance could just see the side of his Squadron Leader's face. He couldn't see the man's eyes, but saw movement from the corner of his mouth. Vance listened.

"Lieutenant Vance O'Brien. You are a good officer."

"Thank you, sir," Vance barked.

"You keep fit. You pilot your retrieval drone admirably. You go above and beyond with hours. Your requisition and expungement counts are consistently high."

"Thank you, sir." Vance said again with a slight crack in his voice. He feared these compliments were the preamble to some vicious personal attack or terrible news. Squadron Leader Strickland crossed to the other back corner in too few steps.

"You maintain your equipment, your uniform, and your personal life with attentive success. I understand your daughter has recently changed schools. An educational level more suited to your in-laws' predilections, perhaps." Vance shifted uncomfortably. *How did he know that?* Strickland appeared back in the door-frame of the gym, facing Vance. Vance concealed his surprise at his superior's sudden apparition. Vance studied Strickland's face, searching for clues to the nature of their current meeting. There were none.

The face was guarded, unforthcoming in its details, angular and severe. He was an older man, but Vance could never tell exactly how old. He had a large forehead that seemed to stretch farther than it should. His head was bald on top with sides of neat-cut short gray hair. A sharp, beak like nose hung down his face below brown-green eyes that looked almost yellow. His whole appearance reminded Vance of the bald eagles Vance had seen in historical nature documentaries.

"Please meet me in one hour in my office in full dress uniform," Strickland said.

"Sir, yes, sir," Vance barked. He saluted, but noticed too late that the squadron leader had already left. Vance stood alone in the gym, unsure about what would happen in that meeting.

Everything he said was positive, but... Vance shuffled back to his quarters. He wanted ample time to ensure his uniform was in perfect condition for his impending meeting. *It'll be fine. Yes this man pretty much holds your life and your family's lives in the palm of his hand, but it will be fine.* Vance repeated the line to himself ad nauseam as he got into full dress.

He pulled on his gray dress shirt and tucked it into his black dress pants. Vance bent down and shined his dress boots, running a microfiber cloth over every square centimeter of black leather. He pulled on his overcoat and fastened each button on the double-breasted jacket. He gave a tug on the front to get out any creases and to ensure the coat hung straight on his muscled frame. Vance put each corner of his clip-on black tie through the buttoned-down collar of his impeccably ironed shirt and clipped the end of the tie with a tie pin. Finally, he put on his freshly shined officer's hat and his silver pin denoting his officer status, a metallic silver silhouette of Arc Alpha with one outstretched leg.

Vance would protect his person from any charge of negligence through uncompromising attention to detail. Vance thought of his wife and daughter and looked back at himself in the mirror. *Whatever this is, it's going to be good. I'll make it good. For them. I have to. For them.*

Vance left his barracks and made his way down a hallway into an elevator, pushing the button that would bring him to the top deck. All officers and enlisted security personnel lived in barracks below-surface, on the first deck above the arc's power plant. Vance left the elevator and strode across the open top deck toward the command tower at the front of the arc.

Security Arc, Arc Ghost's design was different. Whereas every other arc had high walls surrounding their decks, Arc Ghost kept only a steel post railing with wired crossbars stretching around the deck's outermost perimeter. Vance could see the outside world for what it was. No illusions on Arc Ghost.

Windswept plains bereft of life stretched far into the distance. Dust clouds and sandstorms clothed a ruined city in red-orange glow as waning sunlight refracted through turbulent air. Further still, heat lightning flashed. It sent silent sparks to illuminate a world that had long since lost any reason to be looked upon for more than a passing glance.

Vance looked around in every direction. He could not see the arc where his family lived. Arc Ghost, stayed far away from the other arcs in the caravan, invisible to the naked eye. It was smaller, faster, and had enough air power to intercept any threat from the wastes. It stayed away, like an eagle circling a wide distance around its nest. Unseen and unknown until it needed to strike. An invisible shield keeping the arc safe, a shield that was for the average arc citizen thoroughly out of sight and out of mind. This suited the security officers of Arc Ghost just fine.

Vance walked into the command tower. He walked straight through the front offices without a word to the two enlisted personnel on duty. Vance did not want any delay for his meeting and suspected discretion may be advisable for this requested conversation. The enlisted said nothing. Vance ascended the central staircase unimpeded. *Officer's rank has its privileges,* Vance thought.

Vance steeled his nerves as he rounded the corner and came to the solid brown wooden door marked 'Squadron Leader Strickland.' He held his breath and knocked twice. The sound of rustling of papers crept under the door before a voice followed.

"Come in."

Vance opened the door and saw Squadron Leader Strickland seated at his desk. He loomed, filling the office with his being.

"Have a seat." Strickland said. Vance obeyed and pulled out the small chair in front of the desk. The Squadron leader slid a manila folder across the desk in front of Vance.

"Open it," Strickland commanded in his usual quiet monotone. Vance obeyed. Inside the folder was a photo of another security officer he knew—one Senior Officer Harold Harkness. Vance winced. Squadron Leader Strickland went on speaking as if he hadn't noticed the younger officer's slight tic, but Vance knew better.

"I understand you and Harkness have a history." Vance nodded begrudgingly. Harkness had trained Vance when he was a cadet, and Vance remembered the brutal education he had received from the man.

Strickland continued,

"There is only one thing that displeases me more than complacency, and that is *sloppiness*. The man you see before you possesses both."

Vance spoke candidly for the first time in the meeting.

"Respectfully, sir, what does this have to do with me?"

Strickland leaned back in his chair and smiled.

"You are aware, of course, of The Circle?"

Vance nodded. A small council of the most senior and decorated security officers in the arc system. Informally, all real decisions regarding arc security were made in The Circle's back-room meetings.

"This man, Officer Harkness, was a member of The Circle until today. He now finds himself in violation of a few, severe rules regarding the comport of Circle members, and he is currently mishandling an important task which has significantly complicated the matter. The last straw has fallen for his continued membership."

Vance began to speak but the Squadron leader cut him off.

"Your assignment is as follows: You will take a heli-carrier to Arc Delta and wait there for it to dock. You will then proceed across the cargo bridge to Arc Alpha where you will apprehend Officer Harkness. You will cross back over to Arc Delta while it is still docked and secure

Harkness in your heli-carrier, then, you will return him here for his tribunal."

"Yes, sir." Vance furrowed his brow. "Sir, if I'm permitted to know, why am I assigned to this instead of one of the other Circle members, sir?" Vance thought he saw a thin smile hatch across the squadron leader's hawk-like face.

"Consider this your audition. One out, one in."

Vance sat back in his chair. Strickland took Harkness' photo from Vance and shuffled it back into its original folder.

"You are to report to the helipad first thing tomorrow. Wake at 0300 hours to carry out this task with—"the squadron leader slowed down as he strained the last two words, "*perfect discretion.*"

Vance immediately understood the gravity of the task. He stood up and saluted the commander.

"Thank you, sir."

Strickland studied Vance.

"Officer O'Brien, I have chosen you for this assignment because you possess qualities that Officer Harkness lacks. You are not complacent. You are not sloppy." He waved Vance away.

"You are dismissed."

Vance saluted again, opened the door, and descended the staircase, beginning the march back to his quarters. *Not complacent. Not sloppy.* Vance knew these words were as much a command as a compliment.

Vance retired to his quarters to sleep. 0300 would come early and he needed some rest. The thought came before he could process it. *Back to Arc Alpha. I can see Kayla and Lizzie!*

Immediately, the wind fell out of Vance as if his lungs had been punctured. The image of the squadron leader's thin lips coalesced in his head as they formed the singular deflating phrase. *Perfect discretion.* Vance looked over to the phone on his nightstand and picked it up. He held it to his ear and imagined Lizzie's babbling giggles and Kayla's sweet, tired voice singing melodies to their daughter. Vance put the phone down on its receiver. *Click.*

Chapter 9

Magda eyed the security officer. His breath drifted from his mouth. It filled her nostrils with rank odor.

"I am almost late for work. Do you mind if we walk and talk?" Magda said. She stepped out of her front door, pushing past the officer leaning across her apartment's threshold. He moved out of her way, and Magda shut and locked the door, closing her apartment to the unwanted intruder. She started her trek to Coconut Joe's, making her way towards her building's elevator. The security officer's face soured as he turned to keep step with the absconding barkeep.

"Laney, she's one of my regulars. Really good girl, couldn't find a more decent soul on this whole damn arc." Magda said.

The officer drawled,

"Well I spoke to Miss Quist this morning as I was checking up on faulty mechanics in her department, and got an uncanny feeling from our conversation. She seemed quite on-edge, as if something was deeply troubling her, but she was unable to talk about it." The officer leaned in to the last words drawing them out.

Magda clocked the man's scheme, fishing for information, hoping she'd incriminate Laney to save herself from whatever hammer security would inevitably bring down. She kept her cool.

"Well, I know Laney is stressed at work. She can't say much on account of the NDA, but there's been a *lot* of items passing through her warehouse lately, and I know she cares so much about maintaining all of them in perfect condition. Being so dedicated to her job and all."

The elevator opened. Magda and the security officer stepped out onto the promenade. The officer flipped his truncheon around in his hand before resting it on his shoulder. His voice softened slightly as he continued his drawl.

"Do call us if you see or hear of anything. The safety and well being of arc citizens is our number one priority."

The officer departed. Magda watched his pompous slink, rolling his boots from heel to toe in an exaggerated fashion as he strutted down the promenade. His words rattled around in her head like shrapnel. *Little fucker thinks he can scare me.* Magda eyed the officer. Waiting until he was a good distance away, she squinted one eye, held up her hand, and flicked at the officer's tiny body, imagining it sailing off the arc and falling to the earth. *Splat!*

With that sunny thought, Magda's mood brightened. She took a swig of hoppy amber liquid from her canteen and continued her commute.

Along her route, Magda spotted a brown-skinned woman with short curly hair in a jumpsuit marked with the Arc Interior Solutions logo. Magda panned her head to ensure the security officer was long-gone and walked toward Laney. Magda got within thirty feet of Laney, who was returning from work, and cocked her head violently to the left whilst rolling her eyes. Laney got the memo and changed course. The two stood against the back wall of a little commissary that served snacks, tobacco, and personal items to the buildings in this corner of C+ Sector.

Magda thrust her key fob into Laney's hands.

"Had to duck out early. They're sniffing around," Magda said. Laney replied, mirroring Magda's same hurried, hushed tone.

"I got a visit from—"

"Little pecker in a uniform with a voice like kitchen grease doing a book report?" Magda said, wiping an imagined smell from her nose.

"Actually, yes," Laney responded. "Fuck me, so he came by your place too? How'd he..." Laney trailed off. She ran through the list of people that could connect her to Magda.

Magda put her hand out, stopping Laney's finger counting. She urged her in a low, clear, commanding voice.

"That doesn't matter right now. All that matters is that it is only a *matter* of time before they concoct some excuse to search my apartment. And yours, most likely. Bloodhound came down to sniff around. He'll be back as soon as he can. Our mutual friend needs to be gone before then."

Laney ran her fingers through her curls.

"We'll have to move him tonight. I just hope he's ready." Magda let out a heaving breath and took a swig from her canteen.

"For all our sakes, he'll have to be."

Laney squeezed her eyes shut and pinched the bridge of her nose.

"Where am I even gonna take him?"

Laney leaned over and rested her hands on her knees, looking askance at Magda, but the older woman didn't respond.

"Mags??? Hey, Red!" Laney snapped her fingers, trying to get Magda's attention without success. Magda kept staring without a word.

Laney craned her neck and turned her head to find the object of Magda's gaze. Back between the buildings, the arc's silhouetted wall loomed untouched by the building lights that brightened pedestrian walkways. Amidst the shadowed steel, the pair could just make out an unused maintenance hatch.

"Huh,...the one place on the arc even security pretends doesn't exist. You think he'll *make* it down there?" Laney asked.

"He will have to," Magda replied.

The two women departed from each other, each knowing exactly what they had to do.

Chapter 10

Tenzing sat on the floor in the closet. He cupped the one-antlered skull in his hands and stared into its empty eye sockets.

"I will do what you ask of me."

Tenzing heard no response.

"I will find the way to tear down this city."

No response.

"What do you want from me?!" Tenzing's voice rose as he threw the skull. It crashed into the wall and fell on the floor in front of his crossed legs. The closet door opened and Tenzing reeled back.

"Are you okay?" Laney said. She met Tenzing's eyes in the dark. "I heard a thunk and yelling. Are you hurt?"

Tenzing saw the corners of Laney's mouth quiver.

"I am not hurt," he said. He stood up and exited the closet. Laney saw Tenzing's deer skull lay on its side on the floor. She bent down to pick the skull up, but Tenzing stopped her hand with a gentle push.

"No. I will look strange. I will stand out. It is not needed," Tenzing said.

"Well, you always look strange," Laney said with a smile. Tenzing chuckled and shut the closet door. He gleaned a troubled look etched on Laney's face hidden beneath her jest.

"What is the problem?" Tenzing asked. Laney ignored him and scurried around, gathering items— clothes, a package of morning biscuits from the pantry, and one of Magda's spare canteens filled with water. Laney threw all the items together in a small backpack she found rummaging through Magda's closet.

"What is wrong?!" Tenzing asked.

Laney stood still over the backpack filled with supplies. She turned around. Fear and anxious agitation filled her face.

"Tenzing, I'm sorry, the...the people after you. They're close! They are *tracking* Magda and I. We are a danger to you, and—"

"And I am a danger to you," Tenzing said.

"I'm sorry, Tenzing," Laney's voice broke and she turned around so she wouldn't cry.

"You have to hide somewhere else. I'm taking you there tonight."

Silence, then Tenzing's voice again.

"When do we leave?"

Laney scanned the room. She tried to see if there was anything she had forgotten.

"Two-thirty in the morning. Right after the night crowd settles down and before any night workers are getting off-shift. That'll give us the best gap with the fewest number of potential witnesses."

Tenzing looked pensive.

"Will I see you and Magda again?" he asked.

Laney's lip trembled and a few tears escaped the corners of her eyes.

"I don't know...security will be tracking us. The more contact we have with you, the more we put you in danger. But I *promise*, I will try and figure something out. Keeping you hidden is the best thing we can do for you right now."

Tenzing put a hand on Laney's shoulder. His eyes reached just up to her chin. He looked up to meet hers.

"Thank you, Laney," Tenzing said.

Laney nodded. Her jaw quivered.

"Why did you come here?" Laney asked. She sniffed away her tears.

"I never thought to ask you before."

Tenzing's eyes darted to the closet.

"I was...pulled here. I...I thought I would know what to do when I got here, but now...I am less sure than ever. I just know that I cannot go back. Not yet." Laney saw indecision and pain in Tenzing's eyes. She accepted his non-answer and decided not to probe further. She looked at the clock.

"Only a couple hours til we have to go. Magda said she briefed you on enough of the arc that you can get around without looking completely lost. Is there anything you need to know before we leave?"

Tenzing thought for a moment.

"Does the arc have weapons?" he asked. Laney blinked a few times and shook her head.

"Why do you ask?"

"I was nearly killed by a dart," Tenzing continued, pointing to his neck. "I want to know what else they can use against me."

Laney sat down and sighed.

"That's fair. Only security has any weapons. All ballistics—any type of gun or anything that explodes is completely and totally forbidden, never allowed on the arc." Laney watched Tenzing's expression. His face remained unchanged when she mentioned guns. *He must... God... I only know about them from movie archives...*

"Why are ballistics forbidden?"

"A stray bullet could ricochet and damage some vital component on the arc. Security has tranquilizer darts, knockout gas, electrified stun clubs, and restraining devices. Everything they wield is engineered to subdue organic life whilst preserving the arc's mechanical infrastructure." Laney shuddered. "God... I never realized how fucked up it all sounds until I had to explain it out loud like that."

"On this arc, people do not care for one another. You are not like this. You are different," Tenzing said.

Laney felt her face go red. she sucked air between her teeth as she spoke.

"Most people live by the culture of divide-and-conquer, look out for yourself and your own, eat or be eaten. Never stop moving.

"You do not live for this," Tenzing said.

"Thank you," she replied. "It took me a while to get there. I got burned getting there, but I try. I still try." The two stood. For a few breaths, no one spoke. Laney laughed nervously and changed the subject.

"I'm taking you to a place called the Side Hull. I wish I could tell you more, but I've never actually been there."

"What is it?"

"Old abandoned maintenance shafts. They run between the inner and outer hull walls. Sometimes people live down there when they don't have any other place to go."

"Will the men with darts, and gas, and clubs look for me down there?" Tenzing asked."

Laney furrowed her brow. She squeezed her hands.

"Not likely. Security doesn't go down there. Policing that section would acknowledge there's a growing segment of the arc that can't find any place to live. The board of directors doesn't want that. Also, they might lose a fight down there in the dark. Too many places to hide and get struck in the back. It's happened before." Tenzing's face squirmed into a grimace.

"And this is the place you are taking me? he asked."

Laney sighed. She checked the bug-out bag she had assembled for Tenzing.

"If there were any other place, I'd take you, but this is the best option we've got right now."

"Then this is where I will go," Tenzing said. His face returned to a determined countenance. He crossed the room and lied on the sofa. His tired body tried to soak in the feeling of comfort for a moment longer unsure when he would next receive such bounty.

"I need rest before we leave. I will sleep now," Tenzing announced.

"That's more than fair," Laney replied. Her words fell silently onto an already dozing Tenzing.

Laney sat in the kitchen, mulling over the situation. Doubt seeped in. *He still won't say why he came here. What if he came here to do something horrible, to hurt someone? The comment about weapons... and I'm helping him? What if arc security was right to stop him? What if they know more than I do? What if he somehow really is a threat?* The faceless image of arc security personnel glopped into her mind. She almost heard the chewing tobacco voice.

No... this is fear talking. Conditioning to submit to armed authority. I won't. His clothes are dirty rags. His only possessions are a bone knife and a deer skull. We have drones, electricity, power, medicine, long range tranquilizer rifles. If there were something out there, something dangerous, we could solve it. We have so much. Whoever shot Tenzing chose to use violence against something so much weaker. They made a choice. It's always a choice.

Laney let the man from the wastes sleep until it was time. She watched the digital clock turn to 2:15 and tapped Tenzing on the shoulder. His eyes opened, and he stood.

"Put these on," Laney commanded. She had combed through Magda's closet, and found a wardrobe of old arc civilian clothes several sizes too small for Magda. Laney stepped away respectfully as Tenzing dressed in a pair of red slacks and a button-up oxford shirt. She spoke to the wall.

"You can thank several of Magda's old girlfriends for the clothes. Must've left them here after bad breakups."

"I'm ready," Tenzing called. Laney turned back around to look at the fugitive. With a haircut and dressed in normal clothes instead of rags, Tenzing looked like a new man, a far cry from the feral wild man she had first rescued.

"That'll do nicely," she said. The pair walked toward the apartment door, but Laney stopped.

"One more thing —and this is important—if anyone asks, just say you lost your job ID and violated your lease."

Tenzing repeated those words. He fumbled through the arcane lines for several clumsy attempts before he asked,

"What does that—"

"Doesn't matter. Just remember that phrase. Now, let's go."

The pair left Magda's apartment in silence and made their way down the stairwell to the deck level. Tenzing spoke the mystery phrase under his breath until it permanently stamped itself into his brain. Laney signaled for Tenzing to stop. She walked out the front door of the C+ sector building and onto the deck and looked around. *Clear.*

She signaled back to Tenzing. He followed right behind her. The pair wound through the alleyways of densely packed apartment buildings until they stopped at a high wall. The wall extended farther left and right than could be seen.

"Here," Laney said. She tapped her foot on an object before turning around.

"Here it is," she said in a hushed whisper. "I can't go any further, but I promise you, if I find anything to help you, I *will* come find you."

Tenzing nodded. Laney pressed the small backpack into his hands. He slung it across his shoulders and spoke.

"Goodbye, Laney. Thank you."

"Goodbye, Tenzing."

Tenzing lifted the maintenance hatch and climbed down into the darkness. Laney shut the hatch behind him. It felt heavy as she released the steel plate from her grip. It rested covering the opening, sealing Tenzing's descent from her view.

Laney turned around and began the long walk back to her quarters below deck. Her steps trudged heavy. Her body felt weary. A numbness in her mind signaled the coming anxiety knot her brain would surely tie itself into. All of this she felt. She walked on anyway.

Chapter 11

Tenzing looked up and saw darkness. He looked down and saw darkness. Shuddering, he held tight to the ladder and climbed down the first rung. Then another and another pulling himself downward.

I can. I must hide. I must protect Laney. Must protect Magda. He thought of his dream, and the voice from the one antlered skull. *I... I must...*

His knuckles wrapped tightly around each rung. They unwrapped only when his other three limbs felt secure in their placement. He counted the rungs as he descended. *Five, ten, fifteen.*

This descent was unlike any climb Tenzing had accomplished before. He climbed alone, without his deer skull companion. No voices save his own sounded in that lightless shaft. He clung to cold, slippery steel that leeched heat from his hands. His palms grew clammy. A sharp, unfamiliar smell corkscrewed a winding path through his nostrils. His skin's oil and grease commingled with the metal held captive in his white-knuckle grip. Their mixture radiated a nauseating scent that filled the dark crevasse below.

Twenty, Tenzing counted. His feet touched a flat surface below the ladder's bottom rung where he dropped to his hands and knees skimming his fingertips across the floor, hoping to discern any details to clue him in to the surrounding invisible terrain.

He felt a pattern across the floor. A grid of uniform square holes—a grated steel panel. He stretched his hands out in front of him and felt a solid wall. Rotating around, he felt nothing to either side. He looked to his right and saw darkness. He looked to his left.

Tenzing strained his eyes. He made out the faintest glimmer far ahead. A few stray, exploratory beams of yellow light crept around a gentle curve in the distance. *It's the only way to go. Probably a couple hundred feet. No way to be sure in this dark.*

Tenzing patted the bag Laney had packed for him. Through the fabric, he felt the outline of each item. *Still there.* He looked back toward the light in the distance. *Nowhere else to go. I must.*

Tenzing took his first step toward the faint light. He forged ahead, hands outstretched, fingers splayed, probing for obstacles in the dark. He moved an inch at a time. With each step, if his fingertips felt nothing, he took another. He dutifully marched forward step-by-step at this crawling pace. Tenzing hunched his shoulders toward his center line. He tried to make himself small, smaller than the width of the narrow passage.

Loose fabric on his sleeves scraped the coarse metal walls that enclosed him as he walked. Tenzing scrunched further in to avoid the feeling of the cold metal bleeding through the fabric onto his skin. Ten paces forward. His fingers found something.

Cold, rough, gritty. The tip of his right ring finger scratched against a small burr notch in the steel. He winced. He felt a little drop of blood trickle down to the adjoining skin between his innermost fingers. His hand drew to his mouth and he licked the wound. The small cut stopped. The trickle staved off.

Tenzing's hands probed further around the mystery object. He stretched his hands to either wall and felt the walls narrowing, that gritty, flat steel stretching from the inner and outer hull walls toward the center. Tenzing's search quickened. Calloused palms flitted about the flat steel until his arm passed through, unimpeded by metal. His hand waved about in open air and darkness. *An opening. A path.*

Tenzing felt around the aperture's shape. The edges felt smooth around the perimeter. The metal extended all around from the sides and from the floor ending in a cut oval hole, much taller than it was wide.

Tenzing turned his body to the side. He sucked in and straightened his spine, aligning his body in one straight direction. He stepped over the metal sill that ran up from the floor and shimmied through the opening one leg at a time. His back and breast-bone scraped the slot. He felt cold metal and then open air as he reached the other side of the object, back in open darkness.

Images flashed from the recesses of his memory. Bodies lay motionless at his childhood village's center. The one antlered skull of his dream wreathed in white mist stared down from above with fiery eyes. Tenzing fell to the floor and thrashed his head side to side.

"*I try to follow your path and you leave me!*" He yelled in the dark. His scream echoed down the corridor to no answer. He curled his fists and grit his teeth. Images in his memory ebbed out like the tide. First his village and its bodies, then the arc, next a shadowy figure and a dart, and finally, the kindnesses of Laney and Magda.

"How? What do I do? They all?"

Tenzing sat for a moment. No answer came. He sat until the cold and dark made him forget the question. He stood back up and looked toward the faint, distant light.

Tenzing pressed farther through the dark. After a while, he found the same object in the dark. The exact same narrowing and exact same aperture. He clambered through with the same sideways hole-shimmying. He repeated this dance every thirty paces.

After five, he grew confident from the repetition. *What are they?* Tenzing gripped the steel which narrowed as he passed through his ninth one. He recalled the video Magda showed him, picturing drawings of the arc. Cross-sectional drawings that showed the space between the arc's inner and outer walls.

He remembered narrowing circles in the video's image. He touched the object in the dark. Tenzing felt the steel against his own rib cage as it just brushed through the opening. *They are the same. Bones. Metal bones make the arc strong. Metal ribs.*

Tenzing passed five more of the metal bones. Steel ribs.

He had followed enough of the corridor's subtle curvature that more and more errant light beams snaked into vision. Their yellow light changed the darkness from pitch-black to deep-gray. Previously invisible details now filled the thin room.

Bundles of wire clipped to the ceiling ran every which way, like masses of thorny vines. Branching pipes split and traveled like the dead, exposed roots common in the waste. Above and below, the wires and pipes hugged the ceiling and space beneath the grated floor. These mechanical veins threaded through slots in the arc's metal bones. Scurrying roaches used the winding structures as highways for their unknowable travels.

Seven metal bones later, Tenzing arrived at the source of the light. Yellow light blinded eyes adapted to low light. Tenzing buried his face within the crook of his arm. He ambled forward and under the light's direct beam, finally learning its origin. A headlamp. Its fabric-fastener wound tight, knotted around a jutting pipe. Carefully pointed to shine light at exactly the right angle. *Someone put this here.*

Tenzing studied his immediate area. The outer wall widened out ten or so feet. Ahead, past the headlamp, lay a massive steel curvature. It ran from the grated floor almost to the top of the ceiling. A curved ladder followed the steel along a curling path up and over the metal bulk. The ladder passed through a tight gap between the sloping metal hill and the ceiling.

Tenzing redirected the headlamp's shining yellow beam and brightened the widened outer wall. He saw another ladder off to the right that led down. He shone the light below him, through the grated floor beneath. Between the tangle of pipe and wires, he saw the same steel curvature.

It stretched beneath the grated floor and continued, the sloping metal hill in front of him down below his feet. *How big is this thing?* He pointed the headlamp toward the ladder heading down. He left it in this position, illuminating his descent.

He found his hand again on his backpack, felt familiar shapes, comfortable shapes. *Still there.*

Tenzing lied down on his belly. He shifted his legs backward until they found purchase on a rung beneath. His hands gripped the grated floor and then the top rung. He climbed down. Nine rungs down, he stretched his foot one more step. It met another grated floor and stepped farther into another dark corridor. The yellowed light above failed to penetrate to this greater depth.

Two steps more. He hit the floor and felt a heavy bash against his skull's right side. Tenzing looked up in a daze, pain surging across his temples. His neck wobbled and shook, too weak to hold his bloodied, bludgeoned head. A trickling dribble of blood dripped down the high side of his skull to the steel grate floor that supported his face.

The iron smell of blood invaded his nose. Its scent combined with the unctuous odor of his cheek-skin pressed against the steel grate. Sweat and blood dripped through the uniform square holes. A foreign hand pawed around his back.

The backpack was ripped from his frame. A shadowy hand retreated to a silhouetted body which ran down a corridor, lost farther in depth and darkness. Then Tenzing saw nothing. He slept. His face pressed against the grated floor. Little, uniform, square holes marked his cheek and bit into his skin as he slumbered.

94

Chapter 12

0300 hours came early.

Vance rose and looked at his uniform, pressed and hung neatly in his closet. He passed it up in favor of regular the civilian clothes he kept folded in a drawer under his desk. *Better to look normal and unassuming. People would talk about one security officer taking in another. I'll find him when he's off duty, alone. Just an altercation between two ordinary men.*

Vance dressed in a light-gray, long sleeved T-shirt, faded and wearing thin. He put on jeans with weathering that matched the shirt. He clipped his officer's badge on a thin chain he threaded underneath his shirt. Vance checked the mirror to make sure the badge showed no lines. A tranquilizer pistol, the only other marker of authority, sat on his hip, concealed within a sleek, unassuming holster covered by the loose fabric of his shirt. It was loaded— safety on—with a clip of two darts and one in the chamber.

Vance laced up his running shoes and grabbed the dossier for his target off his desk. Shutting and locking the door to his quarters, Vance began the short journey up to the helipad from which he would depart. Few security personnel were up at this hour. Vance saw only the junior officers made to stand watch on deck as he passed by. Never had there been any kind of security breach on this arc. Secrecy protected it. Most people on the main arcs either didn't know of its existence or were only vaguely aware that it was out there somewhere well-beyond the few sight lines not covered by walls or a VerchLife helmet. Those that knew, knew well enough not to talk about it. The security arc, Arc Ghost as it was called, housed only those who had undergone the rigorous selection process to become Arc Security.

Vance observed one junior officer. The younger man stared iron-eyed at the empty deck. It seemed all-the-emptier before morning started, before drills, before drones. The junior officer stood with his back turned to the heli-carrier that would soon take Vance to Arc Delta. He recognized the junior officer by face and knew the junior officer recognized him as well. This man had served him many times in the commissary. It was customary for officers-in-training to serve higher-ranking officers during mealtimes, bringing food and cleaning up afterwards.

Vance remembered his own times of having been put on these types of posts—woken up at odd hours and being made to guard empty rooms with no one around, the temptation to sleep, goof off, or leave forestalled by threat of surprise inspection. Vance remembered Officer Harkness' fondness for placing Vance and the others on long guard duties for any perceived slight. Other times, the training instructor had done it just because he'd wanted to.

Harkness claimed it was "Good for the nerves of the officer." Vance understood now; it was an exercise in obedience. *If you can stand to guard nothing for hours with full attention, the barriers of what you are willing to do are gone. You no longer look for reason or importance with your tasks— only successful completion.*

Vance passed the young officer wordlessly and ascended the small flight of stairs that put him on level with the helipad. He pushed a button and the front windshield slid forward, revealing a cockpit with a single deep-reclining seat. Behind the seat sat a small space for allotted cargo. Vance looked at the space and visualized his target. He saw Harkness' body secured and comatose within the space.

Vance remembered Harkness during his training days. He remembered the joy the man took in his abuses of trainees, the cruelty that lurked behind the man's eyes. That cruelty transmuted into sadism directed at those he deemed his lessers. Vance gritted his teeth.

He climbed in, pushed a button, and the heli-carrier shuddered to life. As the opaque windshield slid back into place and shielded him from sight, a small, sly grin curled at the corners of Vance's lips. His eyes rested once more upon the cargo space behind his seat. In less than two hours, that cargo space would be occupied with the detained body of the officer who had for so long made his life hell.

The rotors on the heli-carrier spun faster and faster, their deafening sound muffled by the aircraft's sealed interior. Vance felt his stomach lurch. The machine lifted off the pad and climbed slowly into the air. He took his badge and slotted it into a device in the heli-carrier dash.

A robotic voice sifted coolly through the cockpit's confines.

"*Officer: Vance O'Brien. Destination: Arc Delta. Flight protocols: activated.*"

Once the heli-carrier reached altitude, it pulled forward in a silent dash. Vance could not see anything of his journey, his eyes shielded by the opaque screen of the windshield's interior.

He thumbed over the singular page of his dossier. Scant information on his target, followed by a single line of instruction. Detain and return. Vance looked at the information, committing it to memory.

Harold Harkness: Arc Security Officer

    Former Arc Security Training Instructor

    Spouse: None

    Children: None

    Address: Sector B - Building 12, Floor G, Room 16.

    Detain and return.

Vance spent the remainder of the thirty or so minutes of flight in meditative silence. He visualized every detail of his mission. Lizzie and Kayla's faces bubbled up into his mind.

I'm so close to them. Closer than I've been in months. But I can't think of them now. Thoughts other than the mission at hand are nothing but distraction. Distractions are sloppy. Strickland hates sloppiness. Strickland has the power to extend my post, forestall the day I'll get to see them. I can't be sloppy.

Vance returned to the task at hand. *It would be early morning when he arrived, still dark. Dark enough most of the arc would have not taken one conscious blink away from their sleep. Only workers processing that day's shipments would see, but they knew well enough not to ask questions when security passed through. Get to Harkness' address. Solve the problem. Come back. No time for Lizzie or Kayla. No time for distraction. No time for sloppiness.*

Vance visualized his success. He saw himself walking back across the loading bridge connecting Arcs Alpha and Delta with Harkness' unconscious body concealed in a crate. He loaded it into the back of his aircraft. His grin widened.

He found his hand caressing the handle of his tranq gun. It felt good in the palm of his hand. Alone, he couldn't deny the joy it would bring him to use it on his former training officer. Vance wondered if Squadron Leader Strickland had anticipated this fact when he'd selected Vance for the job. *Of course he did. Man thinks of everything. That's why he is where he is.*

For a moment Vance pictured himself in the Squadron Leader's chair. *Maybe one day.* Vance checked the darts in his gun. *Three darts. Two more than I'll need.*

Vance felt the familiar lurch in his stomach. *Descent.* He braced his body for the small, thunking impact of the heli-carriers touch-down. It came, but Vance was surprised by the smoothness of the landing.

Finally, someone's improved flight control programming.

Vance pushed the central button on the console. The whirring rotors started their slow wind-down into stillness and the cockpit opened. Vance drew on his core strength to extract himself from the cockpit seat's near-supine position. He stepped out of the aircraft onto the helipad and looked out at the horizon—mostly black with the tiniest hint of blue-gray creeping in from far-off in the distance. High winds rustled and stirred.

Vance walked down the helipad onto the main deck of Arc Delta. He couldn't help but reminisce. One of his first active-duty security responses had been about a year ago on this very arc. A deranged machine shop worker had snapped. The man had gathered power tools and locked his coworkers in an annex. He threatened to kill them all if 'the machines' were not turned off. The man screamed and screamed about the machine's noise. He screamed that everything was too loud. Vance had deployed with a small strike force. They subdued the altercation with surgical precision.

Vance took the shot. The man went down. His screams stopped. The mission's success brought Vance's name across his superior's desk.

Vance surveyed the deck. Arc Delta was designed for manufacturing. It docked with Arc Golf, which handled natural resource acquisition, and then docked with Arc Alpha, where finished goods were sent. The many competing machine shops on Arc Delta took the copper, steel, glass, and silicon procured by the loader drones on Arc Golf and rendered them into usable products for Arc Alpha.

Vance considered all the arcs together and their functions. *We scout ahead, clear out hostiles, and bring back treasure. Arc Golf sends out its plodding machines picking up materials from cleared zones. Arc Delta turns those materials into things for Arc Alpha to buy. One of the many little loops that keep this last little happy caravan in the world running.*

Vance walked farther down the top deck, drawing closer to the loading zone. He eyed a sleepy-looking dock worker just reaching topside from a stairwell down below. His face looked unready to start the loading procedure, but the man trudged on. The outer arcs kept vastly fewer people than Arc Alpha. They held only the minimum number of semi-permanent residents to keep the machines running. Vance turned to the worker and spoke in a low-but-commanding tone.

"Keep docked for one hour, and I'll need one of those" Vance flashed his badge at the worker and pointed to a nearby auto-jack, "with an empty crate." The worker offered a silent nod and obliged, pulling the loading apparatus up to the front.

Vance gripped the auto-jack in hand and stood. He waited for those crucial few minutes where Arc Delta and Arc Alpha connected. Like clockwork, two massive telescoping loading ramps extended from either arc toward one another and locked together in the middle. Vance gave the dock worker a curt nod and walked across the ramp ahead of queued shipments. He pulled his cargo-carrying device in tow.

Vance reached the end of the bridge and paused for a second, acknowledging that this was his first step on Arc Alpha in many long months. *Soon, I'll finish my rotation and see Lizzie and Kayla every day.*

It will be better then. It will be better soon.

Vance resumed his mission. He hurried through the aft loading dock and its warehouses and descended an elevator toward the transit deck to the Underbelt.

He eyed a nest of tunneled openings and selected the tube that would take him closest to Harkness. He pulled the empty auto jack onto the winding, snaking rubber that gripped the moving walkway stretching the length of Arc Alpha's interior. His rhythmic, marching steps carried him only a little faster than the continuous railed momentum of the Underbelt's always-on conveyors. The gentle whirring of the moving pathway filled the soundscape of this tunnel and every other tunnel. Arc Alpha circulated its silent passengers through its transit system to every part of its mechanical body.

Vance looked through the translucent plastic walls of the Underbelt branch he traveled. He saw few commuters about at this hour. He didn't see their faces. They whizzed by too fast to see. Their faces were only fractions of his view. Vance looked up. A gray, plain, trussed ceiling concealed and supported the city that dwelt above. The plate the city sat upon, from this angle a ceiling, was as opaque as it was strong. It divided an arc already sectioned into sectors into above and below.

Vance moved forward, his exit terminal drawing closer. He stepped off onto the B Sector platform closest to his destination. He took an elevator up and stepped out walking across the deck toward Harkness' building. Towing the auto-jack, Vance's eyes drew down towards the deck on which he walked, the inverse of the ceiling he considered. The plate's solidity hid all that permitted the arc to live, the toil and movement, the people and machines that kept lights on and parcels moving. Vance stepped into the lobby of Building 12, the dwelling of his quarry. No one about—pure silence. *Perfection.*

Vance pulled the auto-jack into the lobby elevator, rode it up, and stepped out onto Floor G. He parked his cargo-carrying device in front of room 16. He pressed his ear to the door and heard only deep, scratching, croaky snores. Vance pressed his badge to the door's electronic lock. The word OVERRIDE appeared in small blue text and the lock clicked open. Vance twisted the doorknob carefully, silently, and stepped into the apartment.

Harkness' dwelling displayed a luxurious space corroded by hedonistic pursuits. Empty liquor bottles, sticky pipes, half-crushed pills, and full ashtrays were strewn about every square foot of the room. A kaleidoscope of pungent chemical smells hit Vance with a fury. He wrinkled his nose and crept through the living room, hands holding the tranq gun in a readied posture, dart at the ready.

He pressed open the bedroom door. The fading twilight of the early-morning sun crawled through cracks in the blinds, illuminating Harkness' pallid skin. Vance moved to the bedside table and picked up Harkness' tranq gun. A pig like snore made Vance's heart pound, but Harkness stayed asleep. His sallow nose wrinkled and his jaw hung slack. As Vance looked at the sleeping man in disgust, he remembered the needless cruelties he had endured at the hands of this sloppy ingrate. He remembered the needless cruelties this sloppy ingrate had inflicted on others as Vance watched, powerless to intercede.

Now who is powerless?

Vance felt an urge, a delicious cry for indulgence bubbling up from the back of his mind. He tapped Harkness on the face with the butt of his pistol. The dazed, hateful eyes Vance had expected opened with groggy vision. Vance looked at those eyes and saw something else lurking behind the hate. He saw fear. Vance realized all at once. It had always been fear—fear transmuted into sadistic abuse by some sick strain of the reclining man's psyche. It lurked like a rabid animal. It was raw, *pure*, but now it was different. Now it was unable to do anything but watch. That fear stayed behind those eyes until Vance shut them. He straightened his trigger finger and stowed his pistol back into its holster.

His hands trembled. Exhilaration surged through his body at the sight of the thin dart protruding from Harkness' veiny, red neck. Glorious adrenaline. Glorious vengeance. Glorious *victory*. He drew in a few shaky breaths and allowed himself one more moment to bask. The moment passed.

Enough.

On the left nightstand, Vance found a small paper scribbled with names he did not recognize. *Delaney Quist, Auxiliary Cargo Bay, Magda Erdos, Coconut Joe's.* All the names had little arrows that drew to another name. *Mr. Interloper.*

Vance folded the paper and tucked it into his pocket. He then got to work, rolling Harkness' unconscious body up in a bed sheet and tying it off at the ends. He dumped Harkness into the crate and clicked the lid's plastic latches shut, sealing its four sides. It was an easy journey back to the aft loading dock. Vance walked across the still connected ramp with his newly acquired cargo safely in tow. He eyed the same dock worker who had loaned him the auto-jack

"Can I get help loading this crate into the heli-carrier? Emergency requisition for excess plasma on Arc Echo." The dock worker shrugged and followed Vance to the heli-carrier. Together they hefted the crate into the small cargo area behind the cockpit.

"Thank you sir." Vance thanked the retreating dock worker's back as he leaned back into the heli-carriers seat and pushed the button to close the cockpit. The aircraft began its climb. Vance looked at the clock at the center console - *only forty-three minutes* - then at the crate behind him. Stillness. He heard nothing but the muffled sounds of the aircraft's rotors. He thought of Strickland's command and smiled as he mouthed the words to himself. *Perfect discretion.* Perfect discretion and all of its perks would assure his family a better life.

Chapter 13

Tenzing jolted awake. His hand flew to his head, still throbbing from the dull pain where he'd been struck. Instead of an open wound on his temple, his questing fingers found a layer of cloth covered in an adhesive plastic. Part of his head had been shaved to affix the bandage. Tenzing probed gingerly around his newly dressed injury. Only a globby bit of dried blood had bled through the fabric and formed a crust that flaked off as he touched it. Any other bleeding seemed to have been stemmed by the dressing. His thoughts ran in circles.

Who... who did this? Tenzing shuffled his body, and found he was no longer lying on the grated floor. He found himself propped up against one of the steel bones, a layer of fabric cushions nestled behind his back. *Odd.* He looked around. He was in a corridor like the one he'd traversed, but about twice as wide, maybe five feet wide at the widest. Streaks of sunlight poured through holes that appeared to have been cut into the exterior wall. The light beams bounced off sheets of pale metal, bathing the corridor in morning light like glowing liquid gold.

Tenzing squinted farther down the corridor and saw two silhouettes approaching. As the figures drew nearer, Tenzing held his head and struggled to stand. He closed one eye against the pain that surged through his head as he threw his free hand up between himself and the strangers. The shorter figure addressed him.

"It's okay. It's okay. We're not gonna hurt you. I'm June and this is Grandpa." Tenzing kept his arm up, frozen in place, tracking every movement the strangers made. The woman kept speaking as she backed up and urged her companion to do the same.

"I found you hurt and Grandpa dressed your head." She pointed to the older man beside her. "We're coming back to check on our patient. Thought you'd probably be wanting something to cope with the pain by now. Nasty wound. Nothing serious, but it doesn't have to be serious to hurt."

Tenzing dropped his arms and sat. He slumped back against the cushions behind him, his head still throbbing.

"Yes...please. Pain..." The man June had called Grandpa crouched near Tenzing and pressed a small steel cup up to Tenzing's lips. Tenzing tensed and the older man drew back slightly.

"It's medicine," he explained patiently. "We grow it. It'll help dull the pain." Tenzing took the cup into his own hands and took a tentative sip. Finding it not scalding but pleasantly warm, he downed it in a quick gulp. The warm, earthy, herbal-tasting concoction coated the back of his throat as it went down. It left a faintly bitter aftertaste.

Now that the strangers were standing in the light coming in through the hull wall, Tenzing could observe them more closely. The woman had long black hair, dark eyes, a generously round face, and pale skin. Her hands shook violently, twitching back and forth, but she seemed to take no notice of these erratic movements.

June saw Tenzing's gaze and answered the unasked question evident on his face.

"Neurological injury. They've got a mind of their own."

Tenzing nodded. The older man—Grandpa—had tan skin, an angular face, piercing light blue eyes, and short gray hair. Tiny circular glasses rested on the bridge of his downturned, pointed nose that reminded Tenzing of a beak. His face was clean shaven and he had a wide, thin mouth that rested in an easy smile. He wore the threadbare remnants of a coat that at one point in time might have been white. The older man coughed, interrupting Tenzing's thoughts.

"What do we call you?"

"I am called Tenzing."

"Well, Tenzing, I know your head is probably still reeling, but you must be absolutely new or absolutely stupid to have come through the corridor you came through, *at night*, and alone."

Tenzing shrugged weakly as June agreed.

"Nobody who knows anything goes *that* way at night, alone. It's contested territory. You're unprotected there. Thief would see you as a mark a mile away coming from there."

Grandpa interjected. "Yes, June, I believe you've made your point. Our guest doesn't need pain from blunt force trauma *and* the pain of a scolding."

June sat down on the floor in front of Tenzing in a huff.

"I'm sorry, I just...I *hate* to see somebody taken advantage of like that. As if we *all* don't have it bad enough down here already!"

In her blustering, Tenzing recognized the tone of a quick temper that stemmed not from ill will, but from kindness and concern for others' safety. *There are many rules I do not know here.* Suddenly, he remembered the all-important words Laney had impressed upon him.

"I lost my job and my lease expired!" Tenzing blurted. June looked at him and cocked her head to the side. She let out a quiet, dejected laugh.

"Sorry, Hon. Story of most of the people here. Everyone's song's got a different melody, but they're all playing in the same key." As if sensing the need to change the subject, Grandpa interrupted.

"By now the medicine should be kicking in. It's a natural pain neutralizer and sedative found in a plant we grow." Sure enough, Tenzing began to feel a buzzy, relaxed calm wash over him like warm sand. The pain in his head became softer, more distant, existing only when he directed his attention towards it. Grandpa continued.

"Would you kindly join us for breakfast? You will likely be very hungry very soon, if you're not already." Tenzing felt a familiar gnawing deep in the pit of his stomach. He fumbled about at his feet, remembering the shadowed figure absconding with his backpack in the night.

"I...I don't have anything to eat," he admitted sheepishly. Grandpa sat down on the floor and put a hand on Tenzing's shoulders.

"It's okay. We always have food to spare for a guest." With that, the old man began to root around in a fraying fabric Duffel bag that bulged at the sides. Tenzing watched as he pulled out a small, flat piece of sheet metal and three steel rods about two-and-a-half-feet-long each, with one threaded end and one hollow end. The old man joined the rods together, screwing each threaded end into another, creating a singular pole about eight feet long. He attached the pole to the sheet metal by threading it through a series of thin metal loops welded onto the sheet metal's bottom side.

Tenzing leaned in, trying to decipher how this strange construction was in any way related to the concept of breakfast. The old man pulled out a small, green glass jar from his duffel and poured a thin layer of yellowy, semi-translucent, viscous liquid across the surface of the sheet metal. With the full surface covered, the old man stood up and thrust the apparatus, flat side first, through a large triangular hole in the hull's exterior wall. He held about a foot's length of the pole on the inside of the wall and tied it to a nearby pipe with a small spool of twine. Tenzing's brow furrowed deeper in confusion.

"What's going on?" he asked.

"Patience," Grandpa counseled, smiling. "It should only take a few minutes."

June chimed in,

"I'd spoil it for ya, but Grandpa's a showman at heart and it's not often he gets a new audience." She punctuated her statement with a hearty slap across the old man's shoulder.

"A man is within every right to be proud of his inventions," the older man retorted.

The three sat for a few minutes, waiting. The silence discomfited Tenzing and he realized just how short a time it had taken him to get fond of the simple act of human conversation. He felt its absence. Finally, unable to stand the silence any longer, he hazarded a question.

"How did you find me?"

It was June who answered.

"I went out to do some late-night patrolling and found your body."

"I thought you said no one should travel that corridor alone."

"I am never alone," June replied. She glanced at Grandpa. "None of us are. Once I found you, I came back and got help. A couple of us carried you here, and now you're having breakfast with myself and our esteemed leader."

"The leader of what?" Tenzing asked.

"The Side Hull Rats!" June beamed as she pronounced the words. Tenzing started to speak, but the question died on his lips as he heard a sizzling sound. Grandpa untied the twine and pulled the pole-apparatus back through the slit in the exterior wall.

"Stand back! Hot pan coming through." The older man brought the flat metal topped with bubbling, crackling liquid into the corridor and sat it at his feet between himself, Tenzing, and June. He turned around to his bag and pulled out eight small white oblong objects speckled with tan flecks. The old man knocked one of the objects on the side of the hot metal and held it above the center of the pan as he deftly separated the two broken halves with one hand. An orange-yellow yolk surrounded in clear white slid out onto the sizzling hot sheet metal. It bubbled up around the edges. *Eggs.* The searing sound and smell comforted Tenzing.

"Long frying pan," the old man said as he shuffled the still-cooking eggs around the constructed pan with a long metal spoon. With his other hand, he picked up the discarded shells and dropped them into a small plastic container within his bag. Tenzing noticed the eggs appeared about half the size of the chicken eggs he had eaten with Magda.

"What are these eggs?"

June answered. "Pigeon eggs. Further down the corridor, there's a huge roosting area. Hundred birds, maybe. Who knows when or how they got in there, but Grandpa scoops up a whole bunch of eggs from time to time."

Grandpa piped up. "They lay more eggs in a day than a chicken even though the eggs are much smaller. Very docile birds. Their roost is one of my many pet projects. Like this one." The older man patted the homemade frying pan. "It takes a little practice, but you stick out the end for a few minutes into the morning sun beyond the shadow of the shade sail and it gets nice and hot. Then you bring it in and cook whatever you've got before the metal cools off."

June pulled a little package out of a backpack. Tenzing recognized the package as the same brand of morning biscuits Magda had kept.

"Got these too," she announced. "Some lady was just throwing them out on one of my last deliveries."

The older man shook the pan gently, ensuring the cooked eggs wouldn't stick. Tenzing hungrily eyed the eight perfect little fried eggs, like miniature versions of what Magda had prepared, as the old man detached the flat metal from his pole and set it between himself, June, and Tenzing.

"Eat," Grandpa said. He and June scooped their eggs onto a morning biscuit. Tenzing did the same.

"What are the Side Hull Rats?" he asked around a mouthful. June leaned forward.

"Side Hull Rats are who you've got when you've got nobody else. Everybody topside always snickers about the so-called *rats* who live down in the Side Hulls. So we took the name with pride. Describes us perfectly. Rats stick together. They're *survivors*."

Grandpa swallowed his last bite of breakfast and cut in.

"We are a mutual aid and protection society," he patiently corrected. June noticed the befuddled look upon Tenzing's face and jumped in again to explain.

"That means we share what we have between us all and we watch each other's backs down here."

Presently, there was a loud, grumbly shout from farther down the corridor.

"Hell of a lot easier to share when you've got next to nothing!"

"Shut up, Jonas, we're trying to onboard a new recruit!" June shouted back. There was more fondness than animosity in her voice. She turned back to Tenzing and shrugged. "He's not wrong. Equality is easier, a *hell of a lot* easier, at the bottom of the heap. Nothing to lord over anyone else if you've all got nothing to start with." Tenzing nodded, moving his eyes to the older man.

"And..." he faltered, struggling with the unfamiliar moniker June had used to refer to the older man. The fellow's blue eyes twinkled in response as he took a small towel from his bag and began to clean up his large frying pan.

"It's okay if you call me Grandpa as well, son. Everyone does. I'm not actually related to anyone here. They just gave me that name on account of how old I am."

"Okay then. So...Grandpa...you lead the Side Hull Rats?"

Grandpa shook his head.

"I am a Leader in name only. I have no power, not really. Giving orders ruins too much. Rats are better left to follow their own whims, usually works out better that way."

June jumped in. "We only ever do what he says 'cause he's the oldest, wisest rat. You gotta humor him from time to time. I mean, who would want to upset El Ratticus Firsticus." Grandpa wiped a hand down his lined face, sighing.

"*No one* calls me that." T

he voice from farther down the corridor - Jonas - chimed back in.

"We do so, Gramps. Hail El Ratticus Firsticus, first of His Name. Long may he skitter!" Grandpa just rolled his eyes as peals of laughter echoed from June and the voice farther down the corridor. Tenzing couldn't help but smile at the pair. He waited for their chuckles to die down before speaking.

"You have treated me, a stranger, with kindness. I will make sure to do the same." Grandpa smiled good-naturedly.

"Reciprocity makes the world turn," June mused.

Grandpa nodded in agreement as he disassembled his frying pan and shuffled it into his bag. "We don't expect you to immediately go out and repay us. Take some time, recover, and the offer is there if you want it. It's a hard life to go through without friends."

"No hard feelings if it's not for you, though," June reassured him, gesturing with her shaking hands to the back of her skull. "I've just got a soft spot for people with head injuries." Tenzing nodded. He thought of Laney and Magda and wondered how they were faring.

"How many of you are there?" Tenzing asked.

June looked up at the ceiling as she counted in her head.

"In our little humble family? Maybe twenty or so."

Tenzing probed further. "There are others who live in the Side Hull that are not part of your group?"

"Yeah, farther down, around the other side of the arc, closer to the front. I know of at least two more camps. Probably where the thief that robbed you came from."

"It is common to form into groups then?" Tenzing asked.

"Oh sure I guess it's just nature when you get down to it. We're animals with language, so it's natural to want to have somebody listen to you and words to hear from outside your own head." June scratched her head. "Don't worry, though. Nobody in our group would be the one who robbed you. You can bet all your inc on that. The rats protect their own. I wouldn't want to see a thief who tried anything after Jonas and Mite get to them."

"Damn right." Jonas echoed once again from farther down the corridor, and Tenzing wasn't sure, but he thought he could hear the faint sound of knuckles popping. Having finished breakfast, June and Grandpa stood up and June addressed Tenzing.

"Please get some rest. You can find us when you wake up."

"June and I have some business to attend to," Grandpa explained as he zipped his Duffel. "Please think over our offer. You don't have to answer til you've recovered. June can give you a tour of the camp later and show you all of our assets."

June nodded.

"We want to put out all our cards so you can make an informed decision on whether or not you'd like to live like a rat."

Tenzing watched the pair leave down the corridor. He saw they had left him a blanket. It was well-worn but soft. He unfolded the blanket and shuffled comfortably against the corner where the steel reinforcement met the exterior wall. Breakfast and whatever medicine Grandpa had given him had brought a drowsy haze to his body, which desperately needed rest.

As Tenzing dozed, the same medicine that dulled his pain allowed his mind to free itself—to think. Through the haze came inspiration. Tenzing's past, the last few days and the last long years, all swirled around in his head. His old village, the bodies of his family lying still, and that great crashing sound in the distance, the same sound had led him to this strange arc. He thought of all the people he had encountered.

The unknown sniper. Laney. Magda. The mysterious thief in the corridor. Grandpa. June. Tenzing weighed it all, but the scales were impossible to balance.

In the great depths of a buzzy, chemically aided sleep, Tenzing dreamed.

I sought to kill a metal beast. I sought to end what killed my people.

I followed the sound that heralded their deaths. That sound I ran from for years.

I listened to the voice of the one-antlered skull. I listened to the voice of the family taken.

That one voice led me, not to a beast, but to a city.

That city marched on six great towers that choked life from an already dying world.

I climbed its tower to be cast down by cowards who deal death from distance.

Saved by souls who live at the mercy of the city's weight.

These selfsame souls bound to those tower's great strides.

I fled from a law designed for my demise. A law that protects itself with death.

I descended, lost in darkness and depth. Unseeing and alone, I was robbed and beaten.

I awoke to strangers who patched my wounds and shared their bounty.

Twice spurned. Twice saved. There is no balance in these scales.

To tear down those towers in revenge would ruin those whose kindness I have received.

I longed for destruction and the voices I followed left me. Silent.
The monster changed when I saw it up close.
It cannot be killed, for it gives life too.
To those bound within its claws.

What do I do now?

After what felt like an unknowable eon, Tenzing began the tired climb from the depths of his daze. Consciousness came slowly back and forth like driftwood washing ashore from a storm-tossed sea. He thought of June's words that had etched themselves in the back of his mind.

"Reciprocity makes the world turn."

Reciprocity. I guess I'll give that a try.

Another voice sounded in Tenzing's mind.

"Y O U A R E L I S T E N I N G A G A I N."

Tenzing woke up.

Chapter 14

Vance pushed the button opening the cockpit on the heli-carrier. He stepped out and opened the side door to the small cargo bay. No sound carried from the crate. *He'll have a few more hours in that state while I find out what the commander wants to do with him.* Vance locked the heli-carrier and practically strutted back to Squadron Leader Strickland's office. He rapped on the door until he heard a quiet voice slide through the cracks where the door met the frame.

"Enter."

Squadron Leader Strickland sat at his desk, attending to documents. The man did not move when Vance entered.

"Assignment completed, sir," Vance barked. He stood in a formal salute, appraising every minute facial movement of his seated commander for some kind of reaction. Squadron Leader Strickland thumbed over the last line of a paper and continued to read for a good minute before stowing the paper in a nearby file and placing it into a drawer. His eagle-eyed gaze met O'Brien's. O'Brien hung on his every word.

"Excellent work, Officer O'Brien."

"Thank you, sir," Vance answered, releasing a short breath in relief. The squadron leader leaned back in his chair and folded his hands over his stomach.

"Your assignment is not yet finished. You will now take Mr. Harkness to the room with yellow walls." Vance felt a small twitch that quivered in the corner of his right eye.

"I thought you said Harkness would be put under a tribunal?" The words spilled forth before he could stop them. *Fuck! Why did I say that!?* Vance thought. He arrested his face muscles into frozen stillness, atonement for words uttered out of turn.

The slightest change in Strickland's expression formed. A keener interest hidden deep behind the man's eyes appeared with Vance's outburst. Strickland answered the question without a singular change in tone.

"I deem a tribunal unnecessary in this matter. Better to remove rot quickly and quietly, before it spreads. We do not want sloppiness, disorderliness, and disobedience to spread, do we, O'Brien?"

"No sir," Vance said. The smallest tremble shook his jaw. He scanned the Squadron Leader's face, hoping the seated man did not notice his tremble, but he knew he did. That little hidden thing in his superior officer's eyes receded. Strickland continued.

"I will meet you outside the room with yellow walls in ten minutes. Officer O'Brien, you are dismissed."

Vance exited his commander's office and made his way back to the heli-carrier. *The room with yellow walls. Whatever assignment Harkness failed must have been absolutely crucial. He* signaled two nearby junior officers to approach the aircraft. The two men loaded the cargo crate from the heli-carrier onto a nearby auto-jack and awaited further instruction from Vance.

"That will be all. Return to your posts," he said.

Vance thought he noticed the beginning of a communicating glance between the two men, a glance that resembled curiosity. Vance interrupted the pair.

"Now, men!"

The two junior officers hustled away. Vance stood alone with the auto-jack. He piloted it toward the nearest freight elevator and entered.

He pushed the requisite button and the elevator began its downward churn.

Down. The room with yellow walls is down.

The elevator dinged, announcing its arrival to basement subfloor one.

Vance stepped out of the elevator with the auto-jack.

The room with yellow walls. Vance put the auto-jack in self-drive mode and gave it a gentle push. It glided down the dimly lit hallway at a controlled walking pace as Vance walked beside. He knew the exact location of the room. He didn't know exactly how he knew, but his feet carried him in a single, sure direction. With every step, he fought an urge to turn back.

It's an order. I have to do it. I have no choice. Lizzie can't grow up with a father in prison.

This subfloor, home to the mechanical heart of the security arc's power-plant, hummed gently. Dim-orange track lights lined the ceiling every five paces casting the hallway in an unnatural glow. Vance led his sleeping prisoner through this glow down to his ultimate destination.

The room with yellow walls. Every single room on this arc has unpainted walls. Metallic gray. This is the only one with any color.

Vance passed the door to the arc's power plant. A smaller power apparatus than the one on Arc Alpha, but he felt its heartbeat nonetheless. The floor itself vibrated, sending prickling sensations spiraling up Vance's legs with every reluctant step.

The room with yellow walls. I'll be in The Circle soon. I'll see Kayla. I'll see Lizzy. She'll have a better life. He's a vile bastard of a man anyway. He deserves whatever will come to him.

Vance reached the end of the hallway, a T junction. He took a left without thinking and stopped in front of a closed door. He grabbed the auto-jack. The slightest pressure yanking the cargo device in reverse stopped its wheels to a halt. The closed door loomed ahead.

The room with yellow walls.

Vance peeked inside the tiny window built into the solid metal-frame door. An acrid, sallow hue enveloped the room's interior. Shadows of unfamiliar objects danced around those yellow walls, cast by a single light bulb that dangled from a strand which swung gently from the ceiling. Drawing closer to the small pane, Vance saw a padded chair with straps. Beyond the chair sat some kind of machine. From this angle, he could only see the very edge. Vance strained his eyes, stretching the bounds of his peripheral vision. Tucked in the corner, he saw goggles similar to a VerchLife helmet, and an IV tube connected to a small tank filled with a liquid that appeared clear, with only the slightest tint of blue.

A calm voice slipped past Vance's shoulders up to his ears.

"I will take it from here, O'Brien." Squadron Leader Strickland stepped forth from the shadowed corridor as Vance spun around. "You are dismissed. You will take Mr. Harkness' former seat in The Circle when we next convene."

The hawkish man pressed a tablet-sized, circular electronic device into Vance's hand. "This will be your tether to The Circle. Through it you will receive orders. It is a secure text based, one-way communication channel. I can send you messages for your assignments. The device does other things as well. Keep it on your person at all times. Expect a message."

Strickland stepped past Vance, unlocking the door by placing his key card to a pad to the left of the frame. The door swung wide and the Squadron Leader gave the auto-jack a little kick. It glided noiselessly through the doorway into the room. Vance's thoughts raced.

The room with yellow walls.

"What will happen to him?" For the second time that day, Vance felt the words slip past his lips before he could stop them. *Fuck.* He stood paralyzed as he gripped the tablet Strickland had given him, fingers clenched around its dark screen tightly enough that he thought the glass would shatter.

To Vance's surprise, his superior officer answered again.

"We will be doing a debriefing with the machine. Afterwards, Mr. Harkness will be transferred permanently back to Arc Alpha. Officially, he will be declared unfit for duty, having suffered a nervous breakdown. He will be stripped of his rank, his salary, and his issued living quarters. What happens to him after that will not be my concern—*or yours.*" With this icy declaration, the Squadron leader approached Vance once again and placed a hand on his shoulder.

"Officer O'Brien, you are now a member of The Circle, the order that stands as an invisible aegis shielding the arc. You stand between citizens of the arc and the destruction that festers and gnashes its teeth outside these walls. *Heed this charge.*"

"Sir, yes, sir!" Vance barked obediently.

Strickland continued,

"Know this: The people you protect will never understand the burden you bear in silence to protect them. They will never know the sacrifices you make or the trials you face. Some may even hate you, but they speak with shielded eyes, eyes that do not know the horrors out there. Your eyes do. You know the monsters that lurk in the wasteland, those gnashing fangs that would bite our flesh, and those scraping claws that would spill forth our blood. Your eyes know the sorrows that we protect the arc from. *Remember what you've seen.* Remember why you walk this hard path."

"Sir, yes sir!" Vance repeated. Strickland took his hand off of Vance's shoulders and patted him across the back, his demeanor lightening.

"Celebrate! This is a great opportunity for you and your family. Your next post will put you aboard Arc Alpha, taking over Harkness' duties. You'll get to see much more of Kayla...and little baby Lizzie."

"Yes, sir. Thank you, sir," Vance responded, touched that his commanding officer remembered his family's names. The Squadron Leader retreated back into the room with yellow walls. As the door began to close behind him, he gave one last wave and spoke.

"Vance, welcome to The Circle. Keep your device close. You will be hearing from me shortly."

Vance turned away, still clutching the device in his hands. He left the Squadron Leader and the sleeping Harkness behind the door that finally swung shut, sealing the room with the yellow walls away from the rest of the arc.

Vance started back down the hallway, away from the room, but something nagged him. Against his better judgment, he glanced back. Through the window, he saw the shadow of his commander cast against the yellow walls.

A figure filled the chair with straps. The shadow of goggles sat upon its face and a tube connected from its wrist to the machine. Wires cascaded down from the figure's head. Its shadow writhed.

Vance heard a muffled yell. He couldn't make out the words through the door, but it sounded most like two separate words repeated over and over. "Forgive...me."

If those were the words he heard, the muffled screams that chased him down the corridor as he hurried away proved that there was no forgiveness granted. No forgiveness in the room with yellow walls.

Vance made his way up the stairs, leaving this subdeck behind. That terrible shade of yellow squirmed behind his eyes, seeming realer than anything he saw ahead. Vance returned to his quarters. He talked to no one on the way there, and he closed and locked the door behind him.

He sat down and looked at the circular tablet Strickland had given him. *I'll see Lizzie. I'll see Kayla... he's a vile man anyway... I did this for them. He's a vile man anyway...*

Vance's stomach churned and he felt watched, even as he sat on his bed alone in his quarters. *I did this for them... If they knew what I do for them, would they still love me?*

Vance picked up the phone and dialed Kayla. He listened through the receiver. His face lit up as he heard happy baby noises. "Lizzie Wizzy! You're home today!" The babbles continued and broke into a little laugh as a second voice came through the receiver.

"Lizzie stayed home today. Slightest amount of fever possible, just enough to keep her home, but not enough for her to notice. Little darling." In the background, Lizzie let out an infectious chuckle. Vance smiled slightly.

"Kayla, I've got some news. I'm coming home soon." Silence from the other end, then Kayla's voice, tinged with alarm.

"Babe, what happened? Is everything okay?" Vance realized he'd delivered his news in the cadence of a funeral dirge.

"No, babe! Nothing's wrong! I got a promotion! I'm gonna be stationed on Arc Alpha for a while. I'll be able to see more of you and Lizzie." Vance heard a slight sniffle through his end as Kayla choked through her words.

"Oh, honey, that's *wonderful*! Whatever you did...thank you. You do so much for this family. I'm so proud of you."

Acid-yellow walls flashed behind Vance's eyes as he heard muffled screams on repeat.

"It's nothing. I'm just trying to do my best for you and Lizzie," he mumbled.

"It is *not* nothing, Vance. We'll be together again. I love you so much for working so hard and bringing yourself back home."

"I love you too," Vance responded, eyes closed against the flashes of yellow that he couldn't forget.

God if she knew...everything. Would she still?

Vance thought of the feral, pained lingerers scurrying amidst the hollowed out rubble that used to be civilization. He thought of every one he terminated as the little ticker on his drone's HUD went up by one. *Euthanization count plus one.*

He thought of the man he'd just kidnapped and turned in. He thought of this man's last words. *Forgive... me.*

He thought of Kayla, and he thought of Lizzie.

We do this—all of this—to protect them. They'll never know. They can never know. I can shoulder that burden...for them. I can protect them from that.

"Dear? You've been quiet for a while. Are you still there?"

Vance snapped back to the present.

"Yeah, yeah I'm still here. How is Lizzie? You said the fever wasn't too bad?"

"It wasn't. Listen," Kayla said as she held the phone to their daughter.

Vance and Kayla said nothing as they sat for minutes on the phone listening to the sound of their daughter's happy little noises. She laughed, sputtered, and blew bubbles.

"She's been absolutely fascinated with her toes today," Kayla said, taking the phone back, extracting it from Lizzie's tiny fingers.

"Does she keep trying to snack on them?" Vance asked. He pictured Kayla rocking Lizzie on her hip as she responded.

"Yeah, it's a full-time job trying to keep them out of her mouth." Kayla was interrupted by the faint ding of a doorbell. "Oh, when did it get to be that time? Say goodbye to Daddy, baby. Gramma is here to see Little Miss Lizard, and I've gotta run out to make an appointment with a client." Lizzie blew one last little raspberry sound into the phone. Kayla and Vance said at nearly the same time.

"Have a good day, babe."

Vance hung up the phone, lied back on his bed, and stared at the ceiling. He stared at his tablet on the nightstand, remembering Strickland's promise that he would be receiving his new orders soon. *Whatever it is, I'll be ready. I'll be ready for them. I'll shoulder that burden. For them.*

Chapter 15

Laney arched her spine and stretched, her bones squeezing the last few drops of exhaustion from her body like a wrung-out towel. She lied still, using every ounce of will and energy not to move her body. An itchy impulse to spring out of bed and sprint down to the Side Hull intruded upon her concentration.

She sat in a mentally taxing stillness, trying to wrestle her thoughts away from anxiety. The panic had resumed as soon as she'd woken up. Laney fell back on the hamster wheel of thoughts that had stolen any respite from her during the hours she tossed in sleeplessness. She remembered every detail of the last night. She couldn't stop remembering. Laney saw Tenzing climb down into an unknown depth, a place she had never seen with her own two eyes. An hour before that, she had told him it was his best option. The Side Hull, Tenzing's hiding place. Laney shuddered.

What had, at the time—spurred by desperation and adrenaline— seemed the best and most perfect solution, had soured the longer Laney thought. That mechanical chasm grew more thorny complications the more Laney pictured it. All her life she'd heard rumors about the Side Hull. Vicious, lurid tales. A place full of desperate people doing anything to survive, happy to pick one another apart. Rats eating each other alive.

We had to.

Laney tried to assuage her guilt with facts. *People exaggerate on purpose. It's all a ploy so people will learn to be happy with their lot in life for fear of losing it. It's just a boogeyman to scare children into keeping their mouths shut and working hard for the arc.*

Laney was losing the wrestling match with her own mind. Still, she persisted. *It was the best place to take him. It is the one place security won't look for him.* The image of a faceless arc security officer bearing down on Tenzing flashed through her mind. The empty uniform Laney conjured trained a dart filled with lethal, proprietary, chemical serum directly over the spot on Tenzing's chest above his heart. Laney imagined the dark corridors filled with-God-knows-what. The two fears competed for her worrying mind's attention with only Laney losing.

Laney tried to assuage herself again. *Better the devil you don't know when the devil you do know is armed, dangerous, and institutionally encouraged to use lethal force.*

Laney tried to force her thoughts to stop chasing each other around like so many demented rabbits. She remembered an old adage from her grandfather: *Worrying is like a rocking chair. Gives you something to do, but it doesn't get you anywhere.* Laney laughed to herself. *Just feels like somebody's glued a rocking chair to my ass. Every time I sit down, I end up back in it.*

Laney rocked for a moment longer. *God I hope he's okay. On top of cherishing human life, he's the evidence that shatters the whole fucking veil of lies I've lived under my whole life.*

Finally, she peeled herself up from the single-occupancy mattress she had been sunk into for the last twelve hours. She dressed and picked up her apartment phone. *My brain's not working. Time to outsource.*

She dialed, waited for a moment, and heard the comforting brassy voice she looked to in times of uncertainty.

"What's up kid?" Magda answered, waiting for Laney's response.

"Ah, nothing much," Laney croaked, lying.

"You sound rough. Did you just get up?"

Laney looked at the nearby clock and saw 2:27 P.M. in blocky red letters.

"Yeah," she confessed. "Couldn't sleep. It's my off-day for the week today. Can we meet up?"

"Absolutely," Magda replied.

"Meet me in the botanical park up in B Sector," Laney instructed. "I need to talk—in person—to somebody with a clear head." Magda's hearty laugh sounded through the other line.

"And that somebody didn't pick up, so you called me." Laney laughed as Magda continued. "There's a particular bench I've got in mind with our name on it. You know the one?"

"Yeah," Laney answered.

"Give me 'bout an hour or so and I'll meet ya there."

"Will do," Laney replied. She hung up the phone and grabbed an outfit at random from her closet. Shrugging into a jacket, she grabbed her keys and opened the front door. As soon as Laney clicked open her door, she heard the loud *slam* of her next door neighbor's door shutting. *Just missed him. Again. Two years I've lived here and two years we've always 'just missed' each other.* She sighed and spoke aloud under her breath.

"I am *never* gonna meet my neighbor."

Laney walked through the cave-like corridor lined with the tiny little below-deck apartments that made up C Sector. *Retrofitted for living quarters from failed commercial space when the original C Sector overflowed.* She walked straight past the exit terminal leading to the Underbelt. *Magda will probably be late anyway, like always. It'll take me roughly an hour to walk the deck to B sector.* Laney could already feel her muscles burning with the anticipation of the journey as she looked back toward the Underbelt.

An old boyfriend's words flashed within her mind.

"If you've got time to walk somewhere, you aren't doing enough with your life." Laney pictured his slicked back hair and his perpetual hustle, knocking things off of lists to impress other list-makers. He had done everything quickly, efficiently, like he was trying to save up vacation days for a vacation that never came. *No wonder we didn't last.*

Laney ascended a set of stairs away from the Underbelt and relished the feeling of sail-filtered sunlight, warm on her skin, as she began her walk. The shafts of light that poked through the giant webbing that draped over the arc's deck crept around the monolithic gray apartment towers that comprised C+ Sector. *Name something "plus" when you invent a worse version to compare it to.* Laney scoffed to herself as she trekked through the narrow alleyways between the rows of identical gray buildings until she finally arrived where the promenade proper began.

A big, open outdoor collection of shops lined the deck. Mostly little food joints, bars, a barbershop, and a little vending machine that dispensed randomized, prepaid-redeemable verch codes. The vending machine was garishly colored, plastered with display screens of all the items and characters kids could hope to unlock with their purchase. Laney walked past Coconut Joe's. Its unlit,neon, tropical-themed sign looked kitschy and cheap in the filtered light of day. The fake bamboo and fake greenery lining the bar itself seemed sadly surreal at peak sobriety.

Laney hurried through the rest of the promenade.

As she approached B Sector, the buildings got shorter. Shops sold more phys goods. Potted plants lined the sidewalks between buildings and people sat drinking coffee on balconies, watching shoppers pass by below. Laney passed a co-working space located next to a tea shop. A man dressed in a blue oxford shirt and light fleece vest yelled loudly into a headset.

"You tell that asshole he wouldn't know the concept of value if it slept with his wife right in front of him!" The man hung up his phone, slammed it onto the table, and slugged back the last bit of tea in his cup before throwing the whole beverage into a nearby bin. Laney watched as he snatched up his phone and started another aggressive conversation. She hurried away, the sounds of his insults trailing behind her.

Laney reached the botanical park just as the sun was coming through the shade sail at just the right angle to bathe the park in golden light. The rows of raised beds and pots surrounded a little field of turf stretching down an artificial hill. Huge square buildings full of cafes, offices, boutique clothing stores, design firms, and perennially shuffling startup companies surrounded the little space of both real and fake green. Above the labyrinthine corridors of this mercantile maze sat loft apartments filled with tech savvy, fashionable, upwardly mobile company champions. A few leaned out on balcony railings, enjoying the carefully controlled temperature afforded by the arc's shade sail.

Laney sat down on a small bench and watched a couple of green-uniformed landscape workers working in raised beds and pots surrounding the turf greenspace that sat between the rectangular border of planters. She watched with interest as they pulled large, tropical-looking plants that had grown too big for their containers out of the dirt.

They placed the mature plants inside orange bags, tying them off when they stretched from weight. A third worker followed behind the other two, replacing the mature plants with identical-looking tropicals of a much smaller size, putting the little seedlings in the big holes left by the developed root systems' extraction. The worker filled the empty spaces with nearly black soil and patted mulch around the new plants. One of the other landscape workers was just dropping a bag of old mature plants in a nearby trash receptacle when a booming voice sounded from nearby. Laney turned her head to see Magda's approaching, red hair wreathed in the gold of the afternoon sun.

"Sorry I'm a little late," she boomed. "Elevator was on the fritz, the Underbelt was crowded."

"No apology necessary. It always is," Laney said as she scooted over on the bench, making room for her older friend. Magda, predictably, got straight to the point.

"So, what are we here to discuss, besides the obvious?"

Laney sighed. "Just the obvious itself. Thanks for always being able to just come out and say things. Thanks for meeting me here. I figured a public place would draw less suspicion than us meeting at one of our places."

"No key fob history," Magda agreed.

Laney's eyes felt heavy as she looked toward Magda.

"Do you think he's...okay? On his own down there?"

Magda heaved a sigh and fixed her vest. "What? Of course! He survived a whole *wasteland* alone. Maybe as a child. He can handle whatever's hiding down in those spooky old tunnels. Hell, he's probably scarier than anything down there."

Laney stretched back.

"I wish I had your confidence," she lamented.

Magda laughed.

"Just comes with age and seeing how things are over time. You really get a sense of what people are made of. That boy you saved from getting squished by ten trillion tons of steel had something in him that I'd never seen before."

"What do you think it was?" Laney asked. Magda pulled out her canteen and took a long swig. It smelled faintly of jet fuel.

"I don't rightly know, but I think we'll see soon enough." Laney looked over toward a crowd of passing shoppers. Words fell out of her mouth.

"I just wish I could have done more. I—"

Magda cut Laney off. "You saved him from *death*. We gave him a crash course on this alien world he climbed onto, and you slipped him into the cracks where Johnny Law wouldn't stick their noses. Sure, it's not *absent* of danger, but neither is the waste. Neither is anything! You bought him more time than anyone else would have. You can't feel guilty for not guaranteeing the one-hundred percent safety of somebody our entire society has conspired to erase from history."

"I guess you're right," Laney replied. "I wish he would have said more before he went under. About where he's from, how many people are out there. Why would the arc hide that information from everybody? I feel like I'm in some crazy conspiracy, and my two options are one, probe a near-silent fugitive's traumatic past, or two, believe a hundred years' worth of propagandized drivel."

"You could go check Lorne Ambrose's personal memoirs," Magda half-joked. Laney laughed as she replied.

"Anything informative or revelatory just wouldn't exist after all this time. Information can be scrubbed, or worse just not written down."

Magda tried again.

"Maybe the hundred-year-old blue-hairs left on the Great Gray Cruise Liner remember the arc's early days. You could ask them."

Laney rolled her eyes. "Don't call Arc Bravo that. Besides, you know the rules. Only family members are allowed aboard."

Magda replied. "Look, maybe the secret history you're looking for exists, maybe it doesn't. But you don't have to go searching ancient records to see that something here is amiss. It's everywhere you look."

Laney looked out once again across the turf. She saw a rail-thin woman in frayed clothing sitting dejectedly in front of the front window of a boutique shop. A VerchLife helmet covered her face and head. The helmet-clad woman clutched a hand written sign:

"SPARE SOME INC SO I CAN ESCAPE THIS REALITY."

Through the window, Laney saw two well-dressed women in pointy shoes eyeing the woman. They picked up a phone.

Laney bolted up and walked over. She scanned her income card directly into the VerchLife helmet, loading up six hours of virtual bliss. Magda followed behind and did the same.

"Somebody's feeling generous," the older woman quipped as they walked back to their bench. Laney sat back down and ran her fingers through her hair, pulling hard. Her face stretched backward, highlighting the deep circles under her baggy eyes.

"You know, that woman's life is my fault," she murmured.

"Whaddaya mean?" Magda asked, taking another sip from her canteen.

"You know I didn't always work in aux bay right?" Magda threw her eyes back trying to recall the many conversations she'd had with her favorite patron over the past few years. Her eyes lit up in recall and she returned to the conversation.

"Yeah, I remember now. You said you used to work up here with all the techies. Always found that odd, seeing as how you actually had some character in you." Laney laughed bitterly.

"That's just it. *I didn't.* I used to be a programmer for VerchLife." Magda's eyebrows raised as Laney continued. "I worked on the auto-adaptive-iterative personalized virtual content-writing program."

Magda stared at Laney blankly.

"Okay at least three of those words have to be fake."

Laney laughed again. "No, really. We trained an existing program that altered video in real time so it could practice producing continuous video-imaging content. We adapted the iterative image generation so it could produce bespoke content mapped to an individual's choices and behavior inside a simulation."

"Sooo...everybody's simulation is unique?"

"Yes. It studies the user as they use it and auto-generates new content based on what they'd find most enticing."

"And that's what's going on in that woman's helmet we just financed? I'm not sure I totally follow. This stuff came after me," Magda admitted, "we just had good old fashioned video-games."

Laney looked up.

"Yeah, it's kind of like video games melded with a personal, spiritual, psychedelic experience."

"Sounds good," Magda said, whistling.

"That's exactly it," Laney protested, "It's *too* good. A few years ago, I helped make literally the *most addictive programming possible.* Now that I look back, I see it was designed that way from the start."

"How much does it cost?" Magda asked. Laney didn't want to look at her friend as she answered.

"That's the thing. It's got entirely personalized pricing. The program has access to your income data, so it's priced based on your willingness-to-pay profile. Basically, it selects the very highest price that every individual would be willing to pay for a subscription and not one cent more to the point where you'd quit." Magda looked back at the emaciated woman.

"How much would she pay?"

Laney looked over. "Well looking at her, she probably hasn't had a Job ID in a while, so the program bases her payments on incoming inc scans and the length of time intervals between when she pays for new content." Magda folded her hands underneath her chin in consternation.

"So let me get this straight. Everybody pays a different price. They pay the highest price they'd be willing to pay based on what the program learns about them?"

"Exactly."

"So basically, you all built a psychic money vampire," Magda mused.

Laney sighed and reached for Magda's canteen. "Honestly, that's a way better description than auto-adaptive-iterative personalized virt—"

"Please Laney, if I ever have to hear that string of tech jargon again, I don't know if we can still be friends."

"Fair enough," Laney laughed, grateful for her friend's levity in the face of such a weighty confession.

The two sat for a moment before Magda broke the silence.

"So, how'd you end up moving around knickknacks and chairs?"

Laney sighed. "I did something stupid and destructive. I told the truth. One day I sat in with the higher-ups in the launch room. The product was almost finished. One guy—an investor in the project—owned a couple of the fabricating firms on Arc Delta. He listened to everything in the project launch description and then got super giddy. I'll never forget what he said. He said that every one of his employees that used this program would effectively be handing him back at least twenty percent of their paychecks. He laughed when he said it. That fucking laugh got to me. I was always enamored with tech. I mean, there's so much we could build, so much we can make and solve, but *that's* what we green lit and finished, in the end. A way to send twenty-plus-percent of people's paychecks back to their bosses."

Laney realized she was almost shouting. She calmed herself and continued.

"It's amazing what people say when they assume everyone in the room thinks exactly like they do," Magda nodded.

"I'd imagine, a lot of the time, they all do think the same. Or they just get a trip from saying something outrageous and everyone having to toe the line because they're responsible for payday."

Laney took one more swig from the canteen before passing it back to Magda. "Later on, I saw the pricing module and crunched the numbers. He was right, the bastard. That twenty-percent figure was dead-on."

Magda snorted. "Some people can only do math if there's dollar signs attached. I had an old boss who was the world's best at counting to thirty-nine." She leaned in, eyes big. "So what did ya do next?"

"At first, I just voiced my concern. Their reply was that everyone was free to choose to use the product or not, and if they so chose, then we must definitionally be improving user's lives."

"Never mind the metric shit-ton of inc that everybody's 'singular and free choice' would make them," Magda interjected.

"Exactly," Laney continued. "So I wrote a letter. I hit 'send all' to the company, even posted it on the front door. I just explained how much of the arc we'd be bleeding dry and why I thought that was wrong. I just wanted them to put in some safeguards. You know, educate people about the project, healthy limits, *something.* I even put in the direct quote from the guy about getting his employees' paychecks right back."

"What happened?" Magda asked.

"I lost my job, of course. Amazing how fast I went from being a 'model worker with big ideas for the company' to a 'surly slacker with a bad attitude poisoning the well." Laney could hear the venom in her own voice. Magda clapped her on the shoulder.

"They're cowardly, weak fucks, Laney. Too weak to look in a mirror, so they lie. Nobody's probably ever told 'em what's what before. Good on ya." Magda raised her canteen in an imaginary toast.

Laney continued. "I guess. Long run, I didn't get anything. Worst part was how many friends I lost. Wasn't good to be seen around me if you wanted to get a raise. Now, it's like...everything I do, I question. I helped build something terrible. It's hard to feel right about anything you do after something like that." Laney gestured at Magda's canteen, fearing it would go empty soon. "Do you mind?"

"Not at all," Magda said as Laney took several deep drinks from the vessel. She coughed lightly and dabbed her watery eyes.

"And now," Laney said, "now I rearrange settees and Tête-à-Tête's around a warehouse for the exact same type of people that rake in inc for the psychic money vampire I helped create."

"Fuck's sake, what the hell's a Tit a Tit?" Magda blurted, pawing the canteen back from Laney and taking a gulp.

Laney burst out laughing. She sobered when she again caught sight of the begging woman in the VerchLife helmet.

"Sad thing is, they're probably right. That virtual bliss probably does make that woman's life better." Magda slammed down the canteen on the bench with a *thunk.*

"No, it doesn't. It just makes her forget how her life really is. You ever notice how the people with the least on this arc end up trading real physical labor or money for temporary, depreciating virtual items and experiences?"

"I mean, yeah, when you put it that way," Laney replied. "What are you getting at?"

"Well I think it's deliberate. Or maybe it's just a happy fucking accident. Doesn't matter. Point is, there's only so much space on the arc. Folks live in small, cramped quarters. Only natural you'd be encouraged to expand into a virtual dimension when your physical space is lacking. Keeps you from comparing the size of your tin shoebox to the mansions you end up working at," Laney laughed.

"The arc is built on the maximization of the individual's potential," Laney pronounced in a pompous voice as she thrust her finger into the air. "Our founder's favorite quote. Do you remember the field trips to his home in A Sector? The one they turned into a shrine? Remember all the little school children clamoring around to get a peek at Lorne Ambrose's corpse sitting mummified in a vacuum-sealed tube?"

Magda grimaced. "Yeah, we had that same field trip in my day, only he'd been dead two decades less when I was craning my neck and getting on my tiptoes to look at all his plastic surgeries."

Laney looked up. "Yeah like the man thought it'd be natural to stare at a corpse filled with surgically implanted permanent youth."

The two women sat for a moment. Laney spoke first.

"Why do you think he did it?"

"Did what, the surgeries?" Magda asked.

"*No.* The arc, I mean. All of it. Why'd he build it?" The rosy red glow filling Magda's cheeks grew a darker shade, closer to purple.

"I know *exactly* why he did it." Magda steeled her gaze. "I watched the little history tape again recently with our mutual friend. His house was the first thing they ever put on this godforsaken arc."

"Way back when, he gets to a point where he realizes the flood is coming, and he just raises up his castle, high enough to escape the waters. Only, flood isn't the only thing he has to worry about, fire, wind, everything's coming. Eventually one of those is going to take him out, so he puts his castle up on legs and teaches it to walk. Makes his house on stilts. Gives it the ability to run away, dodge every act of God's natural vengeance for decades. He sees a couple of his friends and they want their castles saved too, so he brings them up here with him and everyone calls him king.

"Only it's no fun to live in a castle and call yourself king if you've gotta weed your own gardens and scrub your own floors. So you've gotta bring gardeners and a maid onto your city on stilts, but you don't want them living in *your house*. That doesn't make it a palace, so they've got to have other places to live. And you've gotta have people to feed you and clothe you, and different people to cook for and clothe your workers, because if we eat the same meals and wear the same clothes, then its only natural to ask why doesn't everyone live in a castle?"

"So the whole thing expands. You've got to have a doctor to keep you healthy and that doctor has to have someone to teach his kids how to read enough to get a job selling merchandise in a virtual world. Soon the thing grows big enough that you've got an entire city on the back of a big mechanical bug, and smaller bugs following it to keep the biggest beetle fed and clothed. You call the bug an arc after the old story, but you change the spelling to rebrand it. You bring all your friends on board and eventually you had to bring on all the other people to help support your new lives as the kings of stilted castles."

"You bring two doctors, two magnates, two risk analysts, and two gardeners. Two engineers, two teachers, two life coaches, two partners. Two mechanics, two accountants, two personal trainers, two laborers. Two escorts, two yes-men, two architects, two headsmen. Two h-vac repairmen, two loaders, two pickers, two packers. Two freight drivers, two claims adjusters, two cleaners, two data mappers. You bring them and all the rest, and they multiply. But it can't grow forever because physical things have a limit that drawings, models, projections and ideas don't have. Cracks start appearing in your plan when it's exposed to gravity. Atoms and bits play by different rules. Widgets don't die, feel pain, sweat or get thirsty."

"Your bug starts belching out its spent fuel, poisoning a sun-baked ground. It shits its mountains of trash on the ground. It gets harder and harder to keep all those people on board busy with their lives, keep all those shelves stocked. Maintain variety and quantity. Shipments take longer, houses get smaller, and you develop tech to put a holographic sheen on the same gray food the hoi polloi eat for every meal.

"Maybe there really used to be a day when you really could maximize the individual's potential. But now we can't. The arc can't grow forever. It's too heavy. Not every person can grow themselves to afford every nice big comfy house. The arc's legs would collapse from the weight. I mean, I don't really see any new construction around here, just all the same people shuffling around all the same old spaces. So, some people get ample space to fill with tit-a-tits and fountains and three living rooms and some people get to sit on the street and beg for one more minute in a virtual world.

"Lorne Ambrose didn't build a city. He built a pharaoh's tomb to bring all his stuff along after the world ended. We're all buried with him." Magda raised her canteen and downed the rest of it. "Long live the pharaoh."

Laney looked at Magda with new eyes. She saw a purple anger pulse on her friend's face that she had never seen before. Magda's fist balled, then unclenched. Laney put a hand on her friend's shoulder.

"Is this anger always there?" she asked quietly. "I've never seen it before."

"Yeah, kid," Magda replied, "it's always been there. You can't live as long as I have and think as much as I have without building up more than a little rage inside." She sighed and looked down at her feet. "You just don't get anywhere talking about it, so eventually you learn to keep your mouth shut. You stay quiet long enough that eventually nobody knows you've got that rage. You make jokes instead."

Laney looked at Magda and spoke. "I'm glad you told me. It's still good to say it. Silence can be a special kind of lie."

Magda rested her elbows on her knees wearily. "Look, I'm glad Ambrose and everyone like them did what they did. I'm here because of it. You're alive because of it. We have all these wonderful inventions because of it. I'm not starving, I have an income, and I have a place to sleep without worrying about snakes or bugs biting my ass. But I've also never taken a single step on the planet that humans were born on. And for that...for that, I'm fucking pissed."

Magda and Laney sat together in silence. They didn't see the woman begging for inc shuffle off when she spotted an arc security officer in the distance. She crept away unnoticed through a hidden mechanical access hatch, descending below to the guts of the hull.

The belly of the beast.

The pharaoh's tomb.

Chapter 16

Tenzing got up and stretched his legs. He felt no throb in his skull. *Good medicine.* He wondered what it was that had produced that miraculous, pain-numbing sleep. He walked over toward one of the nearby light holes, and ran his finger around the rough surface of its cut triangular opening. The metal was thin where the holes were cut, and thick in vertical and horizontal lines where multiple sheets of the thin metal joined in little ridges.

He rapped his knuckles against the thin metal near a cut spot. He felt the hard surface and understood the wall's strength. *"I could never cut this,"* he mused, thinking of the bone hewn-knife he'd used in the wastes. *"It is clear these rats possess many talents."*

Tenzing probed farther down the passageway. He ducked under a few large burlap tarps suspended from thick steel pipes higher up in the corridor's ceiling. One of these tarps swung gently, occupied by the sound of a snoring, sleeping, bearded man with wild ginger hair. Tenzing crept past the sleeping occupant as quietly as he could, following the regular midday sunbeams that lit up the corridor, bouncing off triangular metal panels affixed to the interior wall. Illumination filled the corridor with alternating bursts of exterior and reflected light. *Much they've built here.*

Farther down, Tenzing saw the crouched figure of a young woman, younger than Tenzing, with short-cropped hair. She leaned over two buckets, performing some task unknown to Tenzing. One bucket was filled with a moist detritus Tenzing did not recognize. The other, larger bucket had heaps of small, stained white bags with little strings attached. Tenzing watched the young woman pick up the white bags, rip them open and dump their contents into the other bucket. She continued working her way through the pile, not taking any notice of Tenzing. Tenzing's observation of the young woman's work was interrupted by a familiar voice.

"Ah, good you're up again. I'm assuming you'd like the tour?"

Tenzing turned and nodded at June. She pointed towards a green area in the distance farther down the tunnel.

"We'll start with the garden."

Tenzing followed behind June. As they neared the area she had indicated, a vining mass of plants growing over and around one another sprouted into view. Spear-shaped leaves decorated the vines, and they ended in either little yellow flowers or small spheres in shades varying from green to pale orange to brilliant vermilion.

"These beauties are cherry tomatoes." Tenzing observed one of the little green globes just barely tinted with little flecks of orange suspended from the mess of crawling plant matter. More light filled this section, bathing the plants in shade-sail filtered sunlight. Tenzing looked over and saw the light holes were different here—large rectangular cuts on three sides, the thin sheet metal bent up toward the ceiling., a crease in the metal showing its upward curl. June commanded Tenzing's attention back to the garden.

"See that red one? Eat it." Tenzing looked over at June, who pointed more enthusiastically for assurance, and he plucked the little red fruit from the vine and popped it in his mouth. As soon as he had applied the barest pressure, the fruit's skin split and Tenzing's mouth filled with a refreshing burst of acidic, faintly bitter juice.

"Good!" Tenzing hummed around the small mouthful.

"You're damn right it's good," June said proudly, "and there's more where that came from." She stepped forward, motioning for Tenzing to follow. The pair walked in tandem down the corridor, passing multiple containers filled with soil and plants that dotted the hallway with varying shades of bright to dark green. They appeared soft, like someone had looked after them with a caring spirit.

Tenzing thought of the dry, spiky, tough plants from the waste that seemed to exist only to spit in the face of an inhospitable, doomed environment. *These plants taste much better,* he thought. *These plants are fragile. These plants were cared for.*

June beamed as she watched Tenzing explore each container fascinated by both the plants and their receptacles. The grow frames that housed the soil and plants were jury-rigged boxes built out of a hodgepodge of scavenged materials. Tenzing recognized thick corrugated cardboard and what looked like disassembled cargo crates from the VerchLife video. Bits of wire held the boxes' frames, and cut pieces of metal and plastic supplied their paneled sides. June named each plant they passed, like a proud mother introducing her children.

"We've got bell peppers, zucchini, cucumber, black beans, cherry tomatoes, sweet potatoes, and the plant that supplied the medicine you drank."

Tenzing looked at the spiky plant June had just pointed out. He bent down and brought his nose toward its pungent, earthy smell. He remembered a similar odor from Magda's apartment. He bent to look more closely at the beautiful black dirt filling each container. He gently ran his hand through the soil, feeling its texture. It did not slide through his palms into the air like the dust of the wasteland; instead, it clumped together in damp little granules of variable size. It felt soft between the pads of his fingers, with little chunks of brittle wood and dried leaves that crackled softly as Tenzing clenched his fist around the clump of soil.

"Where did this come from!?" Tenzing asked, incredulous at the fertile, black earth in his hand.

"The plants or the soil?" June asked, standing up from where she had bent down to observe some little yellow spots on the cucumber plant's leaves.

"Both? All of it?" Tenzing said. He let the soil's rich, non-uniform texture sprinkle through his fingers.

"The dirt comes from Jonas," June said. "You just missed him. He's out doing a job right now. He works a few days a week landscaping. He brings home a little dirt at a time whenever he comes back from work, along with dead plants, leaves, any organic matter he can get his hands on. We use it to enrich the soil. It all goes into the big sifter and we let it 'cook' til it's fertile." June slapped a nearby cargo crate, then gestured back down the corridor to where the short-haired woman was still busy at her task.

"Mite helps with bringing in soil nutrients as well. She's one of our requisitioners. Likes to scour shop trash cans topside to retrieve anything valuable. Finds a fortune in tea bags every time she looks. That's what she's doing down there, emptying the used leaves from the teabags into the compost," June explained.

"So, some of the Rats have jobs?" Tenzing asked.

"Oh, sure. Some firms on the arc will hire people without a Job ID. Mostly low-paying labor positions. They don't have to pay as much to people without the proper documentation."

"I see," Tenzing mused.

"As for the seeds and botanical knowledge," June continued, "those were my contributions to the Rats."

Tenzing remembered June's discussion of reciprocity.

"Where did you get the seeds?" he asked.

"I used to work in the hydroponics factory on Arc Charlie. I parted ways with my old company on...unfortunate terms. Coupla' work friends knew how much I loved tending to the plants, so they snuck a few thousand seeds out from the vault as a 'parting gift."

"What did you do?" Tenzing asked.

"I was a greenery worker. Spent all day planting, pruning, packaging, watering, attending to every different type of plant you could think of. I loved it. Until my last day, when I...well, I lost my ability to work there."

June's eyes fell. Tenzing considered her dejected stare. This was the first time he'd seen anything but unbound optimism from her.

Tenzing matched June's somber tone.

"What happened?" June looked back at Tenzing and saw a caring sadness in his eyes.

"This tour is about the rats, not me."

"But you are a rat, are you not?" Tenzing insisted. June huffed.

"All right, but I'm going to try and tell this quickly so we can get back to more important things." Tenzing nodded as June resumed.

"Okay, so I'm back working in the greenery on Arc Charlie. One day, an order of orchids for somebody gets left off a shipment, and the docking period between Arc Charlie and Arc Alpha is almost up. The shipment was apparently for a very important customer, so our supervisor is furious that somebody left it off. I get tired of her yelling, so I say something. I don't even remember what I said. Anyway, she tells me to go hand-deliver the orchids up to the loading dock and make sure they get put in their own fragile goods crate. At that point, I was just tired of her scolding everyone, so I just decided to do the damn thing even though I had never been in an active loading zone and never had any training to load cargo. I stepped in the wrong place and BAM! The boom arm of a loader drone whipped around and caught me in the back of the head. I hit the floor and so did the orchids."

"Came to in a hospital bed on Arc Echo. Had a screaming headache and my hands wouldn't stop shaking. They still don't. When I got out,

I had a new mountain of medical debt that I couldn't even begin to pay for because my hands couldn't do the fine motor skill work they used to, and I couldn't afford the surgery that would fix that. So, I'm out of a job, and the people I worked for won't foot the bill. They claimed 'I didn't have any documentation that my hands were fine before I worked there." June spat out the last sentence with venom. Tenzing wondered aloud.

"People that you worked for —people that you *trusted*—did not help you when you needed them?"

"Yep," June answered, voice brittle.

"Not reciprocity," Tenzing stated.

"Not even a little," June agreed. "Anyways, I've got no way to repay the debt, and my lovely little C+ dwelling goes to the next-highest bidder. I'd heard rumors about the Side Hull, and I ended up here."

"I'm sorry," Tenzing offered, unsure of what else to say. June shrugged.

"It is what it is. My story isn't unique. At least now I've got my own garden. I can plant what I want, when I want. Although Grandpa and Mite do most of the actual planting these days, and the pruning. I just tell them what to do."

Tenzing sat for a moment with the revelation of June's sad background. *Something stops working the way you think it ought to, you throw it out.* The concept was foreign to him. The only way to survive in the wastes was by using every tool at his disposal. When something was broken, you fixed it, or repurposed it in a way that better-fit its new shape.

June's voice broke Tenzing's reverie.

"Told you I had a soft spot for people with head injuries," she teased, pointing to the bandages that still wrapped around Tenzing's swollen head. "Now you know why I've taken a liking to you." Both of them laughed. June changed the subject.

"You seemed enamored with the dirt earlier. What's up with that?"

"Just...just never seen dirt like that up close. I-it's..." Tenzing stammered, struggling to find any words to describe its quality without saying how different it was from the dust of the waste.

"It's *real*," June supplied. "It's not from here. The arc, I mean. You can fabricate, 3D print, program, or genetically engineer a lot of things, but a good old-fashioned handful of dirt can still only come from the Earth itself." Tenzing peeked out of a nearby light hole. He craned his neck and looked straight down at the ground that lay at the bottom of a shudderingly high drop.

"How do they *get* the earth?" he asked.

"Arc Golf," June said. "I know a guy who used to work that gig. He said some parts of the earth aren't as dead as the rest of it. Grandpa's tests confirmed that for us. Little pockets of stubborn green still hold out. Arc Golf finds those places - where the trees, grasses, and animal shit have nurtured the soil—and it sends out bushwacker and bulldozer drones to scoop up the topsoil and bring it back. Ends up supplying rose gardens and annual beds in Sector A mansions, tropical plant pots and containers outside B Sector cafes, those sorts of things."

"So, Golf..."

"Destroys what's left of the natural world? Absolutely."

June and Tenzing continued their journey down the long hallway. Out of the darkness before them came a loud, whining, grinding sound. They rounded the corner to the sight of near-blinding sparks filling the corridor ahead as a figure in a large metal mask held a loud power tool against the exterior wall. Tenzing plugged his ears as they neared the figure whose ministrations were filling the vicinity with smoke, sparks and noise. The tool finished etching out a triangle shape and the figure clicked a button on the machine, which whirred to a halt.

The masked figure set the tool down at their feet and picked up a hammer. With two solid *whaps*, the machine operator nearly knocked the triangle from its place in the exterior wall. It held on stubbornly from one minute metal thread still affixing it to a corner. Gloved hands twisted the triangular sheet metal until the last sinuous bit of steel gave way. The figure stowed the large slice of sheet metal in a nearby pile as sunlight flowed freely through the new hole, further illuminating the tunnel.

"This is Roark, our resident machinist," June introduced the figure as they took off the welding mask, revealing a dirty, long haired man with straw-colored hair and a patchy beard. Little pock-mark burns covered the man's face.

Roark pulled off his right glove and reached forward, taking hold of Tenzing's hand. Tenzing hesitated, unfamiliar with the action. He tried his best to match the machine operator's iron grip. He closed his fingers around the sweaty, dirty hand outstretched in front of him. Tenzing's fingers slid around more of the man's hand than expected. He looked down and noticed Roark was missing the two outermost fingers and half of the middle finger on their right hand.

"You make the light," Tenzing said. Roark's mouth bobbed up and down as he chewed on a plastic straw while he talked.

"True enough. Not all of 'em were me, though. Just the good cuts. Some were here when it was just the old-timer down here by himself."

"How do you decide where to put the holes?" Tenzing asked.

"Well, the angle grinder's a bit of a sacred artifact 'round here. Only grabbed so many blades from the fab shop on Delta. So, we vote on whereabouts to put 'em."

"And then you disregard the vote and put them where you think is best, because it's your angle grinder and you don't trust anyone else to use it," June scoffed.

"Yeah, that's about the size of it," Roark responded as he turned to June. "You gonna show the newcomer how we see at night?"

"Uh...yeah, later," June responded, changing the subject with her own question. "So...this hole for light or wind?"

"Just light right now," the long haired man grunted. He wiped a bead of sweat off his brow.

"Guess there's still no success in retrieving our arc welder...?" June asked.

"What is an arc welder?" Tenzing asked.

"It's a machine," Roark answered. "Uses electricity to super heat a rod. You can use it to join metal together. If you're savvy, you can use it to cut metal too. They're heavy but portable. Just a happy coincidence it's a welder also used on the arc."

"So this attempt didn't fare any better than the last?" June asked.

"Naw, that goggle-headed techno-cult recognized Jonas and Mite soon as they set foot down there. Gonna be a little toastier than we like down this section fer a little while longer."

June saw the look on Tenzing's face and answered his question before he had a chance to voice it.

"You're wondering how we're not already roasting alive in a metal tunnel without conditioned air. Come look at this."

Tenzing decided to pretend he knew what June meant by 'conditioned air' and looked to where she was directing his attention.

"Look here. See the funnel welded on the outside?" Tenzing stuck his head out a large light hole in the wall and looked to the side. He saw sheet metal bent into a conical form covering the outside of a cut hole.

"Passive cooling. One of El Ratticus Firsticus' better ideas. First, Roark makes a hole cut through the steel. Later, whenever Spark figures out how to get his welder back from those techno-zealots, he'll come back and weld one of these big funnels onto the outside."

June gave Tenzing's shoulders a light push and guided him to a spot right in front of the hole with the cone. "Stand right here, tell me what you feel." Tenzing waited for a minute before he heard a rushing sound. Concentrated wind blew through the cone, cooling Tenzing's skin.

"I feel air," he confirmed.

June leaned against the metal wall as she explained. "We're high up, so there's more wind to catch. The same wind the walls surrounding the deck block, we let it right in. Wind runs through the funnel and passes through the corridor. Creates air circulation. We got holes where it exits further on down the tunnel. More air tunnels, better circulation. Combined with the shade sail, it can be at least twenty degrees cooler than it is outside at any given time. It'll be better when we make more. We still feel the heat; it's not as good as air conditioning by a long shot-"

"Feeling the seasons makes you pay more attention," Roark interrupted.

"A fine point," June replied. She walked back to a nearby hole cut with the same conical apparatus and struck a dramatic pose, throwing her arms wide across a thin wire mesh. "And here's the best part. Roark, if you'll do the honors."

Roark rolled his eyes slightly, but pulled the wire mesh apart, revealing a little catch-basin filled with dust.

"Here, take this," June commanded, thrusting the catch basin into Tenzing's hands. "Bring it to Grandpa farther down the corridor."

"What is it for?" Tenzing asked.

"You'll see. It's the proof we've been waiting for." With that, June turned around and started to leave. She called back over her shoulder.

"I've got to go check up on some things before I go make some deliveries topside. Don't keep El Ratticus Firsticus waiting. He'll be eager to have today's results. He's right farther down, can't miss him. Bye-ya!"

June departed and Tenzing started in the opposite direction, carrying the catch-basin filled with particulates down the tunnel, looking for the older man. He came to a widened area of the corridor and did some mental calculations. *Must be the support structure for the arc's back leg.*

Grandpa sat at a desk in a beat-up chair. The chair's stuffing poked through several seams in its orange upholstery. The desk was cluttered with a myriad of arcane objects. Dusty, yellowed papers scrawled with odd symbols that Tenzing did not understand, old computer monitors spliced into nearby electrical conduits, and an army of little glass bottles filled every square inch of the desk where Grandpa busied himself. Some were large and filled with fizzing liquids of various colors. Others were small and contained what looked like the same kind of dust that Tenzing held in his hands.

The wiry old man loomed over the desk, going back and forth between aged papers, charts, and a thick red book full of handwritten symbols. A little puff of white fluff fell out of the ancient orange desk chair as Grandpa leaned forward to greet Tenzing.

"Wonderful, you've brought today's sample." Grandpa took the catch-basin and turned around, dumping its contents through a funnel into a few of the smaller glass jars. He wrapped tape around each tube and marked the tape with symbols written in blue ink. Tenzing watched Grandpa work, fascinated. The older man poured various liquids into each of the different small glass jars filled with dust. He watched them silently fizzle, change color, or do nothing at all for a few minutes at a time and wrote symbols in his red book after each observed interaction.

This strange array of precise rituals baffled Tenzing. His brain simply could not conjure any explanation as to the man's alien behavior. Grandpa didn't offer any explanation as he plodded on. Tenzing suspected Grandpa enjoyed this.

"What are you doing?" Tenzing blurted when he could no longer stand his curiosity. Grandpa turned back around and faced the new-comer. He stood up and made a grand gesture with his arms, similar to the one June had made earlier.

"Welcome to my lab!" he announced. "Well, what's left of it anyways. Much less than I used to have as head environmental scientist on Arc

Golf, but what can you do? It was my job to study the earth. Study the health of the very thing you're put in charge of killing— ha! I gave them the proverbial finger, told 'em they'd have to find someone else to do that."

Tenzing offered a nervous grin, feeling it was the right thing to do. Grandpa mirrored Tenzing's smile with one of his own and turned back to his work as he spoke again.

"But enough of ancient history, and back to your question. Simply put, I'm checking the soil's health. Like a dirt doctor," he chuckled.

"How do you do that without touching it? Tenzing asked.

"Little particulates blow up in the high atmospheric winds outside the arc. We collect them in our catch-basins ,and I check for pollutants in ppm— that's parts per million— and I cross-reference that with weather patterns to try and guess where the dust came from."

"Weather patterns?" Tenzing's face furrowed. Grandpa elaborated with the elation that can only come from explaining one's true joy in life.

"The arc is always connected to a series of high atmospheric weather balloons that help predict wind patterns and that sort of thing. It's wildly approximate, of course— no one can do that kind of math with any serious degree of accuracy. Too many variables. Nevertheless, it's all we have, so we use them anyway. Best we can do in these post-satellite days."

"Satellite?" Tenzing asked, falling further into dizzying incomprehension. It seemed for every answer he got, two new questions popped into his mind unbidden. Grandpa waved a hand.

"Yes, according to arc history, in the last days before the arc's completion, Waymon Munch lost humanity's dream of space forever when his orbital colony, 0rbz, collided with one of his own satellites. Easy to do when you put so many up there. One collision can easily turn into more because the shrapnel from each collision multiplies exponentially."

Tenzing stared blankly as Grandpa continued, totally oblivious to the younger man's complete lack of understanding. "Terrible way to go. You spend all your time and energy dodging little missiles traveling at orbital velocity, 'til eventually you're shredded to bits by your own uncompromising vision. I just feel bad for all the employees he demanded to relocate up there."

Grandpa turned back to Tenzing. So overwhelmed by this inundation of incomprehensible information, he lied down still across the metal floor. Grandpa looked at the supine newcomer as a wry grin curled across his wizened face.

"Oh yes, back to soil health. Point is, the farther away the dust is from the arc, the healthier it is, and the healthy soil has started to improve, if only a little. More than we ever thought it would. We're almost ready for the real thing."

"The real thing?"

Grandpa folded both his hands together and his lined face split in a mischievous grin.

"Tenzing you've seen the humble little world we've built in the cracks of this arc?"

"Yes. It is impressive," Tenzing responded.

"It's nothing but *preparation*," Grandpa confided, leaning in. "We're just waiting for the right moment for Phase 2."

Tenzing echoed his lean. "What is Phase 2?"

Grandpa pulled a smaller chair from nearby and put it out in front of Tenzing.

"Please, have a seat." Tenzing obliged and sat in the small chair as Grandpa rifled through the bag under his desk. He pulled out a metal cylinder that extended in discrete sections when he pulled the ends away from one another. Each end of the extended cylinder ended in a circular glass lens. He held the smaller side of the object up to his eye and aimed the far side out of a hole in the wall that was pointed in the direction of the arc's titanic middle legs. Grandpa looked down the corridor and saw no one close before he leaned in and spoke in a gentle tone.

"Tenzing, I saw you climb this arc. I know you came from the wastes."

Tenzing's body flashed hot, then cold. He said nothing. His eyes blinked in panic and his breath quickened. He bolted up from his chair, ready to turn and run, but Grandpa stretched out a placating hand.

"Don't worry. I'm not going to give you away. Tenzing, please stay. We have much to discuss."

Chapter 17

"You are not the first I've seen," said Grandpa.

"What do you mean?" Tenzing's head spun. "You have seen others? People not from the arc!?" Tenzing realized he was almost shouting.

"Lower your voice," Grandpa exhorted. He folded the telescope and adjusted the lens. "I will answer any questions you have. I'll tell you anything you want to know. Please, just take a seat."

Tenzing overcame his urge to turn and run. He put one hand on the small chair beside him as he pulled it closer to the desk. He sat down, but shifted half his weight to the balls of his feet, ready to sprint away if the older man's words did not satisfy. Grandpa crossed the corridor Tenzing had come from and moved a big, thick cloth in front of the corridor.

"This will help dampen the sound. I promise this will be a private conversation. I haven't told a soul about you. I'm the only one down here who knows your true origin. The rest of the rats just think you're another down-on-your-luck arc-dweller. I will keep that story as long as you want."

"How did you know?" Tenzing asked. He ran his fingers around his cut hair, and his arc clothes. "How did you know?" he said again. his fingers tightening around the chair leg where he sat squeezing the metal til his hand blanched pale.

"Please, I will tell you everything I know. I owe you that much."

Grandpa extended the telescope. He walked to the light-hole that illuminated his ramshackle lab and held the spyglass up to the aperture, gesturing for Tenzing to follow. Tenzing released his grip on the chair leg and followed. Grandpa held the lens up to Tenzing's eye as he trained its focus on the horizon.

"Look out there," Grandpa suggested.

Tenzing saw the waste, the treacherous landscape he'd traversed to find this strange city on legs. He saw the gutted ground cracked with windswept ravines. Clouds of polluted air hovered over the horizon like fetid curtains. A thick pool of glowing, green sludge stuck to the earth like a scab of almost dried-blood. A hazy corona refracted light around this sludge. It sent deep reds and deeper violets cascading through the walled prism of dust dredged up by the arc's great strides. Tenzing stared at this pool. He'd never seen anything like it. Tenzing studied its alien form.

"Discharge from the arc's power plant. Spent fuel. It's a rare phenomenon, doesn't need to happen often, but it lasts for quite a long time. From the land at least, the arc takes much more than it returns.

'Not reciprocity," Tenzing said. He stared at the sludge and the arc's craterous footprints. Grandpa pushed the telescope in view of the arc's legs. Tenzing saw where he had climbed. He saw where he fell. He saw where Laney had saved him.

"Could others have seen?" Tenzing asked. The older man took the telescope and compressed it. He stowed it in his bag.

"It's not likely," Grandpa said. "High walls all around the deck keep people looking inward. The tallest buildings have small windows facing only other tall buildings. Balconies face streets instead of the horizon. The mansion dwellers are so enthralled by the perfection of their sanctuaries, they don't look beyond the ornamentation of their interiors. Grandpa looked with naked eyes back to the Arc's discharge.

"Why rest your eyes on an eyesore when you can look at all the pretty things money can buy? Unfortunately, those with less, now have their eyes buried in a helmet swaddled in images of other realities. That was a more recent innovation, but it carries the spirit of my grandfather's design. One has to travel below down to the Side Hull or crane their neck from the aft deck to see the earth below.

My grandfather did well when he designed all these architectural blindfolds. A place's independence and self-sufficiency must preclude the possibility of looking elsewhere." Tenzing remembered the Verch-Life program he watched and asked.

"Your grandfather was the founder, Ambrose?"

"No, he wasn't Ambrose. He was the man Ambrose woke in the middle of the night in a cold panic begging and raving to start this ludicrous project. My grandfather made the drawings, and countless others built it. Ambrose funded it," Grandpa sighed.

"Only some of those countless who built the very floor we stand upon were rewarded a dwelling when the Dry Flood came and killed the earth.

"What is a Dry Flood? How do you know this?" Tenzing asked.

"I know because my grandfather told his children. They told their children and so on. Memories, especially bad ones, are harder to expunge than documents if a person chooses not to forget them."

Tenzing nodded. He remembered the stories and warnings his mother had passed to him, things he would never forget. Things that had kept him alive.

"The Dry Flood was a tabloid name for complete ecological collapse preceded by a great drought. A cheeky, gawky name for a dryness that swept the earth, sending all the things that depend on water into a slow lingering death. Most things depend on water. Amidst that long drought, there were fires, earthquakes, tornadoes, crop failures. Some places even got hurricanes and flooding seas that spilled far inland. Plagued by thirst and inundated with saltwater.

"The arc was built by then. Finished just before the turning point when things stopped getting better. It was built to be independent of all that. Free from harm, free from adaptation. Free to walk on and persist.

"On its maiden voyage, the very first day the arc took its first steps, my great grandfather learned why the practice of looking inward was etched into the very heart of the arc's design. Built into the very structure of its many walls. As the arc left the city where it was built, a mass of people tried to climb its legs."

"Why did they try this climb?" Tenzing asked. He remembered his own attempt at the same act.

"It was the only place left with water," Grandpa said. "The climbers were shot down with darts by a small phalanx of Ambrose's personal security. One by one, they fell to the ground left behind as the arc marched away."

Grandpa's eyes fell over Tenzing.

"Not much has changed," he said.

Tenzing ran his fingers over the raised patch of skin that had scarred over the minute puncture wound on his neck.

"That was the day the arc died for my grandfather. He learned that Ambrose never wanted to save humanity, just keep his own life and surround himself with enough people to pretend life hadn't changed til the day he died. In that regard, the founder couldn't have been more successful. He kept his abundance till his end."

Grandpa got up from his chair. He twisted a little valve attached to a pipe. He held a glass underneath a spout. A trickle of water filled the glass. Grandpa shut the valve.

"Siphoned water. In addition to welding, Spark is an excellent plumber. They don't notice the minuscule amount we use. The arc recycles what water it can, but a great drill on Arc Golf pulls water up from dwindling aquifers and keeps our tanks full and wet. The arc cannot continue this way forever. It's like a tick on a corpse. One day the corpse will stop bleeding."

Grandpa sat down and took a sip of cool, clean water from the glass. He poured a second glass and handed it to Tenzing. Tenzing drank deeply, finished his glass, and asked.

"What did your great-grandfather do? How did more people not see, not remember what happened on that day? The day they shot down the climbers?"

Grandpa finished his drink, and set the empty glass down on his desk.

"To answer your second question, I don't fully know. Perhaps they really were all looking inward and didn't see. Perhaps the survivor's guilt erased their memories. Maybe they feared that saying anything would void their spot on the arc and they'd end up no better than those dying of thirst out in the wasted land.

For whatever reason, societal memory forgot to remember the unpleasantness." Grandpa ran his finger around the water glass.

"But my grandfather was different."

"What did he do?" Tenzing asked.

"He used that day and the contents of Ambrose's first crazed phone call as leverage. Above all, Ambrose cared about his reputation, his celebrity, so Ambrose gave my grandfather what he wanted to keep him quiet. My grandfather's requests were never so much that Ambrose considered anything harsher to silence him. It was easier to give in. Ambrose was used to paying for things. My grandfather just learned to ask for exactly enough and no more. So he always got the only thing he really wanted."

"What did he want?" asked Tenzing.

"He knew he couldn't save the world so he decided to do the next-best thing: provide well for his children. He ensured his children were always well-taken-care-of. Nepotism runs deep on the arc, and the Strickland children have always held prominent posts for that reason.

It continues to this day with the last two of us. I became head of Arc Golf, a cushy job in charge of natural resource acquisition, and my younger brother became head of Arc Security. He leads the spiritual descendants of those men who shot down the thirsty masses clamoring for water on that fateful first day that the arc first took stride."

"Your brother is the man that tried to have me killed," Tenzing asserted.

"Yes. Yes, he is," Grandpa answered. "Much of my life has been a regret, but he is a bigger regret than most. I am sorry I could not put him on a better path, and I am sorry you've paid the price for my mistakes. Heinous deeds done by blood you share puts a taste in the mouth that never leaves."

"Why does he do it, your brother?" Tenzing asked.

"I suppose he believes he is protecting the family legacy, the arc and all its citizens. Or perhaps in some twisted way he believes his actions will keep the arc safe and going forever. But, the things he's done. The things he *does*... it begs the question of how much it is worth."

Grandpa stood up near the light-hole and gazed out toward the arc's legs.

"I saw a woman I did not recognize save you through my telescope. I was all-but-ready to call the top side of the arc done, incapable of producing anything but malice and selfishness, greed and domination, but then this woman saved you. She didn't know you, and she saved you. You were a perfect stranger, and she risked her life to save you. It has been a long time since I've seen someone outside of our little family down here perform such a selfless act. It gave me hope."

"She gives me hope." Tenzing felt a pall of guilt fall around him. His shoulders felt heavy. He fought the urge to sink down to the metal floor beneath him. *She does not know if I'm okay.*

"This woman, can I send a message to her?" Tenzing asked.

"Yes," Grandpa answered. "I will have June deliver it on her next round of deliveries. Grandpa grabbed a small, worn scrap of paper and a pen as he asked. "What do you want it to say?"

Tenzing dictated the message. Grandpa finished writing and folded the paper up four times as he asked, "Do you know where to send this?" Tenzing thought for a moment.

"Coconut Joe's. Loud red-haired woman. She can reach the one who saved me."

Grandpa scratched the address on the folded paper. He moved over to the curtain and opened it. He placed the message on a little shelf just outside the curtained area.

"June will know what to do with this. I believe she has already left, but she will make more deliveries tomorrow."

"What did you do after you saw I was saved?" Tenzing asked. Grandpa shuffled back to his seat and answered,

"I was at a loss. I didn't know what to do other than hope against hope that you would evade my brother's jaws and henchmen and eventually make your way down here as all unwanted, lost, or betrayed things eventually do. I suggested that June and the others patrol entrances to the Side Hull under the guise of defending our contested territory. We've had increasing conflict with other groups in the walls recently. Grandpa pointed to the bandage around Tenzing's head.

"I am sorry that someone else got to you before we did."

Tenzing felt around his bandages. He remembered something the old man said at the start of their conversation.

"What makes me different? You said you have seen others—that I was not the first you have seen. Of outsiders. People who live outside the arc?"

Grandpa answered.

"Distant lights in the cities, flickering on and off. The occasional sound of thunder in the distance that I know to be gunfire. I watch the drones in the distance go into the horizon empty and come back with treasure. I can see their arms through the telescope. Darts and poison gas. They would not have weapons if they did not intend to use them."

Tenzing recounted the adage of his parents, a piece of information he believed that had kept him alive.

"There are no people left in the cities. Only monsters.

"A curious statement, but monsters do not turn electricity back on," Grandpa said. "Something human turned on those blinking lights. Something human discharged those distant shells that the rare listening topsider believes is thunder."

Tenzing felt his blood boil.

"You say there are still people out there, and you saw these... these... flying machines hunting them, *and you did nothing?!*" Tenzing shouted. He stood up.

Grandpa stared at Tenzing. He sat in silence blinking. His voice grew quiet.

"Your anger is correct. I am a weak man. I am a scared man. I am not a good man. All of these things are true. But the question remains, what could I have done? If I were to say anything, do anything, I would just be eliminated and the problem would remain."

"That is not an answer!" Tenzing growled.

"Correct again," Grandpa answered. "I didn't know how to stop it then. I still don't know if I should..." Grandpa reached under his desk and unlocked a combination padlock on a footlocker. He opened the locker and stared at something Tenzing could not see. Grandpa shut and re-locked the case. Grandpa's voice carried this time firmer than before.

"I can't change anything for us, but you can."

Tenzing studied the older man. He saw not malice, not confidence, not the doddering, exuberant showmanship of earlier, but dejected brokenness. Grandpa's head hung as if unattached to his shoulders. Tenzing unballed his fist and sat back down.

"What do you mean I can change things?" Tenzing asked.

"You have so many gifts, Tenzing. You are an accelerant, a catalyst. You are the thing that finally slipped through the cracks in the arc's walls after all this time! All the holes in its defenses finally aligned and you climbed through! That's what makes you different from all the others. You are here. You are living proof of the lie this arc was founded upon! But most of all... most of all, you are still untouched by this arc untainted by its pull, you understand a way to live outside its clutches."

"What do you mean?" Tenzing asked.

"I've lived well from the arc. I've suckled at the teat of its abundance for the better part of my life. I've successfully ignored its chaos, its destruction, its injustice, and its pain for far too long, and I've hated myself for it. That weakness to cling on to what's comfortable kept me uncaring despite everything I'd seen. Loss, betrayal, injury, and debt drove everyone else down here, but guilt brought me down to these tunnels. It was the best thing I ever did.

Grandpa threw his arms across the small confines of the tunnel.

"I will do everything I can, to prepare the others to leave this arc. To make a new life in a new place that will not eat away what's left of them, but I will not go. These walls are the cell I deserve for all I've witnessed and all I've ignored. In these dark tunnels, I can see farther than when I lived draped in prestige and fineries.

"We will need you," Tenzing said. "June and Jonas and all the rest will need you. Do not take that from them. Others still need you when you do not see it."

Grandpa sat for a long moment with Tenzing's words. He leaned forward and asked,

"Tenzing, what do you see in the arc?"

"I... I... don't know. It killed my parents and my family. I remember the smell. It smelled like death when I found their bodies. I heard the arc's steps in the distance."

"Likely a lethal formulation of the very same serum used in the dart you were shot with," Grandpa said.

"I've seen the arc take so much from so many. Still, the people here do not know of starvation or thirst, said Tenzing.

"The arc, it feeds the body, but starves the soul," Grandpa said. "You will see in time. It takes more than it gives. It can't last forever. Nothing designed can. It was designed to walk and feed. It was designed to run away."

Tenzing choked through his words.

"At first, I thought of this arc as a monster. It ate and stomped across the earth."

The refracted mess of glowing sludge reflected light off the waste sending rays of heat through great clouds of dust trudged up from Arc Alpha's steps. Errant, particulate clouded rays snaked through the nearby light hole bathing the two seated men in uneasy light. "It is this monster, but that is not all it is, " Tenzing said. "It still gives life within its claws."

"Why did you come to this place?" Grandpa asked.

"I tracked this arc for years. Far behind the horizon I listened. I always followed tracks. I always heard steps even when I did not. I hated those steps. I wanted to destroy what made them. Years passed. I could not draw close. Fear kept me far away. Hatred made me return again and again to that sound and those tracks. That push and pull gnawed and bit, scraped and clawed. The monster hurt me even when I could not see it. The monster hurt me even when it could not see me. I wanted to destroy it, or let it destroy me. I climbed to make this happen."

Muscles in Grandpa's neck tensed as if a knot formed in the back of the throat that could not be dislodged. He coughed lightly, closed his eyes and pinched the bridge of his nose in a tight, cutting grip.

"Yet here you are alive, and the arc is wholly unscathed," Grandpa said.

Tenzing nodded. He sank his weight off his feet back into the chair, where his body slumped.

"People aboard saved me. They fed me. They clothed me. They patched my wounds. They cared for me and returned to me something I'd forgotten.

"What is that?"

"To survive is to be on your own, but to live is to care and be cared for. I need others to live."

Tenzing stood. The waste outside the light hole stretched desolate and lifeless, an unyielding panorama scorched by a century of waterless flood.

"If the arc did not exist, all these others would not live. They would not even survive. The hungry emptiness of starvation would tear them from within until they tore at each other trapped in this metal beast. I will not do that. I do not want that."

"Nor do I," said Grandpa.

Tenzing stopped. He dropped to the metal ground beneath his feet. His knuckles rapped against the hard steel feeling its smoothness, its strength, the durability of refined things.

"There is no point to speak of this. There is no way to stop something this big anyway."

Grandpa concealed his face, stone like and unforthcoming. He touched the foot locker beneath his desk jostling its lock. He made sure again it was well fastened. He hid this motion from Tenzing.

"Destruction is a totality often unneeded," Grandpa said. "Perhaps there is a middle way, and perhaps this is not your role. Perhaps your role is to teach those who wish another way to live. To give those who wish a life outside of the beast's claws. Change only occurs with options. You could allow the arc to adapt rather than only march and eat. This would stave off that day when it has eaten all that is left and all the little people that live in its body starve with it."

"What do you mean?" Tenzing asked.

"There are things that fall into place that only one person in a lifetime can do. You have a unique gift, Tenzing, a gift that no one else on this arc may give." The wasted lands reflected again in Grandpa's pale-blue eyes. A steely expression scrawled across his face. It battled with the lament Tenzing saw in Grandpa's eyes.

"You, Tenzing, can teach us to live out in that wilderness as no one else can."

"How?" Tenzing asked. "It is empty of life. I survived all that time on scraps, morsels." Tenzing pointed to his ribs. They etched out farther than they should have, papery skin stretched too far over a jutting, skeletal frame. Tenzing continued. "I scavenged. The land I survived off was a carcass. It is now picked clean. There is nothing left but bones. Many cannot survive out there. A group cannot live outside these walls."

"You are right," Grandpa replied. "A group cannot survive in that waste." Grandpa stood up and crossed the tunnel. He opened up the curtain that led out to the Rat's territory. In the distance green stems, and leaves bobbed against their steel wall backdrop.

"It doesn't have to be a waste forever," Grandpa said.

"The garden?" Tenzing asked.

"Yes, but bigger," Grandpa said. "A swathe of green in the waste with roots that grow deep enough to last, enough to make a foothold, roots deep enough to change things. It can be done. We know how. All that is left is someone to guide us, to give us that chance.

"Deep-enough roots will not grow through a metal plate," Tenzing said.

"No. No, they will not." Grandpa's foot rested gently on the secured footlocker beneath his desk.

Chapter 18

POWER ON. Vance held the circular device Strickland gave him in his hands. The dark, blank glass turned to a lit touchscreen. Large font text flashed on the screen in red lettering.

REPORT TO ARC ALPHA IMMEDIATELY. PRESS ICON FOR PERSONAL TRANSPORT. REPORT DIRECTLY TO ARC ALPHA PRIVATE HELIPAD. NO INTERMEDIARY ARC.

A small icon appeared on the screen in the shape of a tiny, stylized heli-carrier with the word TRANSPORT inside. Vance pushed the icon.

CALLING HELI-CARRIER. REPORT IMMEDIATELY TO HELI-PAD 3.

Vance gathered his scant belongings. Every single item of his spartan existence fit in one small suitcase, uniform and all. Few personal effects, clothes, uniform, and a small munitions case, Vance's 'War-Bag.' Vance had packed all his belongings after his last meeting with the Squadron leader, ready to depart as soon as he had the orders.

I'm coming home. I did well by Strickland and he sent me home so soon! He thought about calling Kayla and telling her the news. *Better to keep it a surprise.*

Vance raced out of his quarters across the security deck and up to Helipad 3. A heli-carrier of the same model Vance used to apprehend Harkness sat at the ready in the middle of the platform. Vance pressed a button and the cockpit door slid open on its track. Vance crouched underneath the aircraft's ceiling and settled back into its confines. The circular device hummed. It put forth more text as Vance pushed the button to start the aircraft.

PERSONAL TRANSPORT FOR OFFICER VANCE GRANTED. ACCESS STATUS PERMANENT.

Thank God. After flying solo on my last mission. I'm ruined for group travel. No more filing in with a whole squad of sweaty enlisted men to hop arcs. No more enduring their stares.

Vance hated the covetous looks others held at his prestige—hungry men gunning for his position without knowing the true costs of his status. The agonized, contorted faces and fading skin of Lingerers he'd put down scraped their way into Vance's thoughts, grasping his brain with splintering, sharp nails. They crawled across the sallow backdrop of the room with yellow walls. Their howls of pain and rage were drowned out by the screams of regret and terror of a man who had failed his oath.

Vance thought of the very few officers permitted to pick through the old world's wreckage and face its horrors, and he thought of the enlisted men ordered to watch, wait, and respond to the petty nothings upon the arc.

Now I'm in The Circle. I am called to lead all these men. The ones who keep secrets and defend the arc and the ones who clamor for that privilege without knowing its real meaning.

The rotors whirred into full-speed as the heli-carrier lifted from the ground. Vance pretended the lurching pit in his stomach came from the takeoff and not the images present when he closed his eyes. All the unwanted thoughts stopped as the heli-carrier floated away from Arc Ghost and began its journey toward Arc Alpha. *I'm coming home.*

I'll finally see them. It's been months. It was heartbreaking when Vance got his orders for transfer only six months after Lizzie was born. He didn't hold her or see her grow with his own eyes throughout that time.

Now he would.

Vance marveled over the new circular device that sat at his fingertips. *This thing, my new rank, is bringing me back to Lizzie. I'm grateful for that.* Vance held both hands on the device for four seconds. The bio-signature lock opened and the screen once again went from dark to bright. Vance remembered Strickland's words: "This device does other things as well."

Time to see what else this thing can do. Vance looked over four icons on the device.

Communication, Circle, Transport, Drone.

Vance clicked on communication. A page opened with an archive of his previous orders. Farther down the page text flashed continually.

ORDERS PENDING.

Vance watched the text flash from a bright red to a dull gray and back again five times until he was satisfied. *This might be an always-on kind of deal.* He returned to the home screen to check the other icons.

Let's try Circle.

The names of eight officers including himself and the Squadron leader scrolled across the screen. He recognized every name. *That... odd. Every other member other than the Squadron Leader is so... young.* "I'm the youngest here at thirty, but..."

Vance ran through the list of names. He saw Santoro's name. *Not a single member of The Circle other than Strickland is an officer more than five years my senior.* Vance thought of Harkness and he thought of himself. *One in, one out.*

I guess ambition and energy wins over experience and complacency. Vance put the observation out of his mind as he flipped back to the home screen.

Already saw what transport does. Time to try drone. Vance clicked the icon. It brought up two options: Operate and Flight Log. Vance selected Operate and received a message. ERROR: OUT OF RANGE.

Vance selected the Flight Log icon. He saw video clips. *Recordings of drone flights I have taken.*He closed out of the tab quickly. *Don't look not today. Not on this day.*

Vance remembered Strickland's words. "Remember what you've seen. Remember why you walk the hard path."

Vance sat for the remainder of the flight thinking of his new life post-promotion. *I can be in my daughter's life again. I can be a better husband to Kayla. We can be together.* The image of the two most important, most loved people in his life coaxed his mind to gentle relaxation. Vance barely noticed when the heli-carrier crested downward, making its descent toward Arc Alpha. He thought of Lizzie and how big she'd be as the aircraft dropped its last two feet and its landing gear bobbed against the helipad below. *Almost home.*

Vance tucked the Circle device back in his bag with the rest of his belongings and pushed the button to release the cockpit door. He stepped out on Arc Alpha, onto a helipad he'd never seen before. It sat tucked in an alcove, outside the hull around the corner from aft dock. *The arc is full of surprises.*

A singular set of metal stairs snaked down from the platform to a gate marked. MAXIMUM SECURITY: AUTHORIZED PERSONNEL ONLY. It opened from the inside and locked as it shut.

Private dock. Hidden. More Circle privilege. Glad I didn't have to transfer from one of the docked arcs, don't think I could've made it. Don't think I could've waited to see them.

Vance walked down the stairs and headed straight for the Underbelt. He stepped on the high-speed conveyor and broke into a brisk walk, then a jog, then a run. He gripped his singular suitcase tight and dodged past all the commuters headed to B Sector who stood to the right patiently awaiting their destinations.

The high speed of the railed conveyor transit combined with his steady running stride. Vance raced to his terminal and ascended an elevator closest to his family's building in B Sector. Vance rounded a street and a block in no time until he saw his apartment balcony. He flew up the stairs to his door. *They'll be so excited I'm home early!*

Vance slammed his key fob into the electronic lock as the door clicked open. He nearly broke the knob off its track as he wrenched it open, bursting through the doorway. "Kayla, Lizzie, I'm home!"

Vance heard no response. His yell echoed through the empty apartment. He moved in and set his trunk down on the living room floor. *Where, where are they?*

Vance waited to hear a returning cry of welcome from his family, but he still heard nothing but silence. The silence broke as the cold, judgmental tone of his wife's mother slithered around the wall that separated the bedrooms from the open-floor plan living space. She tipped back a glass of red wine.

"Kayla didn't say you'd be back."

"I'm home early," Vance returned. "Where are Kayla and Lizzie?"

"Eliza's fever cleared up nicely, so I arranged an interview with a new school. Kayla and Eliza are there now."

"We just selected a new program for our daughter," Vance said.

"Well frankly, you chose poorly. Kayla never could be trusted to make important decisions, and you're no better."

Vance quieted his urge to erupt. In a calm tone he offered.

"Lizzie is one year old. It doesn't matte—"

His mother in law spoke over him. She swirled around the wine glass held tight between manicured nails.

"It's high time you put Eliza on an educational track more appropriate for someone of her status. She is my granddaughter, after all. The right infant development program gets her into the right preschool.

The right preschool carries all the way to the right professional life. Every leg of the journey is important. I thought you would *care* about your daughter's life, but apparently not." Vance sucked air through his teeth.

The woman continued.

"I had a fruitful conversation with Roderick the last time I visited him on Arc Bravo. We decided our decisions regarding the financing of our granddaughter were rash and unfair. Just because Kayla has made mistakes, that is no reason Eliza should be punished as well. We will happily pay to ensure Eliza has the correct opportunities going forward."

"What mistakes?" Vance asked through gritted teeth. He knew she was drunk and just wanted a fight. Lizzie and Kayla's absence and her belligerence almost put him in the mood to give her one.

Sharon scoffed through pursed lips.

"My daughter followed in my footsteps. She became successful. Hell, in spite of you, she might end up on the board of directors one day! How she ended up with a struggling rent-a-cop from the arc's backside is simply beyond my comprehension. When you finally moved up the ranks and became an officer, you were gone from your infant daughter's life, absent. Of what importance could you possibly be up to anyway?"

Vance seethed beneath a cool exterior. He would not rise to her bait.

"The decisions about Lizzie's future are mine and Kayla's to make," Vance stated calmly and coolly.

A little smile curled around the woman's thin lips. Vance saw her wine stained teeth as she formed the words.

"Yet Kayla and Eliza are already at the interview without you."

Vance turned back towards his front door. There was no conversation here, no discussion. It was just another encounter with a fountain of verbal poison. This time, Vance chose not to drink.

"I'm leaving," Vance said. He closed the door behind him and descended the winding stair down to his building's ground floor. Festering anger bludgeoned his senses into a dull whole.

He didn't see any distinct sight or hear any single sound. The neon of the arc's signs and light projections melted together into beige sludge. Every pedestrian's footstep, every conversation near and far, and every crier beckoning customers to spend their inc suddenly became too loud. A cacophony of senseless racket beating his skull in pulsing waves—fifty different symphonies played in fifty different keys.

Vance reeled about in the street. Powerlessness transmuted to stinging anger within every fiber of his being. That anger kept his stride in place and his eyes open against this world that was suddenly too big, too loud, and too much. This same world he'd sworn to protect suddenly held no shape.

Tart words by a woman without a shred of understanding became the last straw. Vance paced through the streets regaining that anger, regaining that focus. He walked for hours until that beige sludge reformed itself into familiar sights, until that symphony played its last note.

Vance crossed the length of the arc and back. He didn't know how many times. As his feet covered every inch of the world he'd sworn to protect, that world stopped being too big. For the first time in a long time, it felt small.

Vance never suffered confinement sickness, as they called it, that indefinable malaise from always being in one place, feeling the arc's movement yet never reaching anywhere new. Most people on the arc had their ways of coping. Vance was no different. He had always buried himself within his duties: A defender, a husband, and a father, he devoted his all to every one of those hallowed roles. He never took any easy escape from confinement sickness. As with all officers, he never touched the VerchLife helmets. To him and the others, a digital infinity beyond space was nothing but a distraction from a reality that needed protection.

Vance grounded himself. He forced himself to look and see the individual sights, the individual people who were his charges. See what lay in front of him. He stood in the midst of the promenade. He must've gone all the way past Sector C to the aft dock and back to the mid section.

Two kids, maybe ten or eleven years old, stood outside a VerchLife code dispenser. They had broken the screen and stood prying the little coolly covered papers out from the machine's insides. Each one coded a unique object accessible within the VerchLife helmet, officially coded by VerchLife designers. Prestige items, one of a kind, considered more valuable than what users could make. Vance watched the two youths. *Vandalism, theft. Reminds me of myself at that age.*

He walked forward and asked. "What are you doing?"

"Busting these codes open. Gonna sell them to the rich kids for less than they cost here. Lot of rich kid parents don't want them sucked into verch, but all those A Sector rich kids wanna do is pretend they're just like us."

Vance couldn't believe the perps had just confessed to everything. He looked down. In his anger, he'd forgotten he stood in his plainclothes. *Uniform changes everything, h*e thought.

Vance rifled through his pockets. He found a little prepaid inc card with about five inc on it. He handed the card to the two youths.

"Here. Let me buy one."

"Which season do you want?" the older looking of the youths asked.

"Doesn't matter," Vance replied.

He pocketed the verch code and walked off leaving the youths at their work. *Uniform. Makes all the difference.*

Vance remembered his youth, *God knows I got up to that and worse.* Funds were always tight. He remembered his parents always screaming about money, about who'd drunk up the rent faster. *They both had.*

Vance remembered cowering in his little room in their tiny little C Sector apartment during those fights. A small space. No place in the home where he could get away from that screaming, and the fear of that screaming. It wasn't big enough. He remembered leaving night after night. The screaming faded into the distance, but the fear still followed.

Vance remembered the petty trouble he'd got into at night away from home, and he remembered the Security officer who'd finally caught him. That perfect uniform and that perfect posture with which the officer stood. Pins of authority decorated the officer's chest and a dart gun sat snugly in his holster. Eyes sat behind opaque, dark glasses, and Vance thought those eyes never knew anything close to fear.

Now I know why he wore those dark glasses. Vance thought of the Lingerer's gnashing teeth. *To hide a tremble in those eyes.*

Light filtered through the shade sail in orange, casting the deck in a brilliant, filtered evening glow. *Kayla and Lizzie should be home by now. Sharon should be gone, back to her world of chaise lounges and marble counter tops.*

Vance took the Underbelt home. He didn't run, just stood and let the conveyor walkway ferry his still-postured body. He climbed back up the stairs to his door's threshold. He pushed it open softly and saw Kayla. Vance burst in and kissed her. She held Lizzie. He held them both as he kissed his daughter's messy haired head.

Everything stopped as the three embraced. Everything went silent. Vance stopped. He was content to live in that silence for as long as the silence would permit.

Chapter 19

Tenzing sat with Grandpa. The old man started to speak but stopped mid sentence. Both men turned their heads to a nearby sound. A little, muffled knock rapped from outside the curtain separating Grandpa's lab from the rest of The Rat's territory. A familiar voice sounded right after the tepid knocks.

"Grandpa, it's Jonas. Can I come in?"

"Yes Jonas, please come in," Grandpa answered. He shot Tenzing a serious, stern gaze as the curtain parted and Jonas stepped in. The old man changed his tone back to the doddering bravado from earlier.

"I was just telling Tenzing a little more about the Rats and our illustrious history. What have you come to tell me? Any good news on the welder front?"

"Yeah, about that. Mite and I had an idea."

Tenzing looked over Jonas. He was sweaty and covered in dirt. His sweat-stained T-shirt bunched around his strong frame. He pulled the damp, clinging cloth away from his midsection and wiped his face while he answered.

"We thought the newcomer—Tenzing I mean—might be able to help us get the welder back."

"How so?" Grandpa asked.

"So those goggle headed pain freaks..." Grandpa raised his eyebrows pointedly in Jonas' direction.

Jonas changed his tone.

"Those unfortunate victims of a sadistic and manipulative man remembered our faces from the first time we went down there to ask for the welder. They just fled farther down."

"Yes, that is what I recall as well," Grandpa said. "Although by this time they've fled about as far down as down goes."

Jonas clenched his fists.

"Man, I could kill Spark for leaving the most important piece of equipment we have down unattended. What was he thinking?"

"Nothing, most likely," Grandpa said with a laugh. "Yes, I believe we have all wanted to kill Spark at some point. Nevertheless, his prowess at joining metal together is unmatched by probably anyone on the entire arc. Those hands, eyes, and forearms know things through time and experience that the written word could never teach. He's the perfect example of embodied knowledge."

"Yeah, Gramps," Jonas said. "Anyway—"

Tenzing bolted up from his seat.

"If there is some way I can help, I want to do it," he said.

"Please, Jonas, what is your plan?" Grandpa asked, "and how does it involve our newest guest?"

"So, the thing is, they've never seen Tenzing's face. They might not crawl further into a hole if he goes down there, somebody they don't immediately recognize. Hell, I don't know, they might even try and bring him in to what they've got. Point is, that gives us an edge—an edge we haven't had the other times. And when the moment's right, we can grab the welder."

"It could be a potentially dangerous situation," Grandpa said. "We don't want to ask too much of—"

"I will do it," Tenzing declared. Grandpa and Jonas fell silent as Tenzing continued.

"Reciprocity. I have not yet given to the Rats. You all helped me. Now

I will do the same."

"Newcomer seems to get it already," Jonas said.

Grandpa's eyebrows knitted, but he nodded nonetheless. The two younger men stood resolute in their plans.

"Jonas. Please ensure you all return safely," Grandpa said.

"Of course," Jonas replied.

"Tenzing," Grandpa said, "We can discuss more later. I'm sure Jonas would like to brief you on the plan and get you low-light-acclimated as soon as possible."

"Low-light-acclimated?" Tenzing asked.

"Come on, Tenzing," Jonas said, "Mite is farther down the tunnel. We'll give you the rundown when we meet up with her."

Tenzing left with Jonas, out from the curtained off area. He looked back and saw his letter for Laney sitting snugly in a little box. *June will deliver it tomorrow*, Tenzing reminded himself.

Tenzing followed Jonas through the entirety of the Rat's territory—a long tunnel, five feet wide for the most of it with more width around the areas surrounding the interiors of the arc's legs. A better-lit, different angle of the massive metal hill Tenzing had first encountered in the dark towered beside the two rats as they walked past the structure.

"What is that?" Tenzing asked.

"The internal ball joint for the leg," Jonas said. "Spans a couple floors. You can see it from a few different spots."

"No one comes down here to work on the arc's legs?" Tenzing asked.

Jonas ducked beneath a clothes line. Several damp fabrics hung on the wire, warmed by the heat coming through the light hole.

"No," he said. "Legs are a work of art, really. They'd have to be to hold everything on the arc up for this long. Firms aren't gonna pay someone to do work that doesn't need to be done. Besides, look how thick that metal is. Nothing's getting through that."

Tenzing ducked under the same clothesline.

"June says you bring soil and plants for the garden. Do you like that?" Tenzing asked.

"Like what? My job?" Jonas asked.

"Yes," Tenzing answered.

Jonas' voice lilted.

"Uh, I like digging. I like using my body to build things, make stuff happen. That part's great. You won't hear any complaint from me on that front."

"But there are other parts you do not like?"

Jonas thought for a bit. He took a moment to chew on the question and find the perfect words.

"I like the work. I just don't like the employment that comes with it."

Tenzing did not understand and Jonas did not elaborate. The tunnel grew more and more crowded with people and supplies as the pair walked.

Tenzing put conversation aside. He struggled to keep up with Jonas who darted through the Side Hull's confines with well-honed ease. The Side Hull was busier than Tenzing had ever seen before. Tenzing kept stopping to avoid ramming into another rat's business.

Tenzing studied Jonas' motion. Every time Jonas came face-to-face with a traveler blocking his path, he and the traveler parted to opposite sides in perfect synchronicity. Tenzing watched these partings as he struggled through the crowded tunnel. It was not a simple rule, like moving to the same side every time based on what direction you were facing. Odd clutter and people in random corners prevented such a simple solution.

To Tenzing, it seemed like an intricate dance, learned by time living in these quarters. *I have not yet learned these steps,* Tenzing thought. He bumped into a man carrying a ten-gallon bucket full of some sloshing liquid. The man instantly corrected his grip and prevented any liquid from spilling out of its heavy vessel.

Tenzing ambled past faces he had yet to meet. Every little space was filled with a different person's activity: washing clothes, drying clothes, taking apart machinery, sorting scavenged metals into bins, sleeping, arguing, drinking, trimming plants in the garden, tying up hammocks, taking down hammocks. One man strummed several wires attached to an odd-shaped box with a hole in it. Harmonious, musical sounds drifted from that box, the likes of which Tenzing had never heard. A sadness passed over Tenzing as those rhythmic notes faded into the distance when he traveled farther and farther down the tunnel. Tenzing bumped, shuffled, and apologized his way through the living space that was the Side Hull.

After many, many "I'm sorry's" later, Tenzing had pushed his way through the bulk of the crowd. Side Hull occupancy thinned back down to just himself and Jonas.

Away from the hive of activity, this space was darker. The last light hole had been a ways back, and the ambient light dimmed the further Jonas and Tenzing proceeded down the gentle curve ahead.

"We're getting closer," Jonas yelled. The tunnel's light turned into a muted, dark gray. Tenzing sped up and cut the distance between himself and Jonas. He remembered the last time he'd journeyed in the dark alone. The memory of his head pain and his unknown assailant started an unwanted conversation with the rest of Tenzing's thoughts.

He started a real auditory conversation to change the subject.

"What group took the welder?"

"It's a sad story. Handful of helmet-heads roughed up by a man who loves the sound of his own voice. Inflicts his sadistic bent on the people Arc Security doesn't care about. When he's done, he scarpers topside before anyone notices. We've only seen glimpses. Hopefully tonight will be the closest we ever have to get."

Jonas sped up a little. "There goes Mite." Tenzing matched speed, following close behind.

He looked farther down the tunnel and recognized the tiny, silhouetted figure whose shape could only just be made out against the last drop of light left in the corridor. *It's the small woman who separated the tea leaves from the tea bags,* Tenzing thought.

"Call me Mite." The woman stuck her hand out toward Tenzing. He grasped the hand and understood this handshake ritual a little better this time.

Mite continued,

"Sorry I didn't introduce myself earlier. I'm very task-focused. I get stuck in my own little world when I'm doing something. I honestly love the tea leaf job. It puts my nimble fingers to work."

"Mite, Tenzing. Tenzing, Mite," Jonas said. "Sun is down. Light's almost gone. Let's get our peepers fixed."

Jonas pulled an object out of his pocket. Tenzing couldn't make out any texture or color in the dark—it appeared just as a squat, cylindrical shape bereft of any details. Jonas took the shape in the dark, grabbed its top and bottom with opposite hands, and twisted. He carefully set the bottom part of the shape on the floor between the three of them and crouched down before it. Mite did the same, and after a second, Tenzing followed.

Jonas whispered as he took a small cylindrical object and dipped it into the squat object. Tenzing heard a very slight sloshing sound blanketed over by the sound of Jonas' hushed tone.

"Me first, then Mite, then Tenzing." Tenzing squinted his eyes in near-total darkness. He could just make out the shape of Jonas bringing up the small cylinder up to where his eyes must be. The tunnel fell completely silent and Tenzing heard a small sound. *Drip, drip, drip.* A pause and then a second. *Drip, drip, drip.*

"Mite's turn," Jonas said. He passed the small cylinder into Mite's hands. She repeated the same set of actions Jonas had completed just a moment ago. Dip the cylinder in the vessel, drip, drip drip. One trio of drips for each eye.

Tenzing felt the small cylinder pressed into his hand in the dark. He squeezed it. The front part felt like hard plastic, but the back part was soft. It bent inward when he squeezed it.

Mite spoke up.

"In case you can't tell, it's a dropper. Dunk it in the jar, squeeze and put three drops in each eye."

Tenzing hesitated.

"Relax. It won't do anything other than reduce your dark blindness." Jonas said.

Tenzing put the dropper in the jar, squeezed, and released. He felt it swell with liquid. He held the end to his eye and squeezed out exactly three drops. *Drip, drip, drip.* It felt cold on his eye as he repeated the process for the other. Tenzing blinked a couple times. The inside of his eyelids pushed the liquid around, coating his eyeball in a thin sheen of this mystery liquid. It had a faint fragrance, sweet and floral.

"How does it work?" Tenzing asked.

"It's the petal juice of a plant that's grown on Arc Charlie," Mite said. "A genetically modified flower. Anyway, scientists found genes to make them deep purple, like a really deep purple. Apparently, whatever genes they switched on to make them like that must have switched on some others too. The plant has a surprisingly useful accidental property."

Tenzing looked behind him, pretending to understand. He saw a dim flicker of light that had not been there before.

"It hyper-dilates the eyes," Jonas said. "Basically, it's a muscle relaxer for the iris. Pupil gets way bigger than it ever does in normal circumstances and lets in more light."

Tenzing felt his eyes start to change. The tunnel turned from a lightless corridor to a shade of dark gray. Faint shapes of pipes and rivets stood out around him where before was only darkness. Little bugs scurried about.

"We call it the Cat's Eye Rose," Mite said. "June grows a couple down here."

"How did you find out about its effect?" Tenzing asked.

"That'd be June again," Jonas answered. "To hear her tell it, one day she cut about fifty-thousand of these flowers for some banquet or something and forgot to wash her hands real well before she rubbed her eyes."

"She said she had to pull her whole cloth uniform over her face to keep working on account of how bright it got," Mite chimed.

"It's super gradual. Takes about an hour or two, depending on the person, to see the full effect. You'll know it's done when you can see the color."

"The color of what?" Tenzing asked.

"You'll see," the other two replied.

A bug skittered into view and disappeared down a crack between the floor and the wall. Tenzing could see the brown color of its carapace

"This group that has taken the welder?" Tenzing asked.

"I don't know what Jonas already told you," Mite said, "but you need to know what we're up against. One guy wearing nice clothes and shiny shoes gets his jollies beating the ever loving-hell out of people so far gone in a drug-amplified verch dream, they don't know what's real."

"Verch dream?"

"Yeah, he's gotta be paying the inc for their helmet subscriptions to keep them hooked on the verch-world. Anyway, after that he narrates his fake doomsday bullshit."

"Fake doomsday?" Tenzing asked.

"Of course it's fake," Mite answered. "You've already looked out there and seen the ground. How can the world end twice?"

Tenzing stared hard at the cylindrical jar at his feet and said nothing. It sat equidistant between himself, Jonas, and Mite. The color in the liquid began to change.

"Do you also see that?" Tenzing pointed to the jar on the floor.

"No," Jonas and Mite answered.

The liquid in the jar glowed a color Tenzing had never seen before. A color he did not have a name for. It shown a blue-purple so deep it stood out darker than the almost lightless tunnel that surrounded him.

"It's beautiful," Tenzing said.

"Okay, new guy, you're freaking me out a little bit. There's no fucking way your eyes adapt that fast," Jonas said.

Tenzing described the color to Jonas and Mite.

"Well shit, that's a good description," Mite said. "I guess you're not bullshitting us." Jonas patted Mite across the shoulder.

"We picked well when we chose him for this mission."

Tenzing sat enamored with the new color's beauty. Jonas and Mite sat in near-darkness. They strained their eyes to conjure the object of Tenzing's fascination.

A groan echoed farther down the corridor. Jonas and Mite rocketed up and pressed themselves against either wall.

"We've got company," Jonas whispered. Tenzing felt a small object pressed into his hand. "Use this."

Tenzing's finger pushed a button on the object. A single point of red light shot forth and bounced off the curving wall ahead. His acclimated eyes saw a tunnel awash with red light—the singular beam was all they needed. Tenzing crept forward. The groan wailed louder.

"No more yellow light. No more yellow walls. Forgive me. No more yellow light. No more yellow walls. Forgive me."

A figure shambled forth. Each step seemed a perilous fall with the figure's unbalanced gait favoring one leg. The other stepped lightly. Tenzing flattened himself against the corridor's wall. Heated, humid, stinking breath slapped like wet fog across Tenzing's face. Words echoed again.

"No more yellow light. No more yellow walls. Forgive me." The figure limped past Tenzing. Deadened eyes took no notice of him or anyone else. Pained footsteps carried the figure between Jonas and Mite, who had split to opposite sides of the corridor. The groaning man trekked on. Solemn cries faded farther and farther in the distance until all again was silent.

Mite quivered...

"Dear God... another one." she said.

Jonas trembled. Heaviness in his breath filled the tunnel.

"Maybe Grandpa can help him," he said. "First Rat says they get a little better after the medicine, after he talks to them."

"They still never get their minds fully back," Mite said. "Just a phrase or two at best. She slumped into a squat against the wall and her knees went limp. She held her face in her hands.

"God..." she said. "One, years ago, I can't forget. All of them mention yellow light and yellow walls. This one said something else too."

"What?" Tenzing and Jonas asked.

"They made me make a meat puppet," Mite said. "Said that over and over and over again. They made me make a meat puppet. They made me make a meat puppet."

"What does that mean?" Tenzing asked.

"I don't ever want to know," Mite replied.

"I wish we could help them more," Jonas said.

"Me too," Mite and Tenzing said at the same time.

"Grandpa does what he can," Mite said. "Gives them food and water at the roost. It's something."

"Enough to survive," Tenzing said. "How many are like that?"

"Too many," Jonas and Mite replied in unison.

Jonas picked up the little jar from the floor. He held it up in front of his face.

"Tenzing can see already somehow. I'm getting little flecks of blue. What do you see, Mite?"

"I see enough," Mite answered.

"Okay then. We move forward. We'll need our eyes for what comes next."

Chapter 20

Vance lied in his bed late at night with Kayla pressed up against him. He held his arm around her, pulling her in as close as he could. His hand gripped under her rib cage. She laid her head peacefully across his chest.

"Lizzie went down so easy tonight," Kayla said. "She missed her daddy. You could tell by the look in her eyes when you held her."

'It was hard to put her down," Vance replied. "All those months of holding her I missed. Really hit me when I picked her up. She was so much heavier than the last time."

Kayla leaned in and kissed her husband on the cheek. The pair said nothing for a while as they relaxed in a moment of blissful tranquility. After a while, Kayla spoke first.

"I'm so sorry about my mom. I'm sorry I went to that interview. I shouldn't have."

"It doesn't matter. It's done now."

"It does matter. Every little thing, I just... I never should have caved in to her. The program you and I chose for Lizzie is just fine, it's just... I just, I..."

Vance tightened the hold on his wife. He gazed into her eyes.

"It's hard to put up boundaries against the person who raised you not to have them."

"You're right," Kayla said. "But I still need to. For all of us. It's not just the two of us now."

Vance circled his hand around the small of his wife's back. Kayla perked up. She rested her head on her hand elbow digging gently into the mattress that supported them both. She spoke as she dragged her finger across her husband's face.

"You were my only real rebellion. The only thing I really ever fought for, fought against them I mean. The only thing I won. They pushed me over on everything else, but not you. I wouldn't let them take you away."

"I must be special to you, then?" Vance smiled.

Kayla twisted around the wedding band on her finger.

"Yeah, it's not like I married you or anything," Vance laughed.

"Thank you for being you," he said. "Always making me laugh. Thank you for fighting for me. Thank you for winning that."

"I wouldn't have it any other way," Kayla said. She squeezed her husband tighter and rested her head on his chest.

"Tonight was wonderful," Kayla said.

"Yes. Yes, it was."

The pair drifted off to sleep. Vance slept but did not sleep through the night. Something pulled him awake. He left his bed and crept slowly out of his room, careful not to disturb Kayla.

He tiptoed into the next room and looked at Lizzie asleep in her crib. Her little chest heaved up and down as she drew strong breaths in the blissful depths of her slumber. *To only know what she is dreaming. The dreams of a child so young—what could they be?*

Vance stumbled into the living room. He looked at his luggage. It still stood in the living room. Unpacking had seemed an unnecessary distraction from the bliss of finally being home; he was here, they were here, that was all he needed. A dim red light glowed from a crack where the zipper on his suitcase hung, not fully shut.

Vance pulled the suitcase onto the counter and unzipped it. The red light got brighter as he uncovered the Circle device. He tipped it over and the screen shone a deep red. Vance held it in his hands and it unlocked. Text shone across the screen.

ORDERS RECEIVED.

Fuck, how long has this been active? Vance wondered to himself. He clicked on the text and his heart skipped.

ARC ALPHA INFILTRATED BY WASTELAND OUTSIDER:
    TIME TO LINGERER MUTATION UNKNOWN; ASSUME IMMINENT
    HARKNESS LIED ABOUT TARGET'S TERMINATION.
    TRUTH EXTRACTED IN RWYW.
    KNOWN ASSOCIATES DELANEY QUIST, MAGDA ERDOS
    INSTRUCTIONS: DETAIN ARC CITIZENS FOR MEMORY EXTRACTION
IN RWYW
    TERMINATE OUTSIDER
    PERFORM WITH UTMOST DISCRETION

Vance sat. He breathed in and thought nothing. An oppressive crystalline stillness enveloped every fiber of his being, encasing the dark of his room in dread. *No time for that.* He remembered the scrap of paper he'd pulled from Harkness' apartment. *Mr. Interloper.* He breathed out and got to work. Vance opened the video file linked beneath the order's text and studied its contents.

A brown-skinned, short-haired woman in a jumpsuit led a lithe man in plainclothes to an entrance to the Side Hull. The two embraced, and the man descended beneath the hatch. The woman departed.

He studied the man's face. Vance remembered the dissected Lingerer corpse the superior officers had shown him. He remembered their pained faces in the wastes. He looked at this unknown man. He didn't know why, but he looked kind. *God... this man... I'll save him from that fate. It's worth it. I'll end it before he gets to that. It's a mercy.*

Vance queued into the audio for the recording. It was quiet—just some caring words, some goodbyes, and the name Tenzing. *Good. Not a name you hear often. That works in my favor.*

Vance pulled up the employee records for Delaney Quist and Magda Erdos.

Delaney Quist

VerchLife Programmer Blacklisted.

Arc Interior Solutions Warehouse Attendant and Merchandise Handler.

Vance studied the picture of her Job ID. It matched the woman in the video file.

Magda Erdos.

Arc Echo Emergency Medical Response Unit: Retired

Coconut Joe's Bartender and Manager.

Vance thought of the Lingerers. He thought of their scowling jaws and pained eyes. His face held a perfect stillness. He broke and he screamed from within. *HOW THE FUCK DID HARKNESS FUCK THIS UP?! NOW THERE'S A TICKING TIME BOMB MONSTER ON BOARD! EVERYONE WILL KNOW!*

Vance slammed his hand on the table. He stopped. *Pull yourself together!* He thought he heard Lizzie stir. He rushed over to look. *Silent. She's still asleep. You do this for them. I have to succeed. Why did Harkness fail?*

Vance remembered everything about Harkness. *The man loved his badge. He loved to make people sweat and squeal. Wouldn't miss any opportunity to throw his weight around.* Vance was sure. *This is why the outsider ran underground. His sloppiness is why the fugitive fled down to the tunnels. I need to be the opposite. I need to act with discretion.*

He pulled the munitions case out of his bag. He grabbed darts, a few electronic devices, an instant camera, and some restraint and interrogation tools. Vance returned to his bedroom and put on plainclothes. *Just an ordinary civilian. Uniform makes all the difference.*

He stashed his badge and all the little, hidden spy trinkets within the inside pockets of a gray sweatshirt.

I'll be quiet. I'll be polite. They won't see it coming. I'll succeed.

Vance imagined the dark, unknown tunnels sprawling the length and depth of the hull. *No. Not on his turf. I'll flush him out. I'll get him before he turns into that. It's a mercy.*

Vance turned back to the video file. He watched the woman, Delaney Quist. She hugged the fugitive. He rewound and watched that small segment of footage over and over and over.

To catch a rat, I just need the right bait.

Vance walked over, passed the wall, and stared into the two bedrooms. He saw Kayla and he saw Lizzie. Images squirmed in his head. Lingerer jaws stretched over each of their throats. He wrestled the pictures out of his mind.

No. I will protect them. I will protect us all. I will protect this arc.

Vance left his front door. He closed and locked it behind him.

First I'll set my trap. Tomorrow I'll get my bait.

Chapter 21

"We're here," Jonas whispered in the dark.

Jonas, Mite, and Tenzing shone their laser pointers across the corridor ceiling. To an outside observer, it would just appear as little, hard-to-see red dots washed away in the dark, but to those who'd taken the drops from the Cat's Eye Rose, the tunnel appeared bathed in illuminating light.

They pressed themselves alongside the wall outside an open doorway. A gradual slope they had followed for maybe forty minutes had taken them down, down around the curving bow of the arc to this deepest pit. A hollow bulkhead nested deep below A Sector's sprawling mansions. It sat down below the floors and floors filled with machinery and life-support systems that made life possible in those gargantuan houses above.

Here below everything, the three rats stood. They stood, they waited, and they listened. The smell hit Tenzing first. The oily, ferrous smell of dried blood on steel and the stronger variant of fresher wounds still. Then came the voice.

"HERE WE GIVE OUR LIVES MEANING. WE GIVE OUR GODDESS FORM. SHE HEARS OUR PAINED CRIES AND SHEPHERDS THIS ARC ACROSS MOUNTAINS OF BURNING GLASS TO PARADISE!"

"He's already started!" Mite whispered.

Tenzing peeked around the edge. He pointed his laser deep into the corner of the room, out of sight and too low for uninitiated eyes. A central figure stood with arms wide aloft over a crude dais of scrap metal. It wore a square mask with a dark glass window where eyes would sit. Its shoes were of shiny brown leather, its button down shirt tucked neatly into slacks that were pressed and cleaned. A beautiful crystal-covered watch curled around the figure's wrist.

Six more figures knelt around the dais lower than the masked, preaching man. Every one of the kneeling figures wore a VerchLife helmet atop their head.

"WE AWAKEN OUR NERVOUS SYSTEMS WITH THAT HOLY PAIN SO OUR LADY HEARS OUR CRIES, SO THAT OUR DIGITAL DREAMS MAY BE FILLED WITH HER SHINING FORM!"

The VerchLife helmeted figure's arms bore scars. Cut's, bruises, burns, scrapes crisscrossed their limbs. They wore loose clothes. Tenzing imagined the wounds that the fabric concealed. He spied an emaciated figure with one arm slung limply in a tattered cloth sling. Tenzing looked and saw another arm on another body in the same broken condition.

He crept into that dark room as Jonas and Mite's whispered words faded behind him.

"Did he just—?"

"This wasn't our plan!"

On hands and feet, Tenzing crawled. A lifetime of stalking prey in the wastes taught stealth to his limbs. He crouched in cover behind piles of jagged metal drawing nearer and nearer to the dais. The masked figure waved an object in his hands. Tenzing could not see it fully.

The booming voice bellowed its sick sermon that blanketed every movement Tenzing made. He approached unseen below the metal dais right behind the metal-masked preacher.

"TONIGHT WE OFFER OUR LADY OUR EYES!"

All the helmeted figures removed their helmets. Their white orb eyeballs glowed exposed in the unlit room in Tenzing's altered vision. The figure thrust the object in his hand up to the ceiling. Tenzing heard a clicking sound and saw nothing but brightness. Nothing but light. It burned.

"GAZE DEEP INTO OUR LOVING LADY'S SHINING LIGHT!!!!"

Tenzing screamed. The preaching voice chased swiftly after his cry.

"AN INTERLOPER HAS TRESPASSED UPON THIS HOLY GROUND... SEIZE HIM!!!"

Tenzing reeled backward. His eyes seared and his head throbbed. He shut his eyes. Violet, neon-green, and scarlet flecks swirled around him. They pierced his skull like thorns. He felt a hand grasp around his ankle. Instinct took over and Tenzing twisted his body around and kicked hard with his free leg. His foot made contact curling around a hard-rib cage into the fleshy gap of an already wounded solar plexus.

"FUCK! TENZING! GET OUT OF THERE!!!" Mite screamed.

Tenzing curled over from his supine position. He sprung onto his four limbs and clambered up the nearest scrap pile, hands and feet shuffling their way up, unaided by sight.

"CAPTURE THE INTRUDER!" the voice roared.

Atop the mountain of scrap, Tenzing tore at his clothes. He ripped a thick sleeve from his shirt and tied the fabric over his eyes, shutting out the light that shone bright enough to bleed behind his eyelids. The arcing, sparking violets and greens dampened enough for him to focus.

Tenzing heard the clank of metal on metal a short distance away, a figure climbed on a scrap pile that was not his perch.

They looked into the light too. They have no Cat's Eye drops. They cannot see.

"THERE! GET HIM!" the voice screamed.

Tenzing leapt off the pile toward the voice. He crashed onto the ground.

"HERE! HE'S RIGHT HERE!" The masked preacher screamed. He swung the sparking light in a wide arc in front of him.

Tenzing ducked and dropped to all-fours. Intense heat and light grazed right over the nape of his neck. The back of his hair was singed. He tightened every muscle in his body and sprung from the floor. The end of his elbow connected with the screaming masked figure, right where the underarm met the body's side. The force of Tenzing's whole accelerated mass transferred through this small, hard bone. His contact dug deep into the sadistic sermonizer's flesh. The preacher was knocked backwards, and e flipped over a railing behind him. The sparking device *thunked* onto the metal floor.

Tenzing fumbled for an off switch on the arc welder's power supply and switched it off. The room returned to its original condition: complete darkness. Tenzing tried to lift the welder. His scrawny, malnourished arms struggled against the heavy, unbalanced weight.

"Help me grab it!" Tenzing yelled. Little red laser lights cast around Tenzing's vicinity. Jonas and Mite sprinted to his location. They dodged around the figures, flailing about in the dark and swerved through mountains of debris to the dais.

Tenzing felt pressure constrict his ribs. Hard crystal edges on a metal watch dug into and cut his skin. Interlocking fingers pulled a fist into his gut, forcing out every breath. The hold shrank tighter and tighter around Tenzing's lithe body.

"HOW DARE YOU DEFY THE SACRAMENT!!!" the voice pummeled Tenzing's eardrum.

Tenzing bent his neck down. His teeth found a soft part on his assailant's upper arm. He bit down hard. Blood gushed into Tenzing's mouth, coating his molars and incisors. He spat the foul fluid onto the metal floor. The oily, unctuous pungency of iron-rich blood mixing with steel wormed its way through Tenzing's nostrils.

The howling, preaching figure released its hold. Jonas and Mite each grabbed an opposite side of the arc welder's power supply. Their elongated arms swung like a pendulum with the welder at its center. *Clang!* The power supply knocked straight into the preacher's metal-masked face.

The leader fell down. Tenzing watched, counted to five. The masked figure did not stir.

"*Let's get out of here!*" Mite yelled. She and Jonas carried the welder between the two of them as they ran toward the open door. Tenzing followed, shining the laser ahead. The trio ascended a gentle slope as the sound and smell of this cacophony faded farther and farther to the distance behind.

They ran all the way back to the rats' territory before they stopped to breathe. The trio's breaths heaved in and out under the moonlight shine of a light hole in the rat's nest.

"I think we made it," Jonas said. *Heave...* "They won't come here." *Heave...* "Too many of us." *Heave...* "Too well-lit."

"Jonas, after you catch your breath, Grandpa prepared three cups of medicine for our return," Mite said.

"I'll go now."... *Heave...* "I'm fine."

Jonas slinked away, dodging through the crowded corner's of the rats' home. He crept silently avoiding waking any of the sleeping rats resting in the night.

"Thank you," Mite said. "Thank you, Tenzing."

Mite sat on the arc welder's power supply. Her tiny frame just fit over it like a chair. "You have no idea how important this machine is to everything. It'd be weeks—months even—before we could scavenge another one or find enough parts to fix one. You brought this back to us."

"You all helped me. I helped you. None of us are good unless we all are," Tenzing said. Mite chuckled.

"You sound just like Grandpa in a way. Anyway, you put those words into practice tonight." Mite leaned back on her impromptu mechanical chair. "Thank you, Tenzing."

Jonas returned with three cups of medicine. Tenzing smelled the herbal scent wafting from each tin mug.

"One for each of us," Jonas said. He handed a mug toward each rat. "I'm gonna drink this and mellow out to the best sleep of my life. And, I'm going to take this welder as far back into the Rats' Nest as possible." He downed the mug's contents in a few sips and squatted down, lifting the welder and gripping it on either side as he walked down the corridor, holding the machine like an over-sized, heavy, square baby.

"Sounds like a great plan," Mite echoed. She slinked off down the corridor. "I'm sure we'll get more of a reception tomorrow when the rest of the rats are up."

"Ah, shit, I have work tomorrow." Jonas' perturbed tone bounced from further down the corridor.

Tenzing smiled as he watched the other two rats move farther down into the nest. He crept through the corridor until he found an unoccupied space along the wall to lay his weary body. He took a few sips of the calming medicine, and the pain in his eyes drifted away like a foggy memory. Tenzing slept and his body knew rest.

Deep within his slumber, just before the waking hours, Tenzing dreamed. He saw the bodies of his family lying still in front of the village. He saw the silhouette of the arc in the distance. Swirling white mist dripped and condensed around his family's dead bodies. A dart pierced each of the corpses necks.

Tenzing dropped to his knees in front of his family. His mother held a one-antlered deer skull in her arms. The multitude spoke. He wasn't sure, but he thought he heard a few new voices join the choir.

"L I S T E N."

Tenzing pressed his ear to the ground. A rustling sound. Vines overtook his family's bodies. Their corpses were brought beneath the earth and flowers grew in their place. Tenzing heard the voice once again.

"B R I N G G R E E N B A C K T O T H I S W A S T E D L A N D."

Tenzing looked up. In the space where his family had lain, a garden sat. Children ate fruits picked from trees.

The voice spoke for a final time as Tenzing woke up. Sunlight crested through the light-hole.

"G I V E T H E M T H I S C H O I C E."

"G I V E T H E M T H I S G I F T O N L Y Y O U C A N G I V E."

Chapter 22

Laney stared bleary eyed through the contents of aux bay.

"Where in the fuck is this stupid fucking cushion?!?"

She had looked through every shelf in the warehouse multiple times.

"Some genius before me stored the chair cushion separate from the chair it belonged to, and now my supervisor is on my ass because the damn thing is up for auction tomorrow..."

"See, the thing is, I don't give two solid fucks about this chair or its cushion, but I have to make inc to pay for my space, which means I am forced to care about this stupid cushion. Do you know how exhausting it is, forcing yourself to care about stupid things like chair cushions?"

"Delaney, who are you talking to?

Laney flipped around the portrait of a skull in front of her. She whirled around and saw her boss Helen, Operations Manager and part-owner of Arc Interior Solutions—wealthy woman, A sectioner, big-wig.

"No one, nothing!" Laney blurted. "Hi, Helen, I didn't know you were coming down here. What are you doing here?"

The woman's pristine, symmetrical, plucked eyebrows did not move a millimeter as she spoke.

"I came to ask you a personal favor," said Helen.

Laney braced herself.

"One of the merchandise handlers for the auction injured themselves at the last minute. The idiot couldn't figure out how to move a three-hundred-pound object up-stairs. Anyway, I was hoping you could pitch in tomorrow night. It's a group effort and we need all hands on deck."

"And, I will be paid overtime for this?"

"It's possible. I'll have to check your hours, but this might push you over," Helen said.

Against Laney's better judgment, the one horrible word slipped from her mouth.

"Yes," Laney said.

"Wonderful, I didn't expect this kind of initiative from you, Delaney, but I am pleasantly surprised."

"Helen?" Laney asked. The woman with perfectly static eyebrows turned around.

"Yes?" she responded. Laney dove headfirst into her unrehearsed, un-thought-out plea.

"Look, I've been here a while now, and every auction just kinda dumps a whole lot on me all at once. Do you ever think Arc Interior Solutions would benefit from having more people in the warehouse? I mean, I think the whole company would benefit, really."

Laney's supervisor sniffed gently. Her nose did not move one iota from the inhale. Laney's aching traps wrenched.

"You've always managed so well before. I don't see why there's any issue now."

Laney stared hard at the woman. *Boom. Perfect verbal Jiu-Jitsu. Now anything I say is framed as my own personal incompetence.*

"Never mind. Have a good one," Laney said.

"You do the same," Laney's boss said as she turned toward aux bay's exit. The hard plastic on her shoe bottoms *click-clacked* all the way to the elevator.

Laney went back to look for the cushion. She shoved this missing item to the back of her mind as she scrambled to finish the rest of her to-do list— process all incoming shipments, requisition and inspect everything headed to auction. A ton of items. The hours toward the end of Laney's shift crawled by. She became more panicked minute-by-minute over the missing upholstery.

Ten minutes on the clock left and she saw it: a little torus-shaped black fabric ring with four fake-metal pins on top scrunching in the upholstery in a diamond pattern. Laney held it in her hands and it felt off, felt wrong. Gutted canyons towered in the distance. They ended Laney's view of the wasteland's crawling horizon.

I don't know where my friend is. I don't know whether he's okay or if he's hurt, and I've spent most of today obsessing about a cushion. I've worried about an inanimate object meant to soften the pressure underneath a seated person's ass. This inanimate object in particular will probably be purchased by some profoundly bored and boring ass pursuing yet another step in the infinite chain of distractions required to massage the fact that we all live in a dead world. I had one brush with answers, one brush with something meaningful, and the law of this arc chased him underground for my own "protection."

Laney looked back at the cushion in her hand. Her back muscles twinged. *Now it's back to cushions. Cushions and back pain.*

A gray, desolate landscape stretched under the arc as far as Laney could see. She approached the railing slowly and raised her arm. She threw the cushion as hard as she could. It sailed out into the open space beneath the arc. The cushion fell. It made no noise as it fluttered down a hundred feet and disappeared beneath the dust cloud trudged up by the arc's steps.

Righteous exhilaration surged throughout Laney's being. She smiled wide, and the grin suited her.

The clock showed five minutes to close. *Close enough.* Laney walked toward aux bay's exit, beaming with every step. Her only thought: *Damn, a beer sounds good right about now.*

Laney plopped down on her favorite bar stool at Coconut Joe's. The bar stool cushion was well-worn with time and use. Laney knew many patrons sat on that stool producing its wear-and-tear, but she liked to pretend it was just her, that her singular rear wore an impression in the leather top, that her many evenings drinking and talking left a physical history on the place, that she had an impact.

"Hey Mags, thanks for opening up a little early for me."

"It's the least I can do. Besides, look around, who else would I talk to right now," Magda replied.

Laney swiveled around on the stool as it squeaked. Laney spun, trying to produce a constant tone of squeak.

"LANEY! Stop that!" Magda yelled in the midst of preparing the taps for other patrons soon to trickle in.

"Sorry, sorry. Just excited. I chucked a cushion straight off the arc today."

"Fuck yeah," Magda said without skipping a beat.

"I also dove into the old program I helped build, the one I told you about. Last night after our talk, I looked at it without wincing, kinda made peace with my mistakes, allowed myself to start that process anyway."

"That's wonderful," Magda said. She tested the tap. She pulled the plug out of the rightmost tap and poured. Nothing but foam spilled forth from the metal spout followed by the barest hint of liquid at the very end of the pour.

"Son of a dammit!" Magda cursed. She slammed the foamy glass onto the counter, muttering to herself loudly. Her kvetching echoed around the empty bar.

"It's connected to the same tank as this other tap and that one works just fine! Don't even know how that's possible."

Laney pulled the foam-filled glass toward her lips and attempted a sip. The airy half-liquid bubbles stuck to the glass in protest as Laney angled the glass farther and farther up. *Slosh.* All at once, gravity beat friction and the bubbly mess smacked Laney in the face. She wiped her face with a cocktail napkin.

"Not the best texture, but it still gets you drunk," Laney said.

Magda turned away from the tap.

"People don't just pay to get drunk. They pay to sit here and meet people. They pay to talk and be talked to. They pay to have a place where they can find somebody that wants to go home and screw. They pay for atmosphere, they pay for ambiance. They pay for a wise, old, beautiful bartender who can make anybody laugh after a hard day, and they absolutely pay for the right texture for the beer they're sipping." Magda paused for a moment before she continued.

"And yeah, they pay to get drunk."

"I didn't mean anything by that," Laney said.

Magda stopped fiddling with the tap. She spread her arms out and leaned across the bar.

"I know you didn't. I'm just frustrated by this thing. It should work. It has every reason to work, but it won't work."

"Tech is like that," Laney said. "You think you've looked at every single part, taken a look at the whole system, isolated every part. At the end, there's always some small spec you've missed. Some little bug in the code. Some little break in the line. Your eyes were just too tired to see it. You're so myopic looking at the same thing a thousand times, you never notice the crack. You forget that you're a part of the system and sometimes you're just too worn out to fix something."

"Well, get on back here, Miss Philosophizer and take a look," Magda said. She swirled a spoon around the foamy glass and took a sip.

Laney hopped over the bar toward the tap.

"My gig is computers, but I'll give it a whirl."

Laney fiddled with the knobs and looked at the compressor behind the wall in the back of the bar.

"Look, Mags, I'm sorry, but I just don't understand pipes and valves and pressure differentials. It's just not my domain."

A billboard scrawled across an advertisement for VerchLife. A helmet-clad child smiled serenely. A thought bubble wisped from their head, filled with Knights and dragons, pirates and, trophies, candy and star ships. Text scrolled across the screen.

"Why have your life, when you can have VerchLife!"

Laney sighed as the billboard cut to an advertisement for Clouseau's, one of the finest restaurants in B Sector.

"My dad was so happy when I worked on that project."

"And he's not as happy that you climb shelves and retrieve chairs?" Magda asked. She went right back to fiddling with the tap.

"He doesn't outright say it, but I know. He's my dad and all, but we just don't value the same things. He's the type of guy, if someone wrote a book, he'd ask how many copies it sold before he'd ask them what it was about."

"I know the type. Tell me more," Magda answered.

Magda leaned in. She lived for gossip about people she did not personally know.

"He makes fun of my mom for how she orders at restaurants."

"How does she order?"

"She always asks the server what their favorite thing on the menu is. He scoffs and says it's ridiculous that she should, coincidentally, have the exact same tastes as the server. So he asks what everyone orders. He asks what sells best. He doesn't get that it's the same question really. Maybe it's more likely that whatever everyone gets is the best thing, but it's still just a guess that his tastes are the same as everyone else."

"Your mom is right in that," Magda said. "Share an experience.

Liking the same thing with an abstract crowd, a faceless, everyone, that is nothing. But ask the person right in front of you, the one who's helping make that meal in front of you possible what they like, show them they have importance and their likes and dislikes are important to you. That is something. Maybe you don't like whatever the server recommends, and that's fine. But if you do, then you've now got something in common with a real person that you can call by name instead of market opinion."

"Now who's the philosophizer?" Laney quipped.

"I'm full of talents," Magda said.

Magda turned around and banged on the keg. *Whap whap whap!* She pulled the tap and a perfect ratio of liquid to foam trickled from the spout.

Laney burst out. "How in the he—"

Magda cut her off.

"Don't question it, and never underestimate the power of brute force." Magda flexed her arms with comedic gusto.

Laney laughed. She reached out for the beer Magda poured her. Perfect texture, perfect ratio of liquid to foam. She took a sip.

"Yeah, when you're right, you're right. Texture really does make a difference," Laney said. She dove right back into the tall glass. Its crisp, hoppy body left a smile on her face when she set the glass back down on the laminate in front of her.

Laney glanced around. The absurd, tropical motifs that had never made any sense to her at once brought on the comfort of familiarity.

Magda waved in the first customers other than Laney. First came an older man in coveralls. He ordered a pint and Magda served him as Laney nursed her crisp, cool drink. Satisfied that the customer was cared for, Magda returned to Laney at the bar. Laney continued her story.

"My dad has more pride for my older sister Sadie. I'm proud of her too. She's a doctor on Arc Echo. Does heart transplants. Saves lives."

"I mean, saving lives can't be beat," Magda said.

"I absolutely agree, but whenever my dad talks to someone about his surgeon daughter, that's never the first thing he says. He tells them how much inc she makes in a year. That's always what he says first."

"Priorities reveal who a person really is," Magda said.

"I guess it's not totally his fault," Laney replied. "My grandfather, his dad, was a real piece of work. He must have picked up some odd habits in that house."

A few more customers piled in. Magda readied a few more glasses. She lined them up in front of the tap and spoke.

"I love your stories Laney, but I have to listen to other people's too. You're still my favorite, so I'll be back as much as I can."

Other patrons started to trickle in, seating themselves among the neon palm trees and tables decorated with plastic-grass skirts. Laney sipped through her drink and watched.

An amorous couple filed in. They couldn't keep their hands off each other. Laney laughed as they ordered their drinks and occupied the same bar stool, oblivious—or perhaps encouraged by—everyone else's stares.

A fit, blonde gentleman dressed in a gray sweatshirt and sneakers walked in. He ordered the first thing on tap and sat at a table in the midst of the crowd. Laney briefly met his eyes. He offered a polite smile, but returned back to his beverage. He seemed to enjoy the quiet people watching as much as she did.

Laney looked at her now empty glass. She glanced over toward Magda, but she was busied by the amorous couple at the end of the bar doing shots and loudly oversharing about their personal lives. Magda was enthralled.

Laney looked back over to the fit blonde gentleman in the gray hoodie—short hair, clean-cut, strong but not bulky. Laney studied the man in short, subtle glances over the next few minutes. She'd never seen him before. Magda dashed back behind the bar in front of Laney.

"LANEY, READ THIS!" she half yelled. Magda thrust a scrap of paper into Laney's hands as Laney read the six words that comprised its message.

"I'm safe. I'm protected. Thank you."

Laney beamed and stowed the scrap of paper in her breast pocket. She breathed a deep sigh of relief.

"He's okay. Thank God. He's okay."

"I told you he'd be the strongest damn thing down there. Probably has every tough son of a bitch down there working for him by now," Magda said. Her loud words fell quietly against the backdrop of conversation filling the crowded bar.

"Where did you get this?" Laney asked. Magda pointed towards a woman with dark hair standing outside Coconut Joe's. Laney noticed the woman's hands shaking as she fumbled with a small delivery satchel on her back. Laney saw the fit, blonde man drunkenly stumble near the dark haired woman with the bag. He bumped into her lightly and seemed to apologize. Laney looked back to the blonde man's table. *That's odd, I only saw him order one drink. I guess blondie is a lightweight.*

Magda broke off and talked with the woman who'd delivered the letter for a while. The pair laughed and joked. Magda was always quick to make new friends. Laney sat at the bar. Gracious relief flowed through her. *He's okay.*

Magda returned and Laney ordered a few more drinks through the night. *He's okay.* Laney and Magda toasted to Tenzing. They never said his name or any words every time they clinked glasses. They didn't have to, as they toasted silent cheers to the man who'd both climbed the arc and survived its depths. After many toasts, Laney announced,

"Alright, Mags, I'm gonna call it an early night. I've got that damn auction tomorrow and I need some rest. I'll take a water for the road."

Magda poured Laney the rejuvenating liquid and Laney downed it in a few big gulps.

"Have a good night, Laney. Safe travels," Magda said as she wiped down Laney's vacated spot." The stool spun gently, still in motion from Laney's leaving. It let out a small squeak, its wobbly swivel well-worn from use that existed from the many patrons who'd paid again and again to be a part of that place.

Laney walked home, pleasantly buzzed. She reached her door, took out her key fob, and pressed it against the sensor, before entering her door code.

He made it. He's okay.

A huge smile beamed across her face. She felt the tiniest prick in the back of her neck. Her heart surged. She fell to the floor.

Chapter 23

Earlier that day

Tenzing woke up. Sunlight filtered through the light hole at a high angle. *Slept late.*

He rose and dusted off his slumber, then walked a short beat down through the rats' territory and saw only a few rats moving about. *Emptier. They must be out.* Jonas' protests of having to work the next day rang through his memory.

Tenzing marched farther down the corridor. A man with ginger hair and beard strutted down the hall heading the opposite direction, carrying a bundle of sheet metal tied together with fraying twine. Tenzing and the man deftly parted ways, moving past each other without losing one bit of momentum.

"Tenzing, come here," June's voice called out.

Tenzing broke into a little jog. He shrank the distance between himself and June in no time. She stood just behind a light-hole. Beaming light shone down on her as she kneeled in front of a raised garden bed. She wore a loose green shirt that bounced from the gentle breeze that puffed through the rat's tunnel.

"You're a real rat now," *June said.*

"Thank you," Tenzing said. A huge smile cracked across his face. He'd never received a higher compliment.

"You don't have any idea how important getting that welder back is for us," June said.

"I couldn't have done it without Jonas and Mite," Tenzing said.

"Of course," June replied. "Those two wouldn't stop talking about how you did it. Everyone gathered 'round this morning. The way they told it you took down fifty cultists at once. Tenzing the shadow, Tenzing the blinded warrior, Tenzing the beast!"

Tenzing laughed a soft chuckle. He dragged his foot across the metal floor as June spoke. His face flushed red, embarrassed at hearing his praises.

"Too bad you slept through the accolades," June said.

"That's not why I did it."

"I know," June replied. "That's what impresses me the most about you." June pulled a scrap of paper out of her pocket.

"I've got your letter. I know Coconut Joe's. I'll deliver the letter when it opens up this evening."

"Thank you," Tenzing said.

"I like to do all my deliveries in one run. So you can help me in the garden during the day, and I'll do my deliveries this evening. I'll make sure your letter is my very first stop."

"Thank you again," Tenzing said. June started down the corridor toward the garden, and Tenzing followed behind. "June I have to say."

"What?" June interrupted.

"The cat's eye tonic is incredible. We never would have succeeded last night without it. Tenzing looked at all the plants in the garden ahead of him. He wondered what other amazing properties any of the vines, leaves, stalks, and petals may possess.

"This garden is amazing, June!"

"You don't have to remind me of my botanical genius. I already know," she smiled. The pair of them laughed. Vines before them bobbed gently in the cross-breeze from a nearby wind-hole.

"Grandpa prepared a new plot last evening after y'all left," June said.

She walked over to a nearby raised bed. The black, crumbly earth sat warmed by the sun, disturbed just enough by Grandpa's tending. The plot's previous plants had been cut down to the soil, roots left to rot and nourish, chewed and changed by small, unconsidered things that lived in life-rich earth. Tenzing wondered at the possibilities for this new patch.

"What will be planted here?" he asked. He passed his hand over the soil's surface, smoothing out some of the divots. His fingers felt the warmth and texture in absent minded-admiration.

"I don't know, Tenzing. What would you like planted here?" June replied.

"I... I can not make such a choice," Tenzing said. He backed up a little and bumped into the wall behind him.

"You're a rat now," June said. "Last night's events cemented it. It's simple. Rat's get to choose what grows out of the dirt we gather."

Tenzing knelt down. He raked his fingers through the soft earth. A memory ran through his mind of his father's sister placing the one-antlered skull above the threshold in their hut. *Home is the place you live when you live beyond surviving.*

"Is the garden the source of all the rats' food? Tenzing asked.

"Oh, no," June replied. "We've got the pigeon roost eggs Grandpa gathers, scraps Mite and a few others scavenge topside, and all the collected things bought by Jonas, myself, and everyone else who has some gig up top, which is most of us. We simply don't have the space to feed ourselves entirely from just the garden, but that's not the point. It brings people together more than sustains us, really. Watching things grow does that."

"Then... could we plant flowers?" Tenzing asked. He held his breath.

June stared at Tenzing for three unbroken blinks.

"I think that's a wonderful idea," she said. "Come with me. Let's go get the seeds."

Tenzing followed June to the space where she made her bunk. A small hammock nestled into the side of the exterior wall swung gently over a big trunk. June opened up the trunk. Tenzing saw it filled with bags and bags of seeds of every shape, size, color, and texture.

"These!" June pointed to the weighty sachets with an excited glow about her face.

Tenzing grabbed the bags and the two hurried back to the garden, back to the vacant patch of earth, back to possibility.

"How do I do it?" Tenzing asked.

'I'll teach you, step-by-step. You're gonna do this right. No half-rooted flowers in my garden—I've got a reputation to uphold."

"I'm ready," Tenzing said.

June started her instructions.

"Drag your finger lightly through the soil in little lines. Sprinkle the seeds one-by-one across the little trench."

Tenzing followed June's every instruction. He'd never been so careful with anything.

"Gently rake the soil over the little rows. Make sure not to cover them too much. The seeds need just the right depth—not too high to be above the ground, not too low to never feel the warmth of the sun."

Tenzing dusted his hand atop the little rows. He tucked in each seed with a blanket of fertile earth.

"Now give them a little water."

Tenzing took a plastic bottle stored near the containers and filled it with water from a nearby spout. He tilted the bottle on its side where a previous rat had poked little holes just big enough for water to drip. Drops of water sprinkled in steady streams to the planted spots, dampening the soil with hydrating moisture in controlled splotches.

Tenzing felt little tears swell at the back of his eyes and his face got puffy. This was the first time he'd planted anything, gave life to anything since distant childhood memories of the village. June watched him.

"I know how you feel. It can be powerful. I feel it too," she said. Tenzing thumbed his hands through the soil.

"I know we will leave this place. All the Rats. Grandpa told me."

"Yes." June replied. "We will be leaving. June sighed. She used her forearm to pat the soil where Tenzing had planted. Little bits of dirt stuck to her arm. She continued.

"It's something we've been working toward for a long time. Our lives are hard on this arc. We've fallen through the cracks. We live in the walls. It's not pleasant." The bare patch of earth where Tenzing had sown the seeds glistened. Wet soil reflected incoming light from the hole cut into the outer wall.

June continued.

"But we have grown together in this place. It is still our place. June stooped down head above the newly planted plot." She smelled the fresh sown seeds.

"What kind of flower did we plant?" Tenzing asked.

"Helianthus Annuus, the Sunflower. They're tough. They grow tall. In a better world, they would feed so many little things." June's face scrunched. She sighed. "But one day, we will plant a whole field of these out there. Enough flowers, you could see it from the sky. Grandpa says the time is coming soon."

Tenzing touched his fingers toward the bare patch of earth.

"If the time is soon, then why did we plant these? They will take time to grow. Won't you have left by then?"

"A thing isn't just beautiful when it's finished," June said. "There's beauty in just the start of it too. Nothing alive is ever finished. That's what growth is. Besides, I want to leave something growing behind. We all want to try and leave this place better when we go. It's the least we can do."

Tenzing took June's words to heart as he whiled away the rest of the afternoon working with her in the Garden. He took great pleasure in the starting. The sun cast downward and revealed the orange light of evening.

"I'm going out," June announced. "Gonna deliver your letter first."

"Thank you," Tenzing said.

Chapter 24

Present time

Laney opened her eyes with considerable effort. A groggy sensation filled her body as she thought she felt cold metal against her cheek. Through near shut eyes she glanced around the room. She could not move her head, only her eyes. Every cell in her body desperately screamed one thought—sleep—but she fought the impulse. She didn't know why, but she felt she had to wake up. She had to remember.

Through the filter of interlocking eyelashes, Laney rolled her eyes to the very edge of her periphery. A blonde man sat crouched in the corner of an empty room, somewhere in C Sector, by the layout. He held something trained on a closed door—a dart gun. He sat, waiting.

Laney remembered. Her mind jolted awake as her body lay still in this puncture induced-chemical coma. Instantly, she understood the snare this unknown man had set.

Tenzing... no... don't come... don't. She tried to scream, but she had no voice. The muscles in her throat lay dormant, asleep. For now, all she had was her eyes and her brain. That was enough to keep her awake. She worked to find more.

Laney searched every sensation in her body. Everything felt numb, no sensation except... when she focused, really focused she could half-wiggle her left little toe. *It's a start...*

***

Down in the Side Hull, Tenzing occupied his time after June left. He worked in the garden, pulling seeds from old, dried bean pods. He shelled the beans and placed their dry, papery cocoons in the compost container along with other treasured refuse. He helped Mite separate tea from tea bags.

Tenzing tried to speak with Grandpa but learned the aged man was deep in focus attempting to heal the mind of the lost wanderer who'd come in the night—the wanderer who moaned of yellow light and yellow walls.

He can't heal them. But he still tries, Tenzing thought. He brought himself back to the present, back to the problems he could impact, back to the garden.

Tenzing worked trying to find every little thing he could do to help down in the rat's nest before June arrived. *I'll surprise her with what I've done.* After the hours and minutes ticked down, it was well into the evening. The last light of day faded behind the horizon and a few rats turned on string lights attached to solar batteries that had charged throughout the day.

June's familiar gait bounded down the corridor toward Tenzing. He ran to meet her.

"I delivered your letter," June beamed. "And I ran into a friend of yours who sent me this," June pulled out a sealed paper envelope."

"It is nice Laney and Magda would send something back," Tenzing said.

"Oh, well, this was from a man. He said he knew you from work—he and some of your old coworkers heard how you lost your job and they took up a little collection. He found me just as I was heading back down to the Side Hull. He asked, since he didn't know how to get down there, if I could take it to you. I actually bumped into the same guy as I was delivering your letter to Coconut Joe's. What a coincidence!"

Tenzing's face went stark-white.

"Hey, you never told me where you used to work, Tenzing... Tenzing?"

June attempted to grab Tenzing's attention but he stood still. A fist balled, then a second.

"Read me the letter, June," Tenzing said.

June fumbled with the envelope. Tenzing's change of tone and scowling face frightened her. She read the letter and understood his sudden change.

An instant photo showed the body of an unconscious woman lying on the floor. The letter contained eight words:

"Come find her. Come alone. Follow the sound."

Tenzing and June stopped. They heard a beeping sound. *Beep... ... ... Beep.* June ran her fingers around her clothes, the beep sounded as if it were right on her. She found a small, black device nestled in the knit of her shirt on her back. She held it in her hands and repeated the letter's words.

"Follow the sound..." *Beep.* June thought. Grandpa had sometimes told the other rats about all the little devices Arc Security possessed. He prepped them so they would know. She plumbed her memory as Tenzing grabbed the device from her hand.

June gasped!

"Tenzing! It's a proximity tracker. It's coded to the other one. It will beep more as you get close! He wants you to find him. It's a trap!"

"I AM GOING!" Tenzing commanded. "She saved me. Now, I'm saving HER!"

"Then I'm coming with you!" June yelled. "Rats stick together."

"The letter! Come alone!" Tenzing screamed.

"Fuck the letter! Rat's stick together!"

Tenzing realized there was no convincing her.

"If we both go, then there is something we need," Tenzing said. The pair went down the corridor and grabbed a heavy metal object. They slung it between the two of them as June navigated Tenzing through the fastest path up to the surface.

The arc's deck at night loomed in front of the pair. Its abundant neon signs cast down a sickly glow, the path ahead bathed in hyperreal light. Tenzing gripped the tracker in his hand and ran fifty feet toward the right and listened. *Beep... ... ... beep.* He ran back to his starting position and then fifty feet to the left. *Beep... ... beep... ... beep.*

"*This way!*" he yelled. He and June sprinted in the direction of C+ Sector.

The pair ran hard and fast carrying an object betwixt them. They looked at nothing and heard nothing save for a steady increase in the beep's frequency as they arrived in Sector C +. Everywhere, big, chunky, gray towers squatted in rows and columns, all the same.

"STAY HERE!" Tenzing commanded. He rounded a few blocks, but the beeps stayed constant.

Tenzing burst into a building and ran up a few flights of stairs. A door sat open. Tenzing saw a family with five children. The screaming children's cries echoed through the confines of a too-small apartment. Tenzing listened as the beeping faded slightly. *Not up, but... down!.* Tenzing ran back to June.

"How do we get down?!" Tenzing yelled.

June and Tenzing linked arms around the heavy object they carried. June led Tenzing down through the nearest stairwell.

"C Sector," June said.

The pair wound down through cavern like hallways dimly lit with fluorescent lighting. The light crackled and sputtered as Tenzing listened to the tracker. *Beep... beep... beep...* Tenzing and June flew around the hallways triangulating the sound until they came to a shut door at the end of the hall. *BEEP BEEP BEEP BEEP.*

Tenzing whispered,

"June! If he sees the two of us, he might hurt Laney. I will not take that chance. Please let me go in alone. Listen at the door. Help me when you can."

Real, desperate fear swirled around Tenzing's eyes. June nodded.

Tenzing stood outside the door and counted. "One... two... three."

He kicked in the door and switched on the arc welder. He hurled its lit end into the dim room. A blinding spark filled the room with flashing light as Tenzing dove over its sparking end. A dart whizzed right past him and lodged into the open, wooden door.

In the time of that one miss, Tenzing closed the distance between himself and the ambusher. He threw both hands around the pistol and jerked it to the side, wrenching it from the assailant's hands. It fell to the floor and skidded just out of reach. Tenzing felt concussive force smash into his rib cage as the ambusher's boot rocketed him back five feet. The assailant dove for the pistol. Tenzing slid and just beat him by a hair. He kicked hard, sending the instrument of death flying away. It slid and bashed against a wall at the room's side.

"TENZING! NO!" a weak voice wailed.

Laney's paralyzed frame lay in the corner. The assailant smashed through Tenzing on his way to the pistol. Tenzing fell, knocking hard into the steel wall. He regained his balance.

"Tenzing!" June screamed.

She flung a small, thin object. It skated across the floor. Tenzing grabbed it. The assailant hurried to load another dart into the pistol. He refastened its clip, knocked askew from the pistol's impact with the wall. *Click.* The assailant drew the pistol and took aim only to find a dart held a millimeter away from his own pulsing neck.

"Get him!" June screamed.

Tenzing started to push the dart.

"TENZING, STOP!!!!" Laney yelled.

Tenzing held the dart a hair's width away from the assailant's throat. The assailant stood catatonically still, knowing he'd been beaten, knowing a lethal dart had not pierced his bloodstream only because the woman he had captured told Tenzing to stop. He listened to find out that reason as every single nerve in his body fired in adrenal panic.

"Why?" Tenzing and June shouted in unison. June turned off the sparking welder. She moved into the room behind Tenzing.

Laney used all her energy to command her voice. Surging adrenaline pulsed through her body. She wrenched her arms about and dragged herself across the floor, legs still in their paralyzed state.

"If we kill this man now, there's just going to be another one tomorrow. And then another one. They'll eventually send one who finishes the job. We've got him at the end of his own lethal dart, and we can finally learn what they know. We can use that. We can't give that up. We finally have an edge."

The assailant opened his hands. He gently, slowly set the dart pistol on the ground and locked eyes with Tenzing as he moved in slow motion, dart never more than a millimeter away from the arteries in his neck. June picked up the dart pistol and handed it to Tenzing. Tenzing stood back out of arm's length. He trained the pistol on the ambusher's center mass, a point, blank shot.

"Tell us what you know!" Laney yelled.

"I'll show you. I'll show you why I have to do this," the ambusher said.

He backed away slowly and Tenzing followed, keeping the same point blank shot trained on his heart with every movement. The ambusher reached for a circular electronic device and thumbed through it. He clicked and a video clip played. He slid the device toward Laney, who lay on the ground scrunching her fingers together in their newly found dexterity.

Tenzing heard a whirring noise come from the device, distant screams, and animalistic growls. Laney watched the video clip.

The ambusher spoke.

"See those? See those things. He will turn into one. Everyone out there. Everyone in the waste eventually turns into one. I've put down over a hundred of them."

"NO!" Tenzing screamed.

Laney scrolled back over the footage. Forward and backward. Forward and backward. Something bothered her. Everyone stared at Laney, panicked by her silence.

Laney realized that she'd seen something like this video footage before—not the content, but its errors. The subtle video mapping errors that one would only notice from staring at the same type of footage for years, changing finger lengths per frame, minute pixel length differences between eye positions.

Laney recognized these errors because they were the same errors she'd spent years dealing with when she worked at VerchLife. She took a base program video-image altering software and trained it to create iterative virtual realities. This footage was a product of that same base program. In the device's most recent video log, Laney found the absolute clincher that assured her beyond all doubt.

In the shards of a smashed glass table top, one shard perfectly reflected the face of an all too human victim.

Small, irregular shaped, reflective surfaces. The image mod software always had trouble with detecting faces in those exact conditions.

Laney hit a few command keys, deep software commands only a programmer would know. She pulled an internal keyboard out of the device and entered a few lines of code. She isolated and found the unaltered footage buried deep within the device's archives, hidden but still there.

"Look at this NOW! You will regret everything if you don't." She slid the device back to the ambusher. He picked it up and he looked with desperate eyes. Tenzing held his shot on his chest. The assailant thumbed through video after video, eyes transfixed.

"They've been lying to you. It's a really convincing fake. Literally nobody but someone who built the program would notice. But it's fake nonetheless." Laney used her arms to prop her body against the steel wall.

"NO! I'VE SEEN IT!" the assailant screamed. "THROUGH THE DRONE! I PILOT IT!. I'VE SEEN IT... I'VE SEEN!!"

"The program alters what comes through a screen on a live feed," Laney said. Her voice was firm and clear. "They manipulated everything you ever saw. Look here." Laney crawled over and took back the device. She changed the footage putting the filter back on.

The assailant kneeled. Laney pointed to the reflective image of the fearful human face, illuminated in the singular glass shard. Even in the doctored footage, a reflection showed the truth that the camera concealed. Laney took the filter back off.

The assailant pored over the video logs of his missions putting down Lingerers in the waste. He looked through a special folder. *Euthanizations.* Strickland made it easy. He wanted his men to remember why they protected the arc. He wanted those pained, animalistic faces on the forefront of his men. He wanted Vance to remember. Vance scoured through the footage of every kill.

In this new footage, there were no longer Lingerers. Gone was the sallow, see through skin, gone were the gnashing teeth. Gone were the scowls of animalistic pain. Instead of crazed agony, their faces showed only desperate fear contorting into the visage of unaltered, un-monstrous, thoroughly *human* faces. Faces that understood the mechanical monstrosity that pursued them. Faces that recognized their impending demise. Vance pored over unaltered video log after video log. A horrid pattern formed before his eyes. Of his human victims, very few fought back. Many ran. Even more hid.

"IT'S NOT POSSIBLE! They showed us a DEAD ONE, a body in an airtight case. It looked just like the ones out there! We saw it dissected, its mutant organs splayed out, corrupted. I SAW IT! I SAW THEM!!"

A flash of recognition crawled across Tenzing's face when the assailant described the dissected body. He remembered the meat-printing room he'd seen in the VerchLife log. He remembered the words Mite said she'd never forget.

"Arc Charlie can produce any bespoke protein," Tenzing said. "My friends encountered a woman down in the depths. Over and over, she spoke of yellow light and yellow walls. She said they made her make a meat puppet."

The assailant collapsed to the floor. Yellow bile spilled from his mouth in a deluge. Steady tears dripped onto the acidic spew. Hunched over that filth, he slammed his knuckles into the metal floor. His bruised fists cracked and turned scarlet with trickling blood. With the mention of Yellow walls, he knew.

"Yellow walls," he whispered. No one knows about that place. If someone—said... they had to be—the dissected one—meat puppet... God...

His voice broke. It fell quiet, low, almost inaudible.

"What have I done? Lies... how was I so... stupid? How... was I so... fucking stupid?... It... must be... yellow walls."

Tenzing set the tranquilizer gun gently on the floor. He crept toward the weeping man who lay shaking, tears streaming, almost hyperventilating.

Tenzing placed an arm across the man's back. The man shook and took no notice at first. Tenzing held him as he bore his pain.

Laney pulled the limp lower half of her body forward forearm-by-forearm across the floor. She reached Tenzing and the man and placed an arm on the pair. June held back.

"It's not your fault," Laney said.

The assailant knelt. Rapid, breaths sucked in and out through the man's bile-stained teeth. He stared at the tarnished floor.

"It's not your fault," Laney said again.

"Not your fault," Tenzing said.

The three held that moment until the assailant let out a deep breath and pulled back from the ground. He rested his hands in his lap and knelt on his shins. He spoke softly, words punctuated by pained sobs. Laney and Tenzing listened.

"The darts, the lethal kind we use in the waste. They don't kill in an instant. They told us they do, but it's not true. I asked a doctor once what happens when you're shot by one. The body shuts down. Breathing stops, but the brain is still awake. It knows it's going to die. It knows it can't breathe, but it can't... do... anything."

The man exhaled another deep breath. His bleeding knuckles scraped across the floor.

"Breath. Sometimes I try to hold my breath for as long as I can, to feel the smallest amount of what that must be like. The pressure, the feeling that my rib cage will implode, that desperation as every... single... cell... in my body screams for oxygen, *screams* to dump the CO_2 poisoning it. It's pain. It's nothing but total pain, but I can end it all. I can take another breath. I can end that pain... Everyone I ever shot with a dart doesn't get to do that. Its all they are until the end."

Tenzing and Laney held the man as he heaved a deep breath into his lungs.

"That suffocation... that breathlessness, its total pain, and its total fear, and it lasts for *minutes*. It lasts for minutes longer than I could ever stand... with only the certainty of death at the end. It lasts for minutes that must feel like an eternity."

Tenzing and Laney held him tighter.

"Every single time before a mission, he told us the people in the wastes had a mutation that caused them terminal pain. Somewhere along the line, years ago, the existing population outside the arc suffered an event that changed them. I never asked questions about it. It didn't feel safe to. They told us the people left out there shuffled around in constant torture, nerves firing every second with biting, burning suffering. Not asking questions—that's probably why I got the job. At least I asked about the darts. I can say I questioned something... but I still swallowed it all.

"They told us to come out to cure that suffering. When I learned the darts didn't kill instantly, I rationalized it. What was a few minutes of breathless agony compared to a lifetime of pain? I got good at that calculation. The math got easy. It shouldn't ever be easy. That calculation ran through my head with every shot I made until those shots felt like the right thing to do."

The man's face burst, and tears rolled down in thick streams.

"And now, I know it was never real: the footage, corpse-printing, meat puppet, yellow walls... it all fits.

"I just dealt out pain and death for nothing. I stole breath and handed out death for paintings and mirrors. I killed to keep the arc alone. I killed for treasure and entertainment. I killed to keep the arc going."

"They used you," Laney said. She held tight. Tenzing did too.

"I was a stupid, useful pawn. I should've figured it out." the former assailant replied.

"You know now," Laney said. "They can't use you anymore." The assailant stared into Laney's eyes and nodded. He breathed in deep.

"What will you do now?" Tenzing asked.

The former assailant pressed himself to his feet. He shook, then he steadied himself. His voice trembled, then it didn't.

"I want to kill the man that sits in the middle of all of this. I want to kill the man responsible. I want to kill the man that made me do all this."

Tenzing stood up. His height reached only to the shoulder of the man, but nonetheless, he stood tall.

"If the death of this man will help people on this arc, I will help you."

"I will too," Laney said, still bound to the floor. "We'll need a plan, and I still can't walk." June hung further back from the group watching the other three.

"A brief moment of respite. Then we will move," said Tenzing. He turned toward the former assailant and asked,

"What is your name?"

The man stopped dead his conditioned impulse to precede his name with his rank and title, and replied,

"Vance. Just Vance."

Chapter 25

Tenzing, Vance, Laney, and June rested their bodies in the empty C Sector room. Each occupied one of the room's four corners. Their backs wormed far back into the space where the walls joined as if the slight cover satisfied some instinctual need for shelter. They rested for a few silent minutes partaking in a wordless conversation of heaving breaths as their bodies processed the conspiracy in which they found themselves.

"You said you'd kill him. Kill the man at the center of it all. Who is it? "Who's the man?" June asked.

"My Squadron Lead—" Vance stopped himself. "A man named Strickland. There's no doubt in my mind. He did this, all of this."

"Strickland ordered my death," Tenzing said and pointed to his neck."

"Twice," Laney said. "He ordered Tenzing's death twice." She couldn't stop her eyes from training themselves on Vance's slouched figure.

"Yes," said Vance. "First by Harkness, then... by me. I'm... sorry, I..." Vance looked at Tenzing. He saw a man, a man who was never a monster.

"There's no words that can make this right. I will kill the man at the head of this," Vance said.

"You were a tool used by another man. Do not grieve for the tool's

actions. The tool had no thoughts. Anger at the tool will not help us."
Tenzing's words reminded June a little of Grandpa.

Vance nodded.

"Strickland is the head of all this. The assignment to terminate
Tenzing came directly from him. Nobody else knows of him. Vance's
voice lifted. "If no one else may know of your existence. If he's gone
then—"

"Tenzing might be free," Laney said. "No more target on your back.
You could live here. "

"How do we know that's true?" June asked.

"I only found out about Tenzing when Harkness failed and Strickland
passed his mission on to me. It hasn't been long. Strickland probably
still believes in my success, that any moment now I'll stroll up to Ghost
Arc with my prisoners. That gives us a window."

"That's a big assumption. Are we sure no other officers know about
all this?" June asked.

"I think so," Vance answered. "The Circle, the small cadre of officers
who take secret orders direct from Strickland, are all so young. They're
all like me. They've all been officers for less than ten years. I thought
it was odd when I first noticed it, but now—"

"Ten years is the same amount of time we've had image-
modification tech for live feeds," Laney said. "First invented ten
years ago, I spent two years training that program to make VerchLife
worlds, and we've all seen how popular those have become in just the
last three years."

"All the officers in this circle, are they the same ones who fly the
drones in the wastes?" June asked.

"Yeah," Vance answered. "There's a handful outside that, but they're
all within that same age bracket. Nobody active has been flying for more
than ten years. Nobody except for Harkness."

"Mr. Chewing Tobacco Voice!" Laney blurted. She remembered his oily smirk and her face drew into a disgusted grimace. Vance noticed Laney's expression change.

"I guess he ran into you too. I'm sorry for that," Vance said. "I took his place in The Circle. Strickland altered his memories."

"Altered his memories, how?" Laney asked.

Vance started. "The room with—"

"Yellow walls," Tenzing and June said in unison.

"What happens there?" Laney asked.

Vance remained silent. He didn't meet Laney's eyes.

"They turn people into husks," June answered. "I might not know what happens in that room, but I know exactly what happens when people come out. They end up in the tunnels. They wander and they moan about yellow lights and yellow walls. You wanna see a real face stuck in pain and fear, look at those faces."

Vance shriveled farther into his corner. Tenzing bobbed his head between June and Vance.

"Do you think Strickland ordered the other young officers in this circle to turn in the other older circle members?" Tenzing asked.

"One out, one in," Vance muttered. "That sounds right." He remembered Strickland's in-depth knowledge of his personal life, his difficulty with his in-laws. The man knew all of this without Vance ever having told him a thing.

"Strickland knew everything. For the mind's he didn't destroy in that room, he probably had enough blackmail to put anyone left in an early retirement. He was thorough."

"So, he changed the guard and buried the old generation's secrets leaving himself as the sole guardian," June said. "Quite the spymaster."

"But why?" Tenzing asked.

"Control," Laney said. "Vance, I met Harkness briefly. Just from that short meeting, I got a foul unease. Something sick about him I could see, I could feel. Am I right? How was he as a person,—as an officer, I mean?"

"He was the most gleefully sadistic man I've ever met," Vance answered. "He loved nothing more than to make people squirm underneath his boots. He had a power complex, reveled in twisting the knife to hide or feed something wrong in him, something weak in him. Where are you going with this?"

"You said when you put the darts in the Lingerers, you felt like you were doing the right thing. Like you were ending suffering," Laney replied.

"Yes—God, I was so stupid..." Vance shrank. His eyes dropped to the floor.

"Look, tranqsnake, you can soul-search all you want later. That's not the point right now!" June scolded. "Who gets to pilot a drone? Who gets to put eyes on the outside? Who gets to know there are 'Lingerers' out there?"

"It's lots of training. You must become an officer and undergo... a rigorous psychological battery. That's the step that filters most candidates out..." Vance answered.

"Before, the leaders must have selected pilots like Harkness," Laney said. Those who'd kill for the fun of it. Evil, violent, bastards. People who'd need little convincing to pull a trigger. New technology enabled a different approach. It allowed them to select a different breed to 'protect' the arc. A breed easier to control."

"They appealed to our desire to protect. They told us we eased pain, told us we were defenders. They knew we wouldn't question that, couldn't question that. We couldn't see those deaths we dealt from distance as anything other than noble. Unthinkable—too painful to see ourselves as the monsters in the equation. So we didn't question," Vance said.

"A boy with the need to be a hero is easier to control than a mad dog kept on a leash. Strickland calculated well," Laney said.

"I'd guess the Board of Directors probably had a hand in it as well," June said. Nothing happens on this arc without their go-ahead."

Laney pushed her arms against the ground and pressed herself to her feet. Her legs wobbled, but she could stand. She threw her arms wide to the sides, swaying with every imbalance. She fell back down to the cold floor.

"How did you fight through that tranquilizer so fast?" June asked.

"I don't fully know. I fought to keep my mind awake," Laney answered. "I just.. I knew I had to wake up. My body is a different story. I really don't know how I'm gaining control of my muscles this fast. Same thing happened to Tenzing when he first got pricked."

"You must not eat a lot of Nutri Logs," Vance said. "And I'm assuming Tenzing must not have eaten arc foods until he came aboard?"

Tenzing shook his head no. Laney spoke.

"No. They're the one thing I could never adjust to after falling from A Sector privilege. I know it's prissy, but I just never could stand the gray wriggling..."

"What does that have to do with—" June stopped. She shot an understanding scowl Vance's direction. "Y'all don't—"

"Trace additives in the Nutri Logs," Vance said. Bit-by-bit, it alters the physiology to become more sensitive to our sedative darts. The darts primarily target the body for immobilization. Security needs the mind intact for interrogation purposes."

"And... I'm guessing veal cutlets and martinis don't get the same special ingredient," June said.

"Most of the crimes we respond to aren't from A Sector. Vance stammered. "The Board never deemed it worth it to put the additive in anything other than Sector C staples."

"People in A sector never have to steal to eat," June said.

"You're right," Vance said. Scant foodstuffs of his youth scrawled through his mind. Tenzing crossed to the room's center.

"What do we do now?" Tenzing said. The question hung in the air like an uncomfortable fog.

'If we kill Strickland, this goes away," Vance said. "I know how to frame his death so it won't draw suspicion."

"Of course you do," June replied.

Vance ignored her.

"As far as Strickland knows, my plan to capture you has succeeded without incident. He'll be waiting for my return with the two of you." Vance looked toward Tenzing and Laney. "I can bring you back to Ghost Arc. He assumes you're captured, then I kill him when he's alone and unsuspecting in the room with yellow walls. We can even destroy the machine."

"Wait a second! How in the ever-loving FUCK do we know this isn't some slick plan to finish your abduction assignment!?" June erupted. "What fucking real reason do we have to trust you? How do we know you're not just a convincing fucking actor? You wouldn't be prince of the prod-pigs if you didn't know how to lie!"

June moved toward the center of the room. She held her foot over the still-loaded dart pistol weapon ready to kick it toward Tenzing or Laney.

"There's no way I can make you trust me. The best I can do is to give you control over me," Vance said.

Vance splayed his palms. He reached within his sweatshirt. June kicked the tranquilizer pistol toward Laney. Vance pulled out a small, ring-shaped object. It fit within the palm of his hand.

"Easy! It's a prisoner control device, to be used on me," Vance said.

Vance held up a circular, flat ring about the size of a bottle cap. He turned it around. Little struts supported a tiny capsule suspended just above the ring.

"The capsule houses a remote-activated dart," Vance said. "With a button push, a lethal dart jabs into the wearer's skin." Vance peeled off the adhesive surface on the bottom of the ring, lifted his shirt and stuck the device beneath his sternum. He pulled out a second, stick-shaped device topped with a red button on its end. He rolled the device across the ground. It stopped at Laney's feet.

"It's the activator. Flip off the safety, push that button, and I'm dead. I won't even draw another breath."

Laney studied every microscopic expression on Vance's face as she held the remote that could end his life in her hands. His face remained unchanged as she held the deadly remote, her thumb an inch from its button.

Laney checked that the device's safety was locked in the 'on' position. She lowered the activator back onto the ground and rolled it across the empty floor to the corner. It fell through slats in a floor vent.

"Don't make me regret that. And take that thing off," Laney commanded.

Vance peeled the ringed device off his skin. Little strips of glue stuck to the hair on his chest. He held the little life-ending device in his hands. He met Laney's eyes.

'Thank you," he said.

Vance dropped the ring device onto the ground and crushed it under the thick rubber sole of his boot.

"Look, I'm a little slower to trust," June said. "Life has taught me that. If you try ANYTHING that hurts these two, just know, you will be torn apart by rats and left in a tunnel so deep on this arc no one will ever find you again." Vance nodded and gulped.

"You're not on the docket for imprisonment and memory-extraction. The plan won't work if you come with us," Vance said. He stared at June, not daring to look anywhere else.

"Fine by me," June replied. "Besides, I need to get this back down to the rats. She slapped a hand on the arc welder and the metal thunked.

"I think the moment Grandpa has been waiting for will be here even sooner than he thought." June bent down and gripped the arc welder in a great bear hug. She struggled with the weight. Vance, and Tenzing got up to help as June heaved.

June set the welder back down in the empty room.

"No. Fuck... you all need to go. From what I hear, the window of opportunity before Strickland's suspicion kicks in is closing fast. I'll stash this here and come back for it with the rats."

June marched over to a large wall vent at the back of the room.

"A little help?" June asked. Vance pulled a multitool from his munitions bag and pried off the rusted, bent grate. June, and Tenzing each took a side of the machine and lifted it into the open vent space while Vance refastened the covering.

"I'll get word to Jonas, Spark, and Mite. They'll help me get it back to the nest real quick. Hopefully this time it won't be stolen by a cult before I get back." June winked at Tenzing.

"What do the rat's need with the welder?" Tenzing asked. "Mite and Jonas never told me after we took it back from that cult preacher."

"Cult preacher?" Laney and Vance looked around confusedly and muttered under their breaths.

"There's a lot more that goes on beneath and between the walls than either of you could realize," June said. "Anyway, as for the welder, I don't wanna ruin the surprise."

June bounded out the door. Vance ran after her. He called out.

"June, please! Can you please take a message to my wife? Her name is Kayla."

June nodded and approached. Vance whispered to her his message and the recipient's address.

"Thank you," Vance said.

"I'll do it for Tenzing. He seems to trust you. I don't, but I'm hoping for the opportunity to be wrong." June departed.

"Laney, can you walk?" asked Tenzing.

"Not well," Laney answered.

She pushed herself back to her feet and took another unsteady step. Her paralysis-weakened muscles buckled, but she held firm and fought through the jellied numbness. She took another tentative step and kept her balance, swinging her arms out wide. "That's all I can manage right now." Vance grabbed his munitions bag and slung it over his shoulder.

"Tenzing, get the other arm," Vance said. He braced himself under Laney's left arm. Tenzing obliged and the pair carried Laney's frame with ease.

"There's a private, Circle-personnel-only heli-carrier dock hidden outside the aft deck." Vance held up the Circle tablet. Now that I've got this, I can charter a flight back to Ghost Arc. We'll find Strickland." Laney stared hard at the Circle device Vance held. She furrowed her brow.

"Will he be up at this hour?" Laney asked, "It's pretty late."

Vance remembered Strickland's shadow as it crackled through the window against the glow in the room with yellow walls.

"Yes. He'll be up for this."

Chapter 26

Vance stuffed the Circle device in his munitions bag. He and Tenzing each took Laney by the arm and hobbled out of the room. They navigated the winding, fluorescent-lit corridors of Sector C. Every few steps, Laney put more and more pressure on her legs attempting to condition her muscles and flush away the remaining sedatives.

The trio approached the end of a hallway where a stairwell would take them to aft deck. A C Sector apartment door opened ahead of them and an older woman holding a cane stepped outside. She looked to be just under the minimum age for Arc Bravo passenger eligibility. Her concerned eyes drew toward Laney, carried by Vance and Tenzing.

"Does she need help? Is she hurt?" The older C Sector woman asked.

Vance pulled his security badge out from under his sweatshirt. He held it up in front of the woman. She backed into her apartment and shut the door. The door clicked multiple discrete clicks, locked firmly shut—homemade, mechanical locks.

"Can you imagine what it's like to be on the other side of that? Laney asked.

"If we don't get to Strickland soon, I won't have to imagine," Vance replied.

The three made their way up the stairwell and reached a locked, barred door.

"Aft deck is on the other side of this door," Vance said.

Vance pulled out his badge and held it in front of the door's sensor. The lock clicked and the door swung open.

"Main receiving dock is not proprietary. Security can get in," Vance said. Laney scrunched her face. She put more pressure on her legs. Her gait evolved into an unsteady limp.

"Almost," Laney said.

"We'll carry you a little further," said Tenzing.

Tenzing and Vance hurried through the warehouse. They guided Laney more than they carried her as they past rows and rows of stocked products midway in their journey from a satellite arc to a store on Arc Alpha.

Crisp air wound through a dark, empty warehouse bereft of any personnel or movement in the night. A cold chill filled the room. It felt coldest near the mass of refrigerated containers filled with thousands upon thousands of gray Nutri Logs.

Vance winced. *There's so many. We prejudge so many, chemical preconditioning for the paralyzing dart I carry.* Vance counted hundreds of crates of Nutri Logs. *I used to eat those all the time.*

"Where do we go?" Laney yelled.

"Over there to the right," Vance said. He drew back to the present. He and Tenzing marched with Laney held between them to a stairwell off to the right. She stepped up to the stairwell unaided. The stairwell bent around the aft deck's furthest corner. It ended in a barred gate not visible from aft deck itself.

A sign hung on the gate. 'MAXIMUM SECURITY: AUTHORIZED PERSONNEL ONLY.' Vance held his security badge to the door's sensor. No click.

"Do something!" Laney said. She stood on her legs. They hurt, but she stood.

Vance rifled through his munitions bag. He pulled out his Circle device and held it up to the door's sensor. The lock clicked open.

Vance, Laney, and Tenzing scurried up the rest of the stairwell. It led to a small alcove helipad tucked in the hull wall of C Sector.

"I never knew this was here," Laney said.

"I found out the first time when I came in," Vance replied.

"The arc was not built for its people to understand it," Tenzing said. Two strange machines he'd never seen filled his view. "What are those?"

Two heli-carriers roosted in this secret alcove helipad, a hidden nest for predatory raptors. Each had a metal frame with a crossbar that ran perpendicular to the length of the aircraft at the top of its frame. A rotor sat on either end of that crossbar, and a third rotor ran vertical, extending back from the machine's whip-like tail.

Vance selected the transport option from his Circle device. The dark tinted, opaque glass on the cockpit slid up, revealing the interior.

"Get in," Vance ordered. Laney climbed into the cargo space behind the cockpit. Her face pinched with each pained step. Tenzing followed. Vance took the pilot's seat up front and keyed into his Circle device.

TRANSPORT FOR OFFICER VANCE O'BRIEN SELECTED: RETURNING TO DESTINATION.

The rotors turned and sped. Tenzing and Laney looked around in uneasy anticipation until the craft bobbed its first hop into the air. The two felt liftoff for the first time and braced themselves up against either wall in the back cargo space. Vance reclined in the cockpit up front, eyes closed.

Tenzing slunk down the wall and lied down. He tried to make his body as flat as possible, bring himself lower, guided by a desperate clinging to the sensation of ground in a machine suspended in the sky. He braced his feet against the interior wall and gripped his hands deep into the cushion of Vance's reclined seat.

"It will level out into a smoother ride in a second," Vance promised. Laney held her breath and waited for the noise and disorientation of liftoff to subside. The heli-carrier pulled higher and higher. Free of the arc below, its flight settled into a smooth, constant pull stabilized by the two rotors up front and one at the back. Their raucous rotation faded to the background—an unimportant distant hum at the most.

"When we get to this Ghost Arc, what do we do?" Laney asked.

Vance pulled out two small palm-sized objects and handed one each to Laney and Tenzing. Laney reared back.

"It's okay. It's okay. I took the darts out. They're completely empty but still look armed from the outside."

Tenzing grabbed the prisoner-control device and tilted it sideways. He saw through the hollow space that had once contained a death inducing dart.

"Put them on your necks. Right side, just below the ear, behind the jaw," Vance explained.

Tenzing and Laney peeled off the adhesive layer and stuck the devices onto their necks. An eerie feeling beset the pair. The small device felt heavy on their necks, its weight pulling their skin down despite the device's empty, lightweight frame. It felt like a strange dissonance, like holding an unloaded pistol to the temple, the forebrain and the hindbrain at war, a quantum superposition in sensing danger.

"When we get there, I'll strap the two of you to a prisoner transport device. It's basically an empty auto-jack with restraints over a metal carriage. You'll both play dead. We'll head to the room with yellow walls and I'll summon Strickland from there. Then—"

"Then we cut off the head of the snake," Tenzing said.

"What if we run into more security personnel?" Laney asked.

"If they're enlisted, I can just pull rank. If they're officers..." Vance held up his Circle device. "I can still pull rank. Just pray we don't run into anyone else with one of these."

"Besides the one we're hunting," Tenzing said. "With Strickland dead, I am free. Maybe the arc will be freer."

"Maybe," Vance and Laney said simultaneously. It was too much to hope for, but they did so anyway.

"How long 'til we get to this secret Ghost Arc?" Laney asked.

"About half an hour. These heli-carriers are designed for fuel economy, not speed," Vance answered. "It's fully automated and can't go any faster. Plus it's designed for two people at most, and we've got three, so expect it to take longer. We've probably got about twenty-seven minutes left."

Laney let out words before she could stop herself.

"Were you going to come back and kidnap Magda after me?"

"Yes," Vance replied. His head hung down. "But I'm not that man anymore. At least, I don't want to be." A dull anger pulsed at the back of Laney's head.

"We got here from the room pretty easily. Like nothing stops security officers from abducting arc citizens and taking them to this Ghost Arc. How many people have been taken? How many people have had their memories stolen?" Laney asked.

'I don't know," Vance admitted.

"What happens in the room with yellow walls?" Tenzing asked. Vance stared ahead as he answered. He couldn't face the other two.

"Memory extraction is another lie. The memories aren't extracted, they're buried. There's a machi—"

Tenzing and Laney's bodies flew across the back of the cargo area. They slammed hard into the right wall. They felt their muscles and bones press harder into the metal. A crushing force pinned them in place.

"WE'RE SPINNING! WE'RE GOING DOWN!" Vance yelled. Everyone screamed.

Laney stretched her arms out and grabbed onto the back of Vance's seat. Tenzing held onto Laney. He entwined his every limb around every scant thing he could hold. Vance buried himself into the seat and reached around to grab the both of them. He pulled them up front, and all three gripped the seat and each other. They fell slowly, spinning faster than they dropped. Everyone held tight. Screams deafened the spinning rotor. Every dropping moment felt like the last. Everyone braced for impact.

Their screams filled the aircraft's interior until a hard landing stopped their fall.

Chapter 27

"Make it quick. June and El Ratticus say it's gonna happen soon." A dusty bearded man tapped his finger on the trigger of an unplugged angle grinder.

"You can't rush a master at work." A wild, red-haired, red bearded man tucked his hair behind a dark mask. He hid his beard under a thick set of coveralls. He checked his arc welder to make sure every component sat in functional order.

"Come off it, Spark. You're just cutting a hole. A Mite-sized hole, at that." Roark absent-mindedly scraped his angle grinder blade against the metal. He pushed with anxious pressure. The blade snapped.

"A hole through the strongest, thickest metal on the whole damn arc. Besides, it's still an art to me." He held up the wand. A single test-spark flashed. "It's about to get bright. You might wanna leave."

"I'm leaving. I was supposed to watch you, but I'm leaving."

"I just have to cut this entryway and then the other one. Won't take too long. Then it's all up to Mite."

"I'll go check on her," Roark said. "She's with the First Rat. He's got the diagrams, showing her the best spots."

"Can't believe he kept 'em in his trunk this whole time. The foresight on that man. Spark looked out a nearby light-hole. "After all this time, we'll finally have some room."

Chapter 28

Ears rang. Blood surged. Heads and limbs clubbed with pain. Only adrenaline wrenched focus back, bit-by-bit to the survivors' dulled senses. Disoriented minds saw haze and heard static. They struggled to catch up to the truth that their battered bodies, breathing air and pumping blood, already understood. Laney, Vance, and Tenzing survived.

Laney gasped and spat out air. She swiveled her stiffened neck and surveyed the scene: Debris littered the aircraft. Refuse was strewn everywhere—flight manuals, life jackets, a fire extinguisher, a box of flares, plastic, papers, metal. Anything unattached rocketed about in their descent, but the heli-carrier's actual structure seemed oddly intact, at least from the cramped view of the inside. The walls seemed unbent and uncrumpled. The opaque, dark windshield had withstood impact, without a single crack.

"How?... We fell so slowly. How?" Laney struggled to make words. She looked toward Vance. He pried the door ajar and crawled outside to survey the crash site. She and Tenzing followed.

The aircraft's frame stood mostly intact. It had sustained only minor scrapes, easy to repair. One rotor spun limply. Its movement conjured a small cyclone of wasteland dust. The vortex was borne and died against the night's moonlit sky as the rotor sped and slowed in a quiet cycle.

The other wheel of blades sputtered a damp squeak as the mechanical innards struggled to push the rotor toward anything resembling momentum. It spun a fraction of a rotation only to recoil against the binds of its twisting restraint. A thick mass of flexible steel cord entangled the blades on this rotor. The netting appeared as if it had been dropped from above. Vance's trained mind understood.

"GET DOWN! GET BACK IN!"

He shoved Laney and Tenzing back in the cockpit and dove inside. From the corner of his eye, he saw three blinking red lights streak down from the night sky. He slammed the aircraft's door shut. Its gears grumbled from manual closing. *Tink*—the tiniest sound of small metal plinked against the heli-carrier's only exit. The minute sound boomed for the confined occupants of the grounded craft.

"Fuck!" Vance yelled. He heard the sound of drone rotors hovering just outside the downed aircraft. Vance listened.

"Three drones. They're flying in sync. That means one pilot. They're all in pyramid formation."

"Can they get in?" Laney yelled.

Vance pictured the drone's tentacled arm snaking around the cockpit door handle. He rifled through his munitions bag and found a wrist restraining device. He slipped it around on the inside handle of the aircraft's door, locking the sole exit firmly shut.

"They can't get in, but we can't get out. He's trying to starve us out."

A pit formed in Tenzing's stomach. *Starvation. I've spent my life...*

"How did he know?" Vance yelled.

Laney stared daggers at Vance's Circle device. She grabbed it in her hands and thwacked the device against an exposed bolt. Screen glass shattered in little splinters.

"Screwdriver, pliers, anything!" Laney commanded. Vance rifled through his bag and handed her a multi tool. Laney unfolded the tool's pliers and raked out the glass, exposing the tablet's hardware. Everything stood in place exactly where it should, except...

Laney plucked out a small black object. Its hardware system ran independently of the rest of the device's hardware.

"Microphone," Laney said. "You were under the intended impression that this was a text only device. It had one-way audio. Strickland heard every single thing you ever said in the presence of this thing. He waited. He wanted us to think we'd succeed." Laney crushed the electronic bug between the ridged, gripping teeth of her pliers.

"He fucking knew we were coming." Vance looked around the mostly unscathed aircraft interior. He's trying to kill us without damaging one of his precious aircraft!"

Tenzing, Laney, and Vance sat. The buzzing hum of small rotors circled around their cramped metal confines. Just outside, the ever present drones circled, clips filled with piercing darts of death. The mechanical whining etched line after line of panic upon the brows of the aircraft's trapped occupants.

Tenzing darted his head around the aircraft's interior. The cushy, orange cockpit chair held his attention.

Vance sank into the faux leather that covered the back of the cockpit chair. "Heli-carrier crash," he said. "Strickland can report every single one of us dead without explaining why he's had a Circle officer killed. Chalk it up to mechanical malfunction, no suspicion. He protects his secrets. He'll probably shed tears at my funeral when he puts in an appearance. He'll probably give a speech. He's thought it all through."

"Fuck," Laney said. She felt nothing. The shock came over in waves of numbness.

"Vance," Laney said.

"What?" he replied.

"I'm glad we tried. I'm glad you tried to help us. Look how much you've changed when you learned the truth. Just imagine if everyone knew. Things would be different. They'd have to be. We got close. Strickland can't hide in the shadows forever. He can't. It's just a matter of time."

Tenzing squeezed the cockpit chair and released it. He watched the foam slowly reform into its original shape.

"My wife's message, the one I sent with June."

"What about it?" Laney asked.

"I told her I loved her. I told her I was sorry. I told her I had to do something, something right for once in my life, something to help put things right. I told her I probably wouldn't come back to her, I... I'm sorry. I never meant to take you two with me." Laney rested an arm on Vance's shoulder. He heaved.

"Endless speeches about protecting the arc. I never once thought of the arc. Just Kayla, just Lizzie. The arc wasn't real. It never was. They were." Shallow breaths and tepid tears dripped down Vance's and Laney's faces.

"We are not going to die here," Tenzing said. The whirring outside grew louder. The drones hovered just outside the only exit, as if toying with the trio who sat imprisoned within the surgically preserved wreckage.

Tenzing reached past Vance and placed his hands on a tear in the upholstery. He pulled out a thick, spongy chunk of foam that lined the seat's interior.

"What are you doing?" Laney asked.

Vance opened his eyes. He couldn't parse the meaning of Tenzing's strange machinations.

"Vance! Give me one of your darts!" Tenzing said. "We are not going to die here!' Vance handed Tenzing the dart who stuck the dart's needle into the foam. It sank in and left a half-inch gap where the tip did not penetrate. The color returned to Vance and Laney's faces. In an instant, they understood. All three spun into action. Their chance at surviving was just brought back to life.

Laney flipped the knife out from the multitool and ripped the seams on the seat, exposing all the cushiony foam underneath. Laney cut the foam strategically—large, thick sections maximized the surface area with the right thickness to stop the poisoned projectiles. She cut all she could from the seat.

"It's not gonna be enough to cover all of us. Look around for anything that can stop a dart!" Laney said.

Tenzing and Vance scurried around, sorting through the debris that lined the heli-carrier's interior. Vance found a parachute bag, a parachute, his armor lined munitions bag, a pair of flight goggles, a fire extinguisher, and a hard plastic box of flares. Tenzing found life preserver vests, a thick flight manual, and the scattered contents of a first-aid kit strewn across the floor.

Laney grabbed the fire extinguisher from Vance and smashed apart the center console that formed the heli-carrier's dash. She pulled apart sheets of metal, plastic and fiberglass that formed the front of the aircraft's interior.

The three gutted the cockpit and cargo space for every single thing they could find. They worked to assemble their own motley, ramshackle armor, a hodgepodge of detritus that combined to form a full body covering strong enough to stop a small, thin hypodermic dart tip.

The three stood with armor constructed of paper, plastic, cloth, rubber, and metal. Vance used the last strip of restraining tape from his munitions bag to fasten together a foam circle around Laney's neck. Laney cut the parachute into three loose-fitting ponchos that covered most of their frames. The billowy, thick fabric, stretched out from their bodies, strong enough to deflect any lithe, stealthy projectile. Tenzing used the last of the parachute cord to tie pieces of broken plastic all around their bodies, a plate-armor of trash over an undercoat of repurposed items. Tenzing finished the final reinforcement and the three nodded to each other.

"Back to the arc," Vance said. "We didn't fly too far before he hit us. Strickland won't bring drones around civilians. We can find cover there."

Tenzing nodded.

"I'm ready," he said.

"One second," Laney said. She took the pliers back to Vance's Circle device and plucked out a small, black electronic component. She stored it in her zipped breast pocket underneath her assembled armor.

"Let's go!" Laney said.

Vance removed the restraining device on the door handle. He threw open the exit and shot a flare into the sky. Hot white-and-red light streaked up through the triangle of blinking drones. An array of trickling bright sparks rained down from the thermally significant projectile.

"Go Go Go!" Vance screamed. The three jumped out of the downed aircraft and began their run. Tenzing squinted through the goggles wrapped around his eyes. He could just see the massive broad side of Arc Alpha poking out through a dust storm at the edge of the horizon.

This way! Tenzing called. Laney and Vance sprinted after him, and the trio bounded head-first into the outermost ring of the swirling storm. The pyramid of blinking lights shuddered and recalibrated reforming into an equilateral triangle flight formation. That hateful shape pursued the escaping fugitives into the storm.

"He's after us!" Vance yelled.

The three ran faster. Fight-or-flight drove their bodies to their highest physical potential. Tenzing felt a small impact on his back. He plucked a dart from the foam padded life vest that covered his torso.

"It's working!" Tenzing called. Laney felt a dart bounce off of the hard plastic plate shielding her shoulder.

"Do something!" She screamed.

Vance loaded the flare and fired a second sparking burst directly behind them. The blinking lights shook and sputtered for a few disoriented seconds. *Fucker's limited to thermal targeting in this dust storm!*

The colossal behemoth grew larger across their field of vision. Laney, Vance, and Tenzing hurled themselves farther into the swirling sand glass cloud. Dart after dart bounced off their hastily assembled armor. Any dart that stuck slumped uselessly, unable to pierce the layered debris that protected each desperate runner's pulsing veins from poisonous, breath stealing death.

"We're getting closer!" Laney yelled, pulling a dart out of her loose parachute poncho and tossing it to the ground. Her sprinting stride crushed it into the dust beneath. Every muscle in her battered body screamed, but that stronger instinct to live and fight propelled her every step.

"The arc's feet!" Tenzing yelled.

Titanic legs suspended the walking city. They rose up to meet thick metal joints that connected the arc's legs to its hull. The arc's skyline blocked the moonlight above. It cast a great shadow on the waste, and the shroud fell over the storm's clouds, darkening the space between flying sediment.

Laney, Vance, and Tenzing sprinted through the wind-filled vortex's final stretch. They reached beneath the arc, the eye of the storm.

Darts whizzed past. One plinked uselessly against the metal of Arc Alpha's foot. Laney pulled ahead, ready to reach those behemoth legs, ready to begin this desperate climb back aboard Arc Alpha. Years of climbing for work had prepared her body for this moment. She stretched out her hands ready to take the first handhold.

A metal object collided with Laney's legs. She tumbled over and fell back to the cracked and dusty desert. Her body rolled down the crater left by the arc's foot as it took another step.

"Laney!" Vance and Tenzing screamed together.

Two darts lodged in her life jacket broke off and fell to the ground.

Drops of lethal serum spilled wantonly into the pit of the crater where she lay. Laney screamed and felt her ankle. It twisted all the way around, foot pointing backwards.

Vance and Tenzing saw the blinking light where Laney had just been.

Tenzing grabbed a heavy rock with both hands and hurled it toward the low-flying drone still recalibrating from its impact with Laney's legs. The rock smashed into the carriage, tearing through to the rotors and hardware beneath. The drone whirred to a stop. It fell to the ground and rolled into the crater with Laney.

Laney realized where she was. She clambered out the pit and rolled away, a titanic foot filling the hole where she had just been. The arc moved and the eye of the storm moved with it. Rings of swirling dust orbited back around, and the trio found themselves encased.

Vance looked around. Millions of little particulates rocketed about clouding his vision. A red, octagonal piece of metal stuck to a long steel pole skated across his view—something that had blown in from one of the cities. It rolled and flipped across the ground, light enough to travel but too heavy to sail into the air. Vance grabbed the pole and swung it like a great two-handed club. He shouted to Tenzing and Laney.

"Go! Now! I'll draw his fire!" Vance pulled out the flare gun and shot directly at his feet. Bright white-and-red light swirled through the vortex of wind and dust.

Now I'm all that targeting system sees, you fucker!

Laney sat up. Tenzing grabbed her hand. She bent over and bit down hard on the cloth that covered her mouth, then nodded at Tenzing. He put all his strength into a twisting wrench. Laney screamed through the cloth grinding it between her teeth. Tenzing twisted her ankle-it popped, cracked, and crunched until it pointed the right way—back into place. Tenzing released her foot and helped Laney up. The pair shambled to Arc Alpha's nearest landed foot.

Vance stood in the center of the flare's sparking light. He waited.

Tenzing and Laney saw only that blurred light as they looked back.

They found the arc's foot. Laney limped. She let her trained arms and uninjured foot do most of the work. She and Tenzing climbed.

Handhold-after-handhold, foothold-after-foothold ,they raced. Their fingers and feet found easy, steady purchase against the mechanical regularity of the struts, rivets, and trusses that formed the geometric strength of the arc's leg. The light filled dust cloud shrank beneath them and the two ascended.

Vance held tight around the base of his heavy metal pole. It felt cracked and corroded with rust. He watched for the blinking light's every flit and flutter, just visible beyond the swirl of dust and wind around him. *He's circling me.*

Vance looked up. High above, he saw Tenzing and Laney up high on the arc's legs. *They made it. They actually made it.* He looked over and saw something else, something he would not let Strickland see.

Whizz! Whirling rotors cascaded to Vance's position. He dropped back a foot and swung hard. The rusted metal pole collided with the drone's body and shattered. The drone went down. Vance held nothing but a stump of a weapon. He tossed it aside and ran to the center of a crater left by the arc's titanic stride.

Vance pulled out the final flare and let it loose at his feet. He picked it up and waved it about with abandon. Searing, sparking heat burned through his armored hands. The red light circled and trained on his position. He lost the flit and flutter through the blinding light as he counted. *Ten, nine, eight, seven...*

"TO HELL WITH YOU STRICKLAND! I'M NOT YOURS ANYMORE! I'M NOT YOURS! I'M... NOT... YOURS!"

The drone shot toward his location. Vance leapt and caught a dusty ledge. He hoisted his body up and out of the hole as the drone bashed against his back. It bounced back and its spinning rotor sliced a chunk of Vance's armor with it. Vance rolled away. The drone sputtered, readying itself for a second impact, but it did not reach him.

Arc Alpha's cold, metal platform-foot landed inches from Vance's face. It crushed the flying death machine and entombed it deep under the earth's clay soil. Vance crawled away. The arc's foot lifted to continue its stride. He eyed the drone flattened to foil at the bottom of a crater stamped by the metal beast's behemoth hooves.

Vance rolled over and breathed. He lay heaving. Two figures descended on a rappelling system. Vance felt buckles snap and a harness being pulled over his chest. Laney and Tenzing hoisted the ex Security Officer from the wasted ground up to the gangway of the arc's undercarriage. The pair pulled him over the guardrail. Vance lay on the ground as he looked up to Laney and Tenzing.

"Thank you," he said. The trio breathed in. The trio breathed out. Laney picked up a heavy metal crowbar and the three of them limped their way up the stairs to the arc's densely inhabited deck.

Chapter 29

Vance, Tenzing, and Laney stood atop the stairwell at the promenade's precipice.

"Strickland will rally every single security unit on this arc in less than a minute. What do we do?" Vance asked.

"We can go to the Side Hull," Tenzing suggested.

"No!" Laney commanded. "No more hiding. No more secrets. Not for anyone!" She pulled the small black electronic device from her breast pocket and held it up to Tenzing and Vance.

"We're going to VerchLife. They run the arc wide emergency broadcast through their system. I've got the hard drive from your Circle device. We're going to patch what's on here through every single VerchLife helmet and monitor on the arc."

Laney held up her crowbar.

"And this crowbar is our key to the front door."

She took a step.

"Fuck!" She fell to the floor, clutching her ankle. "Endorphins just ran out," she gasped.

"Here," Tenzing said. He scooped under her arm and Vance followed suit. Between the two, they hoisted Laney up and sped forward, carrying her between them. Laney pointed the way to VerchLife with her crowbar.

A few nighthawk arc civilians dodged out of the way and exchanged strange looks as the motley trio dressed in trash armor passed, speed-hobbling their way the quarter-mile to B Sector. Neon sign light pollution conjured a hazy glow along the streets as they passed. Laney's ankle screamed with pain with every step the three bounced, but she didn't care. Fire surged through her nerves and she gritted her teeth through the journey there.

"Here!" Laney shouted. She yelled louder than the agony her body felt.

A stylistically unique building constructed of glass and clean lines filled the space between two industrial-style multipurpose buildings that looked like every other building in B Sector. The headquarters for the firm that produced the most popular communications and entertainment device on the arc stood empty. The last employee had vacated after a lengthy aftershift just an hour before.

Laney peered through the glass and saw the ground-floor open workspace she used to inhabit. Burnt orange backed rolling chairs perched near open desks made of dark faux wood. A neon sign loomed above the work space, illuminating the otherwise-dark, empty office with a pink hue glowing from its retro-cursive letters. It read.

"Why have your life, when you can have Verch Life?"

The letters reflected in the massive monitor screen hanging beneath the sign. It dominated most of the space on the beige wall. It had broadcast employee productivity stamps minute by minute every year Laney spent there. The screen turned on. Text flashed across its width:

"Employee 17 D. Hawkins has entered thirteen lines of code."

Laney used her crowbar as a cane and shuffled up to the door while Tenzing and Vance followed. She raised the crowbar above her head and brought it down.

CRASH!

Never underestimate the power of brute force—Magda's words rang through her mind. A smile beamed across Laney's face.

Glass shards spilled over the gray, geometric-patterned carpet. An alarm blared. Repeating, deafening screeches traded for seconds of anticipatory silence. Both the noise and its absence bludgeoned the ears that listened. Searing, washed out lights flashed. The office pulsed in a glow akin to lightning.

"That alarm will bring every single member of arc security right here!" Vance said.

"Good, they'll need to see this too," replied Laney.

Laney limped through the hole in the door she just opened.

Vance followed. Tenzing stopped and whipped his head around. Hyperaware, Tenzing's wasteland trained body ran on instinct. In the seconds of silence, he heard footsteps approaching.

"Behind us!" Tenzing yelled. Vance's head swiveled around. The approaching uniform of an Arc Security ensign, the first of many, darted into view.

Vance drew his tranquilizer pistol from his belt. He fired. The dart pierced a young, green ensign right in the chest.

A platoon of security ensigns drew closer to VerchLife.

'They're setting up a perimeter!" Vance called. He shot toward the crowd. Two officers fell. His dart pistol clicked empty.

"I'm out! ... Laney!"

Laney hunched over a computer. The backlight from the monitor cast her determined, resolute gaze in a blue glow. Her fingers flew. She linked the hard rive to the computer. Furiously, she typed.

The platoon of officers drew closer across the street. Tenzing sprinted to the downed young ensign. Darts stuck in the foam life jacket, protecting his chest. He grabbed the downed ensign's pistol and tossed it to Vance. Vance checked the darts.

They're still using tranqs. Good.

Tenzing dove to the ground. He clambered low and moved back into the building. Vance loaded the new clip and returned fire toward the platoon. One-by-one they dropped, but the mass steadily approached, vastly outnumbering his darts.

"There's too many!" Vance yelled. Laney didn't dare look up as she worked. She attached the hard drive's contents to the emergency broadcast.

Crash! A window on the far side of the building exploded. Shattered glass rained down. An armored ensign stepped through the opening armed with an electrified truncheon. It sparked and cracked with neutralizing electrical menace. Volts could tear through flimsy armor where darts could not.

Tenzing flipped up a table to shield his body. He sprinted into the line of incoming security personnel, dug his heels into the ground, and pushed. Explosive, surprising impact knocked back the squad's entry for another second.

Crash! The pane next to Tenzing exploded. An arm burst through. Another electrified truncheon struck Tenzing across the face. Tenzing screamed and convulsed. His hands flew, covering his eyes that took the brunt of the scorching blow. He fell to the ground. The table he had used to shield himself fell on top of him. His face throbbed, his eyeballs seared behind shut eyelids.

Vance whirled around. A blue, crackling truncheon tip wielded by armored security battered the table covering Tenzing. Cheap, shoddy wood split and splintered, cracking with each smashing blow. Tenzing lay trapped underneath, body still convulsing. Vance aimed a shot at the offending guard's neck and pulled the trigger. The guard stayed upright bashing again in furious rage almost through Tenzing's cover. Vance checked the pistol end. The dart lay jammed and useless, lodged inside the thin barrel. The table splintered to pieces, Tenzing's head bounced against the floor. The ensign brought the truncheon up high for one more blow.

Vance moved faster.

He found a soft spot on the ensign's exposed neck, an unarmored space between the helmet and the shoulder pad. Vance jammed the dart pistol's barrel into squishing flesh. Cold, thin metal plunged deep into soft tissue. Vance's hand pushed until blood spurted. The ensign fell. The truncheon dropped. Its electricity crackled across the ground. Vance scooped up Tenzing's limp body draping him over his shoulder and grabbed the still sparking truncheon. *Crash! Crash! Crash!* Windows exploded all around. Cutting glass shards rained down from the ceiling.

"We have the perimeter surrounded!" The words sounded from a megaphone piercing through the alarm's screech. Guards everywhere, Vance whipped the buzzing baton around in wide arcs backing up slowly. Guards formed a semicircle around him looking for their opening.

"Doooooone!" Laney screamed louder than everything. She clicked the last keystroke. Vance chucked the stun baton into the crowd of guards and turned around. He dove, carrying Tenzing's body over a line of cubicles. He ripped open a door at the back of the room.

"Laney in here!"

Laney grabbed her crowbar and vaulted over a row of tables and chairs. She crawled into the room and Vance slammed the door shut. The line of security guards drew close to the closet.

"I'll buy us some time!" Laney screamed. She thrust her crowbar into the door's crack and yanked hard. The heavy door jammed shut against its frame.

The door-knob wiggled from the outside, but the door held shut.

Laney and Vance checked Tenzing. His body shook. Weak, shallow breaths puffed in and out, the only motion of his otherwise still body. Striated burns ran across his face from his forehead to his cheeks. His eyes held shut.

A legion of security guards stood just outside the door.

"Go get the battering ram!" the muffled words slipped under the wedged shut door.

"Look at that," another guard interrupted.

The television monitor just below the neon VerchLife sign flickered on.

Text preceded video. The text read,

"They've been lying to you..."

Loops of footage played. Just a few seconds each.

Raw, undoctored footage showed the face of a young woman clearly outside the arc. Her face turned to fear as she ran from the camera's point of view. A dart pierced her neck. She fell to the ground. Pain filled her face.

More footage, this time an elderly man, then a young boy. The videos continued. Human bodies pierced by arc security darts, then lifeless corpses. Text overlaid the footage.

"Humans outside the arc. Humans killed by arc security. We are not alone."

The footage broadcast through the emergency channel to every screen and every single VerchLife helmet on the arc. Arc citizens saw the emergency channel they knew, the same one tested every month, and on it they saw the dying bodies of people that should not exist. Confusion, paralysis, disbelief, shock, vindication, longing, hope, fear, paranoia, and worst of all, from the very few in positions of high power, feigned surprise.

A myriad of responses, a cacophony of emotions. No one knew what to do, so they did nothing. A blanket of silent stillness fell upon the arc. Arc dwellers described it as lasting from seconds to hours.

Chapter 30

CCCCCCCCCRRRRRRRRRRRRRRRRRRRRRAAAAAAAAAAAAAAAAAAASSS
SSSSSSSSHHHHHHHHHHHHHHHHHHHHHH!!!!......

The loudest sound anyone had ever heard echoed through the arc. Tenzing, Laney, and Vance huddled in a tiny supply closet. They felt a pit lurch in their stomachs. They were falling once again—a slow fall, a slow, gentle, deliberate descent followed that incomprehensible noise. Everyone on every part of the arc felt this lurching sensation at once until they heard another deafening crash. This crash was much deeper and much lower.

The sound stopped. The falling stopped.

Everyone everywhere stood up unscathed, unsure of what had just occurred.

"What happened!?!" Laney blurted.

"I don't know," Vance said.

"Grandpa's moment," Tenzing mumbled. His weak voice puffed out from pursed lips. He opened his eyes.

All was shaky, a fizzle of swirling, floating specks hummed and vibrated filling his gaze. All else appeared as if a veil had cloaked over Tenzing's vision. Familiar shapes appeared curved, blurred, and changed.

His hands felt around his eyes. He felt new roughness on his face that stung when he touched it. Pain and fear filled him at once. Tenzing's torso peeled from the closet floor rocketing up with panicked force. Vance and Laney wrapped their arms around him. He heard their voices.

"It's ok. We did it."

"It's ok."

Tenzing opened his eyes again. There was no time now to process it. Vance scavenged the closet interior and found gauze and a numbing solution in a first aid kit. Laney held Tenzing's head while Vance wrapped layer after layer of tight bandages across Tenzing's face. Adrenaline and pain faded into a medicated numbness.

Tenzing heard again the voices of those that saved him.

"It's ok. We think the guards left. We did it."

The three sat there for a while and listened to the silence that dwelt outside the door until they became convinced no one waited outside. They found handholds on the nearby shelves using them to pull their bodies upright. Spray bottles, paper towels, rags, and all manner of cleaning supplies sat tucked in their cubbies still in neat, orderly piles.

"What were you talking about, Grandpa's moment?" Laney asked"

"Do you know something about what just happened?" Vance whispered.

"I have an idea. Let us go find out," Tenzing answered.

Both he and Laney leaned on Vance who yanked the crowbar from the spot where it was wedged, cracking the door open. Vance took a furtive glimpse outside the closet. The room was empty save for one corpse.

"I need to see something," Vance said. Laney and Tenzing nodded. They held back. Vance knelt down near the body of the dead security guard. A pool of blood dripped from the spot where the pistol barrel punctured the corpse's neck. Most of it soaked into the carpet, but a thin layer slid over itself on top—slick like oil.

Vance pulled down the face shield and removed the goggles from the deceased ensign. He stared at the man he killed. Vance knew he had seen him before. He was young, too young for this. Vance parsed his memories from where he'd seen him. Vance shook. Laney and Tenzing approached. They found him still shaking.

"You didn't have a choice," Laney said. Vance spoke without turning around. His gaze never left the pool of blood beneath the dead ensign.

"Neither did he," Vance replied. Disparate noise, a smattering of voices far outside the office building, roiled into a soundscape of helpless confusion.

"We have to go," Laney said. She braced against Tenzing whilst guiding his steps. He helped her take the weight of her injured ankle.

"Vance," Tenzing said. "Thank you."

Vance nodded. He got up and continued to help the others walk. He still shook while he walked. They all did.

The three marched slowly over broken glass. It crunched over itself when piled up and sunk into the carpet when nothing hard lay underneath it. Laney's ankle swelled and buckled when she attempted to put pressure on it. Vance found her a now dormant truncheon. She leaned on it, and it helped a little.

The three inched down a gentle slope realizing at once the arc's new tilt. Rolling chairs had all collected all in one corner of the office-turned-war zone. Most of them still stood upright.

The cacophonous discord outside grew louder. A crowd had formed across the street, not of security, but of civilians. They were dressed in nightclothes, or hastily assembled wardrobes. A few rushed out barefoot, not even taking the time to put on their shoes.

Laney, Vance, and Tenzing plodded forth. They joined that crowd and together stepped toward the unknown with everyone else.

Everyone everywhere stepped outside to see. To see what had happened. They followed that gentle slope, and a massive migration ensued. A crowd ambled toward the back of the arc.

A timid repairman donned his green coveralls. His only thought was *Gosh, I'm gonna work weeks to fix whatever this is. Better get a look now.* A waiflike woman, head buried deep in a VerchLife helmet, led the crowd at the front. She hid the burns on her arms under a loose, dirty coat. She had scurried to the surface the moment the emergency broadcast proclamation had first scrawled across her screen only an inch from her eyes. She moved fast. She suspected something monumental was about to occur.

"Bro, let's check it out! Look, everyone's going!" A lanky sibling egged on his older brother, a mountain of muscle. The muscle looked at his wife. She held two small children and looked scared. "I'm gonna go with John, make sure it's safe. Lock the door. I'll come back. Keep Annie and Kyle here."

A junior non-fungible virtual merchandising programmer scanned his head around the empty fusion bar where he sat. He realized everyone had left, and no one would bring him his drink. He hopped behind the bar and served himself. With liquid courage, he joined the forming crowd.

A woman with perfectly symmetrical, plucked eyebrows sat in her pointed shoes and drank wine amongst her bevy of fashionable auction-purchased fineries. When the proclamation of truth interrupted her media program, her face soured. *End of an era.* Neither her eyebrows nor her nose moved. After the crashing sound, she locked her door. She lounged on her eggshell tête-à-tête and finished her wine.

The crowd wandered to the back of the arc. Laney, Tenzing, and Vance followed amidst that crowd. Everyone everywhere craned their necks as high as they could to see if they could see anything. Anything that would explain that noise and the accompanying gentle descent.

People got higher to see above the crowd climbing stairwells and looking out on balconies, but they still could not see. The arc was designed for this.

Families gripped small children tight. They couldn't bear to leave them, but they couldn't bear not to see what had happened. Older unaccompanied children and teens ducked under legs and through gaps to move faster to the arc's back side.

A game of telephone trickled through that massive crowd. Scattered fragments of information moved from stern to bow, from Sector C to A. The rumor spread.

"The legs! The legs! Something's happened to the legs! At the aft dock, you can see the legs! The arc's on the ground! The arc has landed!"

The crowd worked to force the bay doors to the aft warehouse open. A security guard witnessed the act of vandalism and gripped his truncheon. Hundreds, upon hundreds, worked in concerted effort to open those doors. He dropped his weapon. He took off his badge. He shuffled into the crowd and helped force the doors open.

Tenzing, Laney, and Vance walked the length of the arc shrouded by the curious bodies of everyone else. They reached aft deck.

"How can this many people fit?" Vance asked. The crowd still shuffled forward in steady waves. When the three reached the front, Vance found his answer.

The aft dock bridge extended. It followed the same gentle slope as the arc. With its length, it reached untouched ground. It landed on the earth. The waiflike woman in her dirty coat stepped onto the new planet. She moved about. Her feet felt something different, something they'd never felt before. A rough surface, an unbuilt surface. It scrunched underneath her feet, reacted to her movements. She took away her foot and saw an imprint in the loose dusted surface, a copy of her step.

The crowd processed this new sensation. They navigated terrain instead of floor. They felt dirt instead of metal. They saw sky, they saw distance, and they saw the space where the two met.

They saw horizon. For the first time in a long time, many wondered what lay beyond it. After the grand revelation that beset their screens and helmets, even more wondered *who* lay beyond it.

Tenzing stooped down to the ground. His hands fell across the earth, feeling its texture— crumbly and light. He was back in the wastes. His fingers found an object. They gripped around something cold, cylindrical, and familiar. *A piece of the legs, one of the many bars I climbed, out here.*

"The right middle and right aft legs—it looks like they exploded out from the joints," Laney said.

A titanic column lay as a severed limb across the waste. Boulder-sized bits of broken metal cast tall shadows in the moonlit night. Pools of blue hydraulic fluid—synthetic blood for mechanical muscle—flooded underneath the downed arc pooling under the great beast's reclining body.

Two legs lay in pieces, broken. The remaining four held the arc's weight, enough to lie but not enough to stand. The arc lay still, tilted down at a gentle slope, its body touching the ground.

Tenzing, Laney, and Vance stood in awe of the wreckage. Everyone did. The crowd thinned. Everyone spread out, taking their own ample space. This too, felt new.

A group walked with purpose weaving through the dispersed crowd. They headed toward Tenzing. Rucksacks heavy at their backs, the group pulled two carts constructed from the remains of decommissioned auto-jacks. One was filled with tools, supplies, crates, and pieces of rebuilt technology. The other held containers filled with beautiful, dark soil. Roark, Spark, Jonas, and Mite pulled this second cart. They struggled with its weight as its wheels sunk into cracks in the uneven earth.

A wizened older man pulled ahead of the rest, reaching Tenzing first.

"Thank you," Grandpa said. Tenzing recognized his familiar voice. Grandpa turned to Laney and Vance nearby. "Thank you all."

"How?" Tenzing asked.

"Every rat took a gift from their work home. I'm a greedy man, so I took two. I took my lab, and I took a few dozen mining charges from Arc Golf."

"Ballistics are forbidden on the arc," Tenzing said. his face lit up.

"Yes. For good reason it appears," Grandpa replied. "We strategically placed them to disable mechanical structures without harming a single cell of organic life. I'm quite different from my brother."

Vance shuddered. His hand touched the softest part of his own neck.

"What about your brother?! What about Strickland?" Tenzing asked.

"Do you know something about Strickland!?" Vance asked.

"My brother will not try anything here. Not now. Not with thousands upon thousands of witnesses. He draws his strength from secrecy, and thanks to you all, that is no longer an option."

"But will he come after you?" Vance asked.

"Perhaps. Perhaps not. Something worse may have already come his way. He's failed in his secret keeping duties. Even he has to answer to the Board of Directors. All I know is, that this is the best moment we will ever have to leave this place, and we don't intend to miss our opportunity."

The recycled, reassembled, and utilitarian assemblage of supplies the rats had gathered lay in a tied down heap across the two carts. Grimy, dirt-covered technology and tools meant for digging, building, and scraping piled high above sacks of dry-bulk provisions.

"On second thought, you might be safe," Vance said. "I don't see a single thing amongst you that any A Sectioner would want to decorate their walls."

"How did the arc fall like that? When it fell down, it was gentle— slow. It felt almost serene, like it just got tired and decided to lay down," Tenzing said.

"My grandfather designed a failsafe in case the arc's legs were ever damaged. It is designed to lie down rather than topple over," Grandpa answered. "It's an emergency measure in case of disaster."

"The beast may at last get to rest," Tenzing said.

"Exactly," Grandpa replied. "It's far from being destroyed. This was never our purpose. Growth with longevity comes from limitations. Even metal things and systems get tired. It is now free to live for as long as it can learn to adapt."

"To live through reciprocity," June said.

She stepped forward. She lightly pressed her wrist to the bandages that covered Tenzing's eyes and face. She leaned in and hugged the man. Tenzing felt the salve of her care and kindness.

Grandpa continued. He called out to the Rats.

"For a time, the arc will no longer trample, no longer spill toxic blood onto the earth, no longer hunt those that live beyond the horizon. It must slow. It must rest. Its passengers must adapt. Perhaps they will even learn to like it. Some may even petition the board to delay fixing the legs."

"The arc. What will happen?" Laney asked.

"That is for them to decide," Grandpa answered. "The vault on Arc Charlie stores the seed of every animal and plant. We intend to go out and find an oasis, grow a space of green in this tired earth, try and make it not so tired. If they are smart, they will do the same. They have much more than we can carry, and they don't have to go far. Imagine the possibilities."

Something caught Laney's eye. The massive downed hull scrunched the surface beneath it.

"AUX BAY! CRUSHED!" Laney yelled. Every antique chair, every mahogany desk, every engraved, silver hand-mirror, smushed into the cracking earth under unfathomable tons of steel.

"Oh, God, what if someone was down there?!" Laney yelped.

"We already thought of that," June said. "Few exits lead under the arc. Spark welded them shut after he cut his openings for Mite to get inside the legs."

A familiar voice boomed over the crowd. A red-haired figure approached Laney and Tenzing. Magda carried two canteens, and a backpack, she held up the canteens as she spoke.

"One is water, one is not," Magda said.

"How.. did... how are you already packed?" Laney asked.

"June came and told me. Glad we hit it off at the bar. She dropped some hints and said I might want to pack a bag for a long, long, long trip. Magda patted another bag bearing the symbol of Arc Emergency Medical Technicians. "Plus, if we run into any trouble out there, I brought my old gear."

"So you're going too?' Laney asked.

"What? Did you think I wasn't going to be a part of the only interesting thing that's ever happened on this arc?" Magda looked over toward Tenzing noticing at once the bandages covering the upper half of Tenzing's face.

"What happened? You alright?" Magda asked. Tenzing felt his face tense. He didn't know how to answer that question just yet.

"There will be plenty of time to tell what happened in our travels ahead," Tenzing said. Magda nodded.

"Oh, I almost forgot!" Magda said. She put down her bag and opened another one. She took out a bony, white object and pushed it into Tenzing's hands. "Here ya go, arc climber."

Tenzing smiled. He felt the roughness of the antler nub. He remembered the exact number of points on its broken end. He felt the skull itself, the familiar smoothness of bone polished by wasteland winds. It felt weighty and familiar in his hands. It felt good to have something he'd thought he'd lost.

"It's time for us to go. Grandpa announced to the crowd. "Please lead the way, El Ratticus Firsticus," Grandpa said. He moved forward, grabbed Tenzing's hand and held it up high. Tenzing paused. It took him a moment to realize what Grandpa meant.

"Me?... I... can not lead... I" Tenzing, said. He started to point to the bandages across his eyes. "My sight is partly gone. I do not know if I can—"

"We're here for you." June interrupted. "You are here for us. That's all there is to it. Grandpa told us where you came from. We know you can survive out there and teach us to do the same. Most importantly, you've already proven who you are. We don't want anyone else to lead us."

Grandpa and the rest of the rats cheered. ALL HAIL EL RATTICUS FIRSTICUS! LONG MAY HE SKITTER! Tenzing's lip quivered. He sniffed in. He smiled.

"Thank you for finding me in that pit June," Tenzing said. "Thank you all for teaching me what it means to be a rat."

"Don't thank me yet," said June. "It's a long road ahead, and I'm not done helping you out yet."

"None of us are." Jonas' voice carried through the crowd."

"And we know you'll do the same for us." Mite yelled.

Jonas, Mite, Roark and Spark and a few others pulled on their cart. They heaved. The heavy soil containers moved slowly as the wheels ground down into the dirt under the cart's weight. The waiflike, emaciated woman approached the motley strangers. She had listened at a distance and now ventured forth.

She tipped her VerchLife helmet upside down and scooped it full to the brim with black earth.

"Can I join you?" she asked. "I can lighten your load. I can help."

"What is your name?" Tenzing asked.

"Yara."

"Yara, welcome to the rats," Tenzing said.

Others followed suit. Every rat filled every spare container they held with life-giving black soil. The cart moved more quickly, but not too quickly. The rats started their first steps.

Laney trudged. Her swollen ankle's burden lessened by her truncheon walking stick and the reliable shoulder of her friend Magda.

"Guess we're fugitives, Magda," Laney said.

"I told you to call me Red," Magda replied.

Laney stopped. One face was missing among the rats. She turned around. Vance had stayed back.

"Come with us," she called out.

"I can't," Vance replied.

"You'll be put in prison at best. At worst..." Laney trailed off.

"I know," Vance said. "Thank you Laney. Thank you Tenzing. Thank you all." Vance left with those parting words. He faded back into the crowd and shuffled back up the ramp to Arc Alpha.

The rest of the rats turned toward Tenzing. A question echoed through the crowd.

"Which way are we going, El Ratticus Firsticus?"

Tenzing heard the chorus of voices from the band who looked to him as a leader. He didn't think of them as followers. He thought of them as a family.

Tenzing took a pioneering step away from the arc. He took another and another, leaving small, human-sized footprints in the crunching ground below.

"June, what do you see?" Tenzing asked.

"Mountains far off that way. Beyond the horizon." She pushed Tenzing's hand in the direction of the distant slopes silhouetted against the starlit sky.

Tenzing held the one-antlered skull high above his head. He remembered its place upon his old hut's threshold and proclaimed.

"Whichever direction we go, we're headed home."

Tenzing walked into the waste land as all the rats followed. They carried many things, but above all, they carried soil and seeds. Seeds that would sprout roots, roots that would pull the dust back to the earth and teach it once again to grow and sustain life.

Chapter 31

The white walls of Vance's cell formed the entirety of his view. No word from the outside; they were the entirety of his world. He was alone, left to the endless cycle of his thoughts. Poor company for a man who'd seen what he'd seen—poor company for a man who'd done what he'd done.

The face of the young ensign he'd killed swirled through Vance's mind in endless repetition. He couldn't see anything else. He wasn't sure if he deserved to. He'd seen the ensign's eager, fresh face on Arc Ghost only weeks before.

He must have finished training and gotten himself promoted. Vance racked his brain trying to remember if he had ever learned his name. He was pretty sure he hadn't. That made it worse somehow.

He was young enough to charge into the fray—young enough to be killed. Vance imagined the young man following the orders of older men who lived in shadows always far away from danger. Vance knew how it was. In that moment, but for the truth revealed to him only a few hours earlier, he and that ensign were the same.

Just a few hours. I killed him. He had to die. I had to kill him because through luck, I found out first. Luck and a few hours. Chance killed him. Chance saved me.

Vance saw it again, the first conscious killing of a human he knew to be human. The other deaths weighed on him but this one weighed the heaviest. The thinned barrel of the pistol. It took barely any pressure to push it through his throat. That was it. He saw the young man's eyes, eyes forever closed only because Vance was lucky enough to learn the truth first.

The door opened. Security Officer Santoro stood outside the door.

"It's been two days," Santoro said. "They've passed your sentence."

It didn't feel like two days. Vance wasn't sure if it had been a thousand days or no time had passed at all. It was as if his life had stopped, like he didn't exist at all, just a loop of thoughts with a body attached by accident.

Vance shook his head hard. Words fell feebly from his lips.

"What will they do to me?"

"The board invented a new punishment for you," Santoro said. He pressed a piece of paper into Vance's shaking hands. A single word leapt from the page.

"Exile?" Vance asked.

"Permanent ban from the arc and its surrounding area."

"I don't understand. Why don't they kill me? Why don't they destroy my mind—put me in the room with yellow walls?"

"Because they're getting smarter. The Board has changed tactics. I've heard things. We've all heard things. Your punishment fits right in."

Vance's hands fumbled, shifting the paper between his fingers.

"You have to remember," Santoro said. "It's strategy not mercy. A photo, a live feed—a real one of your corpse— drying out in the sun off the arc. It sends a clear signal to everyone here."

There is nothing left but the Arc. Vance thought. His thoughts wandered to the rats out in the waste. He remembered something. He remembered the man who'd hunt those who'd escaped.

"What happened to Strickland!?" Vance asked. Santoro paused. He said nothing for a moment. He leaned in close, his face inches from

Vance's own. A knowing glance sprawled over Santoro's face.

"After the footage came out... after we learned... a few of the other officers found him dead. Aneurysm, or stroke or something. We found him like that."

Vance noticed as Santoro lingered on the last part of the sentence a little long.

A guttural wish anguished Vance deep from within. His face grew hot. He pictured his own hands wrapped around Strickland's throat. He saw his own knuckles turn white as they tightened, fingertips pressing deeper into his former commander's flesh.

He felt Strickland's windpipe—such a delicate thing—flatten between his clenched fingers, so flat that not a single molecule of breath could escape. He yearned to see the life drain from Strickland's eyes— see helplessness be the last thing that man ever knew. Vance knew he wouldn't get that. The chance had forever passed. Vance knew he would have to live with that.

He breathed in. He breathed out.

"I'm taking you to the aft dock." Santoro's voice interrupted Vance's thoughts. "There's someone much more important than me who would like to speak to you there."

"Why do you do it?" Vance asked. "Why do you still work for them?"

Santoro stood in the door frame. His face fell as he leaned against the open door.

"The Board has people who answer to them even still. They know where my family lives—know where my family sleeps."

Vance knew the vulnerability Santoro spoke of. The arc's rulers did too.

He followed Santoro all the way to the aft dock. His feet felt heavy and pained, but he didn't care. His body didn't feel real. Nothing did. Nothing felt real until he reached aft dock.

Kayla stood there holding Lizzie. They were real, and then everything was. They brought him back.

Vance moved in and stumbled. His legs almost collapsed, feeling the pressure of everything. He fell into the sweet embrace of his wife and child. He hugged them both.

Tears streamed down Kayla's face. Lizzie babbled her happy little noises.

"I got your message. I love you too. I'm glad you made it back."

Vance held her tighter until she spoke. She fought through her sobs until she produced words.

"I love you more than anything. I can't imagine a life without you. But I can't imagine a life without Lizzie, either. She can't go where you have to go."

Tears streamed down Vance's face as he held them both tight. He looked out toward the waste land. Dust blew in the wind and heat lightning crackled in the distance beyond the horizon.

He held them for as long as he could, wishing the moment would never end.

It did end.

The waste land loomed and stretched beyond the horizon.

Lizzie babbled. Kayla spoke.

"Vance, I love you. I want to hold you again and be held by you. I want to grow old with you and watch Lizzie grow with you, but... I can't bring her out there. Vance sobbed. He stared into his wife's eyes. Kayla spoke. Her tone changed, hardening from gutted to defiant.

"So go out there and change it. Bring life back out there. Make a world safe where Lizzie can run and play and grow. Where she can feel safe and loved. That new world will be fragile while it grows. Fragile things need protection. This is what you were made for. Protect it while it grows. I will try and help here. We'll build a bridge to each other from opposite sides of the world—you out there and me back here. One day, Lizzie and I will walk across that bridge to meet you."

Vance kissed Kayla. Vance kissed Lizzie's head. Tears fell from his face. He walked down that gentle slope into the waste land and followed the footprints of those who would bring back green, those who would put down roots.

Vance looked out at the small, human sized footprints. Their trail stretched before him to beyond the horizon.

I will protect them.

He cast one gaze back to his wife and child as they faded from his view.

I will protect them all.

Vance walked, and with every step, he thought of building that bridge.

The End.